THE MECHANICAL MIND OF JOHN COGGIN

THE MECHANICAL MIND OF JOHN COGGIN

ELINOR TEELE

ILLUSTRATIONS BY
BEN WHITEHOUSE

WALDEN POND PRESS

An Imprint of HarperCollinsPublishers

Walden Pond Press is an imprint of HarperCollins Publishers.
Walden Pond Press and the skipping stone logo are trademarks and registered trademarks
of Walden Media, LLC.

The Mechanical Mind of John Coggin
Text copyright © 2016 by Elinor Teele
Illustrations copyright © 2016 by Ben Whitehouse
Library of Congress Cataloging-in-Publication Data
Teele, Elinor.
The mechanical mind of John Coggin / Elinor Teele ; illustrations by Ben Whitehouse. —
First edition.
    pages cm
  Summary: "When Great-Aunt Beauregard announces her intentions to bring budding
engineer John into the family business of coffin manufacturing for the rest of his natural
life—and, worse, to teach his sister Page to embalm—John decides enough is enough, and
the two of them head out on the lam, maybe joining the circus"— Provided by publisher.
  ISBN 978-0-06-234510-3 (hardback)
  [1. Brothers and sisters—Fiction. 2. Runaways—Fiction. 3. Great-aunts—Fiction.
4. Orphans—Fiction. 5. Circus—Fiction. 6. Family-owned business enterprises—Fiction.
7. Engineering—Fiction.] I. Whitehouse, Ben, illustrator. II. Title.
PZ7.I.T43Me 2016   2015015307
[Fic]—dc23   CIP
                                                                               AC

Typography by Joel Tippie
16 17 18 19 20 CG/RRDH 10 9 8 7 6 5 4 3 2 1
❖
First Edition

For John & Katie
Seize the carp

And for my grandfather
A true and gentle man

THE MECHANICAL MIND OF JOHN COGGIN

THE BEGINNING

"*Tell me a story.*"

"*A story? Not now!*"

"*My dear boy, if not now, when? Seize the carp, John. Seize the carp.*"

John sighed and rolled over onto his back, just in time for a large, lukewarm glob of goo to go SPLAT in his left eye.

"*I can't feel my legs,*" *he said.*

"*Pah!*" *the voice on the other side of the wall bellowed. "That's no way to begin a story!*"

John reached up to wipe the muck from his eye, and a bolt of pain cracked through his right arm.

"*Why don't you tell one?*"

This time it was the voice that sighed. "Now, now, you know I have neither the facility nor—let's face it—the faculties; nutty as a maggot-infested fruitcake. No, I am merely a player that frets and struts his hour upon two arthritic limbs. You, on the other hand, are incurably optimistic and still breathing. The perfect job description for a storyteller."

John looked through the bars of his window. The sun was setting, casting a steamy glow over the door of the cell. He could feel his sweat mixing with the dried blood on his shirt and returning it to liquid.

"I don't know how."

"Balderdash," the voice retorted. "It's very simple. You begin at the beginning and end at the end."

"And what's the end?"

"My dear boy, I haven't a clue."

John sighed again and closed his eyes. "Once upon a time there was a boy who made coffins. . . ."

The voice chuckled. "Now that is an excellent way to begin."

CHAPTER 1

ONCE UPON A time there was a boy who made coffins. His name was John Peregrine Coggin, and the Coggin family had been manufacturing wooden caskets in the city of Pludgett for over a hundred years.

"Depressing way to make a living."

"Aren't you even going to let me start?"

"Sorry."

"Supreme Craftsmen of Death" was how John's Great-Aunt Beauregard referred to the family business. She liked the phrase so much she had it inscribed on the workshop sign:

COGGIN FAMILY COFFINS
Supreme Craftsmen of Death

Great-Aunt Beauregard was John's only surviving relative. She had been granted this honor upon the death of John's parents, who were struck down by virulent consumption when John was five. Great-Aunt Beauregard was so angry at their lack of forethought that she almost refused to make their coffins.

"Waste of perfectly good lumber," she told her great-nephew on his first day in the workshop.

Along with John, his newborn sister, Page, was also entrusted to this termagant's care. Though, truth to tell, over the next six years it was John who did most of the caring.

"What use do I have for girls? Give me two cords of pine over sugar and spice any day."

"But Great-Aunt Beauregard, weren't *you* a girl?" John once asked as he was laboring away.

"Never!" Great-Aunt Beauregard roared. "I went straight from birth into the family business. And that's enough impertinence from you," she added, whacking him soundly on the head with a T square. "Ask a question like that again and I'll clamp your eyebrows together."

"The family business." Those were the first words John heard when he woke up in the morning and the last words he thought of before falling asleep. Great-Aunt Beauregard was determined to make him the finest coffin maker in the history of the city. And if that meant John spent seventeen hours a day embedding splinters in his palms, then so be it.

"One day, you will be known as Pludgett's pint-sized Grim Reaper. Stick that in your ear and dream on it."

Pludgett was where the Coggins had always lived—a grim, grimy, respectable city on the edge of a grim, grimy, respectable bay. It had originally been a swamp, but that did not bother the settlers who decided to make it their home. They simply spent three years dismantling a neighboring hill and depositing the dirt in the mire.

And when that didn't work—and granaries and grannies took to mysteriously disappearing overnight—the settlers began building hovels *on top* of the ones that were sinking. The whole city was a layer cake of decay.

Of course, living in a city built on a swamp meant the air smelled like rotten eggs and mosquitoes were the size of pumpkins. But no one ever complained. Pludgett citizens were terribly proud of Pludgett:

"Did you know we have the most rat-poison factories per capita in the world?"

"Have you heard? Our clock tower has been voted the most egregious edifice in the country!"

"My sister-in-law said the town where she grew up had more personality than Pludgett, but then I told her about our sewer snakes and she took it back."

Great-Aunt Beauregard was the worst patriot of all. Though she generally detested celebrations, she always made an exception for the annual observance of the city's founding. In addition to subsidizing the fireworks finale, she insisted on opening the family workshop for Bring Your Own Parent morning.

Each year, residents were invited to tote along their ancient mother or father for a trial fitting. Customers could preorder a casket and still have time to get a front-row seat for the parade. BYOP was one of the most popular events of Pludgett Day.

Nobody thought this was strange except John, who sometimes wondered aloud why people in the city were so interested in death.

"Bleakness builds character! Now start priming six Maple Number Fours for the Gorfers."

As much as Great-Aunt Beauregard loved Pludgett, John hated it. He hated their three-story workshop perched on pilings on the edge of the harbor. He hated the cramped room that he shared with his sister on the top floor. He hated the lumber wagons that rumbled down Main Street at dawn and the hearses that fetched their goods at night.

And he hated the family business.

Unfortunately, he was extremely good at it. Upon his arrival in Pludgett, Great-Aunt Beauregard had pulled him out of kindergarten and pushed him into handcrafting the Pine Economy line. By the time he was ten, John had perfected the entire process.

With sixty feet of one-inch-thick lumber, an aging

mallet, and a trusty handsaw, he could build a casket that was the envy of the neighborhood. He knew that the head panels should be ten degrees from vertical, the toes only six. That the holes for the handles must be drilled next to the ribs, and not through. That the floorboards were trapezoids and the head ends near squares. He was a lean, unkeen coffin machine.

That's not to say John was an expert from day one. During the first few years, his products were often sent back for refunds. On one memorable occasion, a casket was returned with the dead man still inside. Great-Aunt Beauregard pointed out that *he* didn't look too pleased with the workmanship either.

"But, sir, we don't have to make coffins," John dared to suggest not long after this occasion. "What if we tried something that doesn't get buried? Like furniture, or boats?"

"Boats?" Great-Aunt Beauregard nearly choked on her tongue. "We are doing imperative work! Even if I did want to make furniture—which I don't!—Pludgett wouldn't stand for it. We are the only casket manufacturers in the city. As long as there is a Coggin living, coffins will be made in this workshop. Besides," she added, "what does a stunted boy with ingrown toenails know about boats?"

"I know that they'd take me far from here," John mumbled.

"Rank insubordination! Just for that I'm demoting you to sanding duties. I don't want to see any skin left on your knuckles when the day is through."

And there wasn't any.

Of course, John was never paid for this work. As chief foreman of

COGGIN FAMILY COFFINS
Supreme Craftsmen of Death

John was expected to labor for the greater good of the family business. Any money that didn't go toward supplies went directly into Great-Aunt Beauregard's personal safe, a squat box of steel tucked in the corner of the ground-floor storeroom. She sometimes hinted that she had great plans for these funds in the future.

Life would have been a lot easier on John if he had been dumb. Unluckily for him, he was cursed with imagination. He was always coming up with incredible creations—Bicycle plows! Amphibious velocipedes! Spaceships that slingshotted around the sun!—anything that would free him from the deadening sight of plank after plank. When he wasn't poring over the engineering manuals that Page found for him in the city trash, he was dreaming of armies of mechanical monsters that ran on internal combustion.

He even went so far as to propose that he might build

a shredder to recycle their copious wood scraps into packing material, but Great-Aunt Beauregard was having none of it.

"Grand ideas end in failure," she scolded. "You'll only end up looking like the wrong end of a donkey when you fail miserably at whatever fool thing it is you've tried to do. The trick in life is to stick to what you know. Then you'll never be disappointed."

Answers like these brought John close to despair. And he would have despaired, if not for one thing: Page.

Page was the most understanding six-year-old in the world. She looked like their mother, laughed like their father, and never held a grudge. Great-Aunt Beauregard got one thing about family right. For his sister, John was willing to walk through fire with a bunch of flesh-eating monkeys strapped to his back.

The best part of his day was the end, when Page would sit at the foot of his bed and ask John to tell her about his latest ideas. He'd regale her with visions of mermaid houses run on volcanic steam and metallic dragons that belched blue fire.

"And do they go boom?" she invariably asked.

"Yes," he would say, tickling her feet, "right before they launch rainbows into the sky."

"Good." Page would nod very gravely at this. "You can't have a boom without rainbows."

When John ran out of rainbows, they talked about

their parents. Having only been a baby when they died, Page was eager for details. What did their mother smell like? Lilies of the valley. What did their father say? Pull up a pew. Where did they live? In an old yellow house on the edge of the sky-blue sea.

At the end, Page always had the same request:

"Tell me one of Dad's stories."

This wasn't tough. Their father had been a poor businessman but a great storyteller. When John was young, there had been new tales every night. Tales about journeys, about danger and daring, about sisters and brothers and love.

"Building a story is like any other invention, John, my lad," he would say. "Guts and gung-ho at the beginning, struggles and surprises in the middle, and the glorious moment when everything comes right."

For John, that moment was his mother's bedtime kiss. After his father had finished his tale, she would tuck her son in, rub his nose, and whisper the same good-night prayer: "May you be happy, may you be healthy, may you be loved."

John's heart always ached peculiarly when he recalled these moments. He realized it was important for his sister to know that not all mornings started with a snarl and not all mistakes ended with a slap, but it still hurt to remember. Even if it did help Page to snore.

More often than not, John would then lie awake and

worry. Page was growing up. Next year she would be seven. Old enough to be sent to boarding school. Or farmed out for work. Or, worst of worsts, expected to play her part in the family business.

He had thought about running away, sure. But, deep down in his bones, John was chicken. Six years with Great-Aunt Beauregard had taken its toll. As much as he loved his improbable ideas, he was convinced he had only one practical skill: crafting the best wooden coffin in Pludgett. With his father and mother dead, and no other means of support, John was in charge of his family. And Page needed a home.

He could see no viable way out of their situation . . . until one morning, just before Pludgett Day, when Great-Aunt Beauregard stomped into the workshop.

"John, put down the hammer. After we wrap up the BYOP, I am taking you and your sister to the beach for the weekend."

Whang! John didn't put down the hammer, he dropped it on the floor in shock.

"You will close up, Master Butterfingers, while I fetch your sister from kindergarten. Then you will pack your bags in preparation for tomorrow afternoon."

"Have people stopped dying?" he asked without thinking. Great-Aunt Beauregard rewarded him with a swinging clip to the ear.

"No, but I can think of someone who will if he doesn't

get a move on. Now HOP TO IT!"

John hopped. And less than twenty-four hours later, he was standing on the beach behind Peddington's Practical Hotel, looking out at the ocean.

Yes, it was an ocean crammed with rusty barges honking like geese and steamships burping smoke rings, but it beat the heck out of the workshop.

And sure, it might be five o'clock in the morning and the water might be freezing and Great-Aunt Beauregard might have dressed him up in a wool sack to go swimming, but he was here, wasn't he? They were actually on vacation!

"Johnny, look at me!" Page yelled as she dove into an underwater somersault. John laughed and splashed his way toward her. When he turned back, he saw Great-Aunt Beauregard perched on a piece of driftwood, her stone slab of a face shaded by a hat crowned with a stuffed raven. She was comparing stain samples for children's caskets.

"Johnny." Page surfaced next to him, spitting water. "I love the sea."

John smiled. "So do I."

"Do you think we're moving out of the city? Is that why Great-Aunt Beauregard took us here?"

John stopped smiling. He wasn't at all sure that was what Great-Aunt Beauregard had in mind, but he answered encouragingly enough. "Maybe. You never can tell with the old trout. She might have gone whackadoodle when we weren't looking."

"I hope so," Page said, hurling a huge splash of water over him. "'Cause I want to beat you back to the beach every day!"

Off she went, dog-paddling like mad. John gave Page a head start and followed with a little more hesitation. Whatever Great-Aunt Beauregard had in mind, he was extremely doubtful she would ever go whackadoodle.

CHAPTER 2

"W HAT ARE YOU gawking at?"

John gulped. He had temporarily forgotten that Great-Aunt Beauregard was sitting next to him on the hotel terrace. Perhaps that was because she'd spent the better part of the hour arguing with the waiter about the freshness of her cocktail shrimp. Great-Aunt Beauregard spent a lot of time arguing with people.

"Nothing, sir."

"Nonsense! You have had your head cocked sideways for the past five minutes. Unless you've developed rigor mortis, you were staring at something."

"Well . . ." John swallowed and gestured hesitantly with his finger. "I was looking at him."

"Him" was a tiny figure, no larger than John himself, who was standing upside down on the wall of the terrace.

Despite his hat being squashed against the stone and his feet waving dangerously in the wind, he seemed perfectly comfortable. In fact, he was grinning—although at this angle it looked like a gigantic frown.

"Cease and desist that immediately!" Great-Aunt Beauregard bellowed.

The feet waved in friendly reply.

Great-Aunt Beauregard rose in a tsunami of fury from her patio chair. The figure—with considerably more flexibility than John would have thought possible—leaped upright and did a two-step along the length of the wall. When he reached the end, he skipped over the saddle of a tethered horse, dipped in and out of the hotel fountain, and disappeared down the drive.

Great-Aunt Beauregard sat back down in high dudgeon and raised a toothpick menacingly.

"If I ever catch either of you two behaving in such a manner, no law will hold me responsible for the consequences."

She stabbed the body of a large shrimp and proceeded to gnaw off the head. "Now, where was I?"

"You were going to tell us something about our future," replied John.

"Ah, yes." She swallowed and picked up her beer. "I had hopes of discussing it in detail before my afternoon appointment. But our addlepated waiter and that . . . thing . . . have ruined my moment. So we will delay the announcement until dinner."

"Are we moving here?" Page asked. John pinched her to be quiet.

"Oh, no," said Great-Aunt Beauregard from beneath her foam mustache. "It's much, much better than that."

For the life of him, John couldn't read what his great-aunt was thinking. Her whole body seemed to be fissuring with excitement. He'd never seen her like this before.

After the beer was through, Great-Aunt Beauregard cornered a brass salesman in the hotel lobby. John and Page were instructed to stand near the palms.

"John," Page whispered, "who was that boy on the wall?"

"I don't think he was a boy," John whispered back. "I think he was a little person."

"Wrong on both counts!" a voice trumpeted from behind a palm. John and Page jumped.

Peeking out from between the leaves was a squashed lettuce of a face. Two blue eyes, spaced peculiarly wide apart, rose up over a nose and mouth so tiny they could scarcely be seen. It was as if someone had punched them in and forgotten to pull them back out.

But what the face lacked in drama, the scalp made up for. In all his life, John had never seen such hair. It sprouted and curled and frizzed and twisted and exploded in waves of orange. Whenever the head moved—and it always seemed to be bobbing—a fire of split ends moved with it.

"Greetings. I couldn't help but observe your predicament and thought it a fitting moment to offer my employment services."

"Who are you?" Page asked. She was hiding behind John's shirt.

"Name is Boz." He emerged from the palm and made a strange half bow, half curtsy.

"Short for?" John asked.

"Short for my size, but strong for my years. I once heard the president of Patagonia proclaim that she had never seen such biceps on the body of a biped." Boz flexed his muscles in a helpful manner.

"What kind of employment?"

"Well, as I was cruising the perimeter of this fine establishment—not for any piratical purpose, mind you, but merely to admire the proportions of the Augustan facade—I happened to observe you and your sister tripping the light fantastic in aquamarine waters."

"You were watching us swimming?"

"And turning some rather impressive somersaults. My dear boy, do you know that you and your acrobatic sister would make a fabulous headline on the touring circuit? Jill and Jackanapes. Or Contortion Cuties. Or maybe Twisted Sisters."

"I'm not a girl," John interrupted.

"Oh, we can fix that," Boz said airily.

"Are you an acrobat?" Page asked.

Boz grinned. He was missing two of his teeth.

"Madam, I am a scholar and a gentleman. I have sailed the seven seas to the sands of Samarrand. I have surveyed the Matopolo Mountains and hurdled the Runyon Canyon in a single bound. I am every man's friend and no man's slave."

"But are you an acrobat?" Page insisted.

"On occasion," Boz said, conceding the point. "At this particular moment, I happen to be engaged in a more varietal occupation under the benevolent dictatorship of a circus impresario."

"You're with the circus?" It was the only word in the speech that John could be sure he understood.

"Correct!" Boz twirled once, the bushel of hair twice. "However, Colonel Joe prefers to call them the Wandering Wayfarers, 'circus' being a rather hackneyed term for a group of their caliber. A roving, rummaging lot with bells on their toes and bursitis in their hearts. You'd fit right in."

John opened his mouth . . . and closed it. It was hard to concentrate on Boz's words with his hair still gyrating.

"So, do I have your considered assent? Shall we sign, seal, and deliver ourselves to the adventures of the open road?" Boz pulled hard on John's sleeve, tugging him toward the hotel's front door.

"Wait," John said, pulling back and sending Boz

sprawling on his bottom. "We don't know you from Adam."

Boz sprang to his feet.

"Oh, that's quite all right. I don't know Adam either."

"But why should we join the circus?"

Boz raised what was left of a scraggly eyebrow.

"Well, my dear boy, forgive my unforgivable presumption, but it seems your mother—"

"Great-aunt," Page corrected.

"Pardon me, great-aunt—may not exactly be the most congenial custodian of filial responsibilities."

"What?"

"She appears to be a hag," Boz explained.

John wrinkled his nose. This was undoubtedly true.

"And correct me if I am mistaken, but living with a hag does not strike me as being all barleycorn and brilliantine hair wax."

John wasn't sure what barleycorn had to do with anything, but he nodded in agreement.

"Then why delay?" Boz shouted, his red head bobbing up above the leaves. "Life and linseed oil wait for no man. Let us sally forth and seek new lands!"

Page looked up at John. "Should we go, Johnny?"

For a moment, John was tempted. He'd heard of the Wandering Wayfarers. Though he'd never been allowed to see their act, they were often in town for Pludgett Day. It was possible that this . . . person . . . belonged to their troupe. And it was alluring to imagine a life free of toe boards and trimming.

Then John glanced at Page's face, her wide-eyed trusting gaze, and he had his answer.

"No."

"You cut me to the pectoral," Boz said, clutching his hand to his breast. "Why not?"

John weighed his words.

"Great-Aunt Beauregard *is* horrible. But she's the only family we have. Besides, she might be changing. She took us on this vacation. And she said she was going to tell us something important about our futures. Maybe we'll be moving away from Pludgett."

Boz was unimpressed. "It has been my experience that a sloth never changes his claws, nor is the future a gift. You make your own luck in this world, even if you have to steal the parts.

"But I can see that I am not going to be able to solder my suggestions of sojournings to your iron will. Au revoir, my little amis, may your hearts be free from sclerosis and your thoughts ever pure."

And with that, he did a triple backflip into the legs of a bearded businessman. The hat went flying, the beard went flying, the businessman went flying. But when the dust had settled, Boz—and the businessman's briefcase—were nowhere to be found.

"Johnny," said Page, "what does sclerosis mean?"

"I don't know."

"Coggins! Where are the Coggins?" came the roar of Great-Aunt Beauregard.

John took Page's hand, swallowed hard, and they both went forward to meet their fate.

CHAPTER
3

FOR DINNER, GREAT-AUNT Beauregard had reserved an enormous table in the dining room. She sat in one chair, Page sat next to her, and John sat next to Page. The remaining ten stood empty.

When the menu came, Great-Aunt Beauregard ordered for all. Page and John received an assortment of peas, carrots, and potatoes. Great-Aunt Beauregard received lobster bisque and champagne.

As the plates were put before them, a thin line of mucus with a fat pearl of snot began to ooze out of Great-Aunt Beauregard's left nostril. John shot a warning glance at Page, who was trying not to giggle, and applied himself to his potatoes. For minutes there was silence, until Great-Aunt Beauregard suddenly banged her knife on her glass.

"Right, that's enough bonding. It's time we come to the reason for our little celebration."

The drop of snot swayed in excitement.

"John, I do not know if you are aware of this, but you turned eleven on Pludgett Day."

John was distinctly aware of this, but couldn't quite believe that they were on vacation to celebrate his birthday. They had never celebrated it before.

"On this milestone, I feel you are ready to learn an important fact about your heritage."

John's heart started to beat wildly. Could his prayers have been answered? Was it possible that Great-Aunt Beauregard wasn't his great-aunt after all?

"John Peregrine Coggin, I am pleased to inform you that I have made you the sole heir to the family business."

In the split second of an instant, the bottom dropped out of John's world. He felt he was falling into a black pit far, far below him. He had a vision of his future self, draped in cobwebs, putting the finishing touches on his own coffin.

"Johnny, Johnny!" whispered Page. "Are you okay?"

"At eleven, you are old enough to appreciate the importance of our glorious family tradition. And unlike your nincompoop father, I know, you will not shirk from duty."

John wanted to stand up, to shout, to bolt. But he couldn't move.

"But I have even better news." The bead of snot was vibrating with ecstasy. "The surplus of deaths in Pludgett has created a demand for transitional establishments that cater to the crème de la crème of society."

Great-Aunt Beauregard paused to admire this turn of phrase, then continued.

"Therefore, for the next chapter in our history, I plan to create the

COGGIN FAMILY FUNERAL HOME
Boutique Interments for the Bourgeoisie

And since you, John, are about as tactful as a bellyful of beetles with customers, I will be working with a new assistant on this branch of commerce while you handle workshop affairs."

Great-Aunt Beauregard raised her glass while the snot thread quivered like a plucked harp string.

"John, please welcome the newest member of the family business."

John scanned the empty chairs in confusion. Then he lifted the tablecloth and peered underneath.

"She's not on the floor, you dunderheaded dingbat. She's right here." And ever so slowly, as the drop of snot fell into her soup, Great-Aunt Beauregard laid a meaty hand on Page's shoulder.

Page's mouth fell open. It was full of peas. John's

mouth fell open, and a piece of his potato went bouncing across the table.

"When we return to Pludgett, Page will begin her career at the Coggin Family Funeral Home. She will start by dressing our customers." Great-Aunt Beauregard flicked her finger under Page's chin to close it. "You'll enjoy that, Page. It will be like dressing up a doll." She winked. "And if you're very good, I'll let you apply their makeup."

Page looked like she was about to be sick in her lap.

"Meanwhile, you, John, will begin work on our new line of Chestnut Deluxes."

Great-Aunt Beauregard reached into her bag and pulled out a stack of papers and a fountain pen.

"Now then, I am perfectly aware that you are not old enough to run a large business like this on your own. So I have taken the liberty of drawing up a partnership plan. I agree to lend you my considerable expertise for the next twenty years, and you promise to provide me with room and board upon my retirement."

John stared in horror at the stack in front of him. On the top page, written in thick ink, was one word:

CONTRACT

Great-Aunt Beauregard seemed to think her great-nephew's silence was panic about losing her. She patted the paper confidentially.

"I wouldn't worry too much about my retiring. If my funeral home plan succeeds, as I believe it will, then the family will have decades of corpses and coffers to look forward to." She raised her champagne glass. "To the Coggins!"

The blood in John's veins was congealing in terror. He tried to raise his hand, but his muscles would not obey. Great-Aunt Beauregard snorted in frustration and yanked the last page from the stack.

"Apparently, there's no need to thank me. You simply sign on the dotted line. Here." She uncapped the pen and pointed to the . . . . above his typewritten name.

John stared at the pen. A tiny blob of ink was pooling on its razor-sharp nib. He knew that this step was inevitable. He knew that it meant security for him and his sister for the rest of their days.

But he couldn't, he just *couldn't*, sign that document.

Great-Aunt Beauregard rapped her knuckles on the table.

"Time is ticking, John! We'll take the six a.m. train tomorrow and start construction on the funeral parlor at eight a.m. sharp."

John looked from the pen to the ink to the paper. Then he drew a deep breath and said something he had never said to his great-aunt before.

"No."

Great-Aunt Beauregard opened her mouth to speak, but only "Whhhh?" came out.

"No," John repeated. "I won't sign that paper." He stared straight into the eyes of his nemesis. "And you can't make me."

There was an ominous pause.

"And what will you do instead?"

RUN, a little voice in John's head screamed. RUN!

Great-Aunt Beauregard read his thoughts.

"May I remind you what happened when your father ran away from the family business?" She stabbed the paper for emphasis. "He died"—stab—"penniless"—stab—"and diseased"—stab—"in a house infested with rodents"—stab. "Is that what you envision as your future?"

What John was envisioning was Page applying a dab of rouge to his cold, withered cheeks. He did not move, nor did he answer.

"Fine!" Great-Aunt Beauregard blasted, shoving the contract back in her purse. "If you are unwilling to seize upon the future, then you will stay in your room until YOU ARE!"

Batting a waiter out of the way, she seized both siblings by the scruff of the neck and headed for the lobby.

They were almost at the foot of the stairs when—

"Excuse me, but I wonder, Miss Coggin, if I could

steal a few minutes of your time."

It was the brass salesman, a scruffy man who looked as if he could do with a lick, spit, and polish himself.

"No," Great-Aunt Beauregard said, stomping her foot upon the first tread.

The salesman stepped neatly in front of her.

"I wouldn't insist, only I've had a letter from my supplier, and it appears that we may be able to reach some kind of"—he leaned forward suggestively— "accommodation."

She paused. John's blood surged into life. If Great-Aunt Beauregard was busy downstairs, maybe they could—

"I have to put these things to bed," she insisted.

"Of course, of course," the brass salesman mewed. "I'll wait for you in the lounge."

"Double whisky," Great-Aunt Beauregard stated, "and none of your wishy-washy rocks."

She tightened her grip on John's collar and continued the march upstairs.

"We will finish this discussion when I return, do you understand?"

John nodded. Page would have done the same, but she was having a little trouble breathing.

"Good." They were now at the door of their room. Great-Aunt Beauregard opened it and unceremoniously thrust them inside. "Then I will be back in one hour. Do you hear me? *One hour.*"

She slammed the door shut. John heard the key twist in the lock and the sound of thunderous footsteps making their way down the hall. He waited until he could hear no more, and then he dove for the knapsack he'd packed for vacation.

"What are you doing?" Page asked as he dumped the contents on Great-Aunt Beauregard's bed and began tossing things on the floor.

"I'm packing. Quick, hand me your suitcase."

Page was confused, but she pulled her suitcase out of the closet and handed it to John. He wasted no time in dumping that on the bed as well.

"Are we going somewhere?" Page asked. John grunted. He was too busy assessing underwear options.

"Johnny." Page tugged on his sleeve. "Are we going somewhere?"

John nodded. "We're escaping."

Page gasped. "Now?"

"We can't stay here," John said, stuffing Page's socks on top of Walter Hancock's steam engine manual.

"But where are we going?" Page demanded.

"I don't know—maybe the circus." John pulled the knapsack cords tight. "But I'm not letting you become a dead man's hairdresser. C'mon." He slung the knapsack over his shoulder and grabbed Page's hand. "We've got to go."

He strode over to the balcony door and turned the

knob. Nothing happened. He turned again. Still nothing.

"Johnny, I don't think this is a good idea."

In desperation, John tugged and twisted as hard as he could, but it was no use. "She must have locked this one too. I can't move it."

Page sighed, more in relief than anything else. "Then we'll have to stay."

John looked at Page. Her face was bloodless and her eyes were drooping. He was almost tempted to give up too. Then he remembered the rouge and the lipstick, and he set his jaw.

"No!" he said, picking up Great-Aunt Beauregard's walking stick. "We're leaving."

And with that, he rammed the end of the walking stick into the pane of the balcony door. Shards of glass twinkled like snowflakes to the carpet.

"Johnny!" Page said breathlessly. "You broke the door."

But John was already battering the rest of the glass out of the frame. "Grab the footstool in the bathroom," he commanded. Page ran for it. In a minute, John was through the window and out onto the balcony.

"C'mon," he urged, holding out his hand for Page. She was looking at him funny.

"Is this going to be scary?"

John paused. Then he smiled.

"Not for the bravest girl I know."

CHAPTER
4

THAT DECIDED IT. Page practically dove out the window. John had to hold tight to her sleeve, otherwise she would have been over the balcony.

"Do we jump?" she asked once they were upright and peering over the balustrade. Underneath them, the back gardens seemed to stretch for miles into the twilight.

John peered around in panic. They couldn't jump. They'd break their legs. "We can tie all our clothes together," he said, setting his knapsack down on the tiles and pulling out one of his shirts. It looked awfully small.

"Or we could try climbing down that," Page said.

"What?"

"That."

She pointed over the balustrade. Wonder upon wonders, a trellis had been affixed to the side of the building, between their balcony and the one next door. The wisteria that was supposed to climb up it was nothing more than an asthmatic bunch of leaves, but John could have kissed each and every one.

"Do you think you can reach it?" he said, climbing over the balustrade and seizing hold of the trellis.

Page smiled and stretched out her hand toward him.

"Don't you know, Johnny? I'm going to be an acrobat."

Whomp! Whomp! Whomp! went a knock on the door.

"Excuse me, Miss Coggin, are you all right in there? One of our patrons thought they heard glass breaking. Miss Coggin?" *WHOMP! WHOMP! WHOMP!* "Miss Coggin?"

"Quick, Page, quick!" John said, seizing hold of her hands and hauling her over the railing. She was heavy, and for a brief moment he thought she might slip through his sweaty fingers. He could feel her going and then—

She caught the slats below him and began scampering down to the ground. John followed, adding a brand-new set of splinters to his palms.

"Now what?" Page asked when they had stumbled onto the gravel walkway.

John glanced to his right. Half the hotel and anyone on the terrace had a view of the entrance, which was full of arriving and departing carriages. And they couldn't go around to the left, or they'd run into the ocean.

"We'll go through the garden," John said confidently,

though his pulse was beating fast enough to burst his cuffs open. "And then we can sneak out the back."

He took Page's hand again and darted through a maze of irises.

"But," Page panted, "what will we do when we get on the other side?"

John didn't answer. He didn't know.

Around the manicured magnolias they went, treading over daisies and frightening frogs. Skirting the water-lily pond, they scaled the outcrops on the rock garden and skipped over a patch of ferns.

They soon came to a wrought iron fence with fearsome pikes stretching into the clouds. A rat could barely squeeze through the gap in the posts, let alone a boy.

"We can't get through there," Page said helpfully.

John began to run down the inside of the fence. Maybe there was a gardener's gate or a spot they could tunnel under. . . .

It didn't take them long to smack into a forgotten thicket of unripe raspberry bushes. John wanted to cry.

"Johnny, look, it's a ladybug."

Page pointed to a fat ladybug that was crawling over John's trousers. In the distance, John heard a shout. Then another.

"Page, we don't have time for this!" He tried to brush off the ladybug.

"No, Johnny, don't hurt it!" She pushed his hand away.

"You have to count the spots."

John tried to double back along the fence. If Great-Aunt Beauregard had discovered their footprints, then they had only minutes before they were found. But Page was not to be budged.

"It's important! You get a wish for each spot."

John yelled, "Fine! My first wish is that we get over that stupid fence!"

"Can I be of assistance?"

A bushel of frizzy red hair appeared in a clump of pink azaleas. Then the rest of Boz's face popped into view, the ugliest example of an exotic in full bloom.

"Salutations. You appear to be damselflies in distress."

"We're stuck," Page said.

"We're running away to the circus," John said.

"Naturally. Otherwise you would have attempted a more public point of departure."

"But there's no way through this fence." John tried to kick a post and bruised his shin instead.

"Not to worry," Boz said cheerfully, straightening up and tucking an azalea behind his ear. "If you follow me, I believe I can point you to a convenient exit."

Skipping, he led John and Page around the raspberry bushes and into a dark patch of firs.

"What are you doing here, anyway?" John asked. The faint murmur of human voices had become an angry buzz.

"Fritillaries!" Boz cried out.

"Fritillaries? What are those?"

"Various members of the family Nymphalidae, especially of the genera *Speyeria* and *Boloria*," Boz said.

John was about to ask him what that meant when Boz stopped short.

"The fruition of our good fortune."

John looked up. A teetering tower of flowerpots, wooden fruit crates, and rocks rose before them. As the tiniest breath of wind meandered through the firs, the whole edifice creaked and swayed in an agony of pain.

"What is that?" asked John, taking an involuntary step back.

"It's a princess castle!" Page cried.

"That," Boz said proudly, "is our method of egress."

"You built that?" asked John.

"With my humble hands. I considered a rope, of course, but I deemed that the young lady might find this solution more accessible."

A piece of crate fell off the side and barely missed striking John's head.

"It's incredible," John said despairingly.

Boz rubbed his nose with mock humility. "I am, as they say, a jack-of-all-shades."

"And what are we supposed to do with it?"

"We'll use it to get over the fence."

"Oh, no," John said, watching the tower wobble in the

breeze. "We're not going up that."

"My dear unfortunates," said Boz as the bellows of men could be heard in the distance, "I'm afraid you have no choice." He smiled and put a hand on John's shoulder.

"Now, if you could genuflect in the general direction of the grass." Boz pushed John down into a kneeling position. "And then plant your phalanges firmly in the plants." He continued to push until John was on all fours. "Then I will be able to ascend unto the celestial heavens."

And with that, Boz sprang onto John's back and launched himself onto a crate.

"Coming?"

Up the tower they scrambled, flowerpots slipping beneath their feet. The stones grew skinnier and the wood got rottener as they neared the top. Then, suddenly, they were there! Standing on a crate and sliding dangerously toward the tips of the spikes.

"*Sequimini me!*" Boz leaped into the air.

John and Page looked over the fence. Their new companion was lounging on the top of a fireman's ladder. A fireman's ladder that was attached to a brilliant red fire engine. An engine that was drawn by a pair of black stallions.

"What is that?" yelled John, grabbing onto Page as the tower lurched sideways.

Boz tilted his head in sympathy. He seemed to think John had lost his mind.

"It's a *fire engine*," he said very slowly and carefully. "They use it to help put fires out."

"I know that!" John almost shrieked. "But where did you get it?"

"Amusing anecdote, that," Boz began. "Involving a constipated Labrador and some elderflower cordial—"

"We don't have time!" Page squeaked as the tower began to keel over backward.

"Oh, well, then perhaps you'd better disembark from the bark," Boz said, hopping off the ladder and into the engine.

John and Page needed no prompting. They were on the ladder quicker than you can say KABOOM! Which is precisely the sound the tower made as it hit the ground, almost braining the approaching crowd and sending up a tornado of dust.

"Might I urge a little acceleration?" Boz called up. "We may have outstayed our welcome."

Down the ladder John and Page slid, toward the beautiful hunk of gleaming brass beneath them. The dust was still three feet thick between themselves and the fence, but clearing rapidly.

"So you stole—" John began.

"Borrowed, my dear boy, borrowed." Boz helped Page take a seat.

"You borrowed a fire engine?" John followed Page, landing with a thump.

"Well, they didn't appear to be using it at the time."

Boz flicked the reins. The stallions reared on their hind legs and came down charging. The engine bell clanged uncontrollably. The ladder fell off into the road. Only Page's hand stopped John from tumbling headfirst under the wheels.

"Isn't this magnificent?" Boz yelled. "Off we go, into the wild blue yonder, soaring high, out on the sly!"

Off they went, careening down the road, sending cats and roosters and barrels scattering before them. When John found enough balance to peek back at the fence, he could just spy the top of the canary in Great-Aunt Beauregard's hat. It appeared to be screaming.

"JOHN PEREGRINE COGGIN! I WILL ROAST YOUR GIBLETS FOR THIS!"

CHAPTER 5

"You know, I've never driven one of these before," Boz confessed. "I had assumed the sheer weight of the internal elements would affect its aerodynamic qualities, but it seems to handle quite well."

Boz yanked the engine around a corner, jolting Page's elbow into John's liver.

"If you've never driven one, then why did you steal—"

"Borrow."

"—borrow it?" asked John.

"Logic!" Boz exclaimed, urging the horses over a stone bridge and sending a flock of ducks squawking in protest. "The last refuge of the enlightened man. What method of conveyance can go as fast as it likes without fear of being stopped?"

"A fire engine—look out!" John yelled, and Boz turned

his attention to the large pile of manure lying in their path. He hauled on the reins and the horses skittered sideways, barely missing the steaming pile.

"Correct!" Boz smiled. "An inspired, if elementary, chain of deduction. And now we are off to find adventure in the evening air. Girls in white in a perfumed night where the lights are bright as the stars."

"How long will it take us to get to the circus?" John closed his eyes against the sight of the rutted road in front of them.

"A couple of hours," Boz answered jovially, bouncing in his seat as they took the first pothole at a gallop. "If fortune favors the brave, we might be in time for the late show. They have two on Fridays," he added, clonking his hand against John's skull, "when the barometric pressure is behaving itself."

"Johnny?"

"What is it, Page?"

"I think I'm going to throw up."

There is nothing like watching your younger sister vomit great quantities of peas and carrots over the side of a fire engine to make you doubt your sanity.

Yet once she was righted, Page insisted on enjoying the ride. She whooped and hollered and waved at the gulls as the engine barreled along the seashore.

John was less excited. He had gained enough breath to question whether being on a runaway vehicle driven by a long-winded maniac was such a good idea. Information was needed. Quickly.

"How long have you been with the Wandering Wayfarers?"

"The who?" Boz shouted back.

"The Wandering Wayfarers! The circus we might join!"

"Ah, yes. The name had somehow slipped the cogs of my mind."

Since they were making rapid progress toward their destination, John had difficulty believing this.

"I go back and forth and back again," Boz said, swaying in time with the engine. "Though I haven't set a pair of retinas upon Colonel Joe and his merry band for some months."

"But you're an acrobat with them," John protested.

"Am I?"

"That's what you said!" John smacked his hand on the seat.

"No need to ping the paintwork, my dear boy. If that's what I said, then that's what I said. Whether it has any firm tether to reality is, as they say, a whole 'nother cauldron of cod."

John chewed on his lip and studied Page's face.

"Are we going to be okay, Johnny?"

"We'll be fine," he tried to say quietly, but the noise from the road and the horses and Boz clanging the bell drowned him out.

"What?" she said.

"We'll be fine!"

Boz grinned and flung his arm around John's shoulder.

"Why, of course you will, my bonny wee bairns! By now, that formidable fortress of formaldehyde—your great-aunt—will have retreated to her discounted digs. There she will assemble the constabulary to pursue you. She will think it a mere doddle to reclaim the genetic remnants of her family.

"But she will be wrong!" Boz shouted, almost strangling John in his enthusiasm. "For she has not reckoned with the life force that springs eternal for the young at heart! Am I not right, comrades?"

"Boz," Page said slowly.

"Yes, my dear?"

"I think you're choking John."

"Oh, I do apologize," Boz said, releasing John's neck. John hacked and sputtered a little while Page patted him on the back. "Are you all right?"

"I'll be fine," croaked John. "In about three hours," he added wryly.

"I'm afraid we can't wait that long. We're here."

Under the slim curve of a crescent moon, a flea-bitten tent rose up from a fly-ridden field. Apart from an odd assortment of caravans and grazing horses, there was little to see except a faded canvas gate marked

Wande ing W yfar rs

along with an ancient cannon and a rusty barbed-wire fence around the entire enclosure. Laughter from within the tent indicated a show was in progress.

"Isn't she a pretty peach?" Boz sighed, reining in the horses. "Though I believe we've missed most of the second sitting."

Since John was finding it incredibly difficult to say anything nice, he responded by helping Page down from the seat.

"This place looks awful," Page said.

Boz feigned hurt.

"Well, I admit that the bloom of her youth has somewhat oxidized, but she is home for many a meandering mountebank."

He gestured to the fence.

"Shall we go under?"

"Why can't we go through the gate?" John demanded.

"On any other evening, I would agree with you," Boz said. "Only it happens that tonight, Alligator Dan is at the box office. And he may still be mad about the incident with the fire ants."

John was going to ask about the fire ants when Page cut him off.

"Alligator Dan is a funny name."

"And he, my fine friends, is only the first member of these self-proclaimed dirty tramps." Boz gallantly lifted the barbed wire for Page to crawl under. "Although I doubt that even the powers of bleach would help," he continued. "They're strung together with twine and a prayer by the good Colonel Joe."

Down came the barbed wire, pinning John to the ground.

"Now, we'll just pop our cerebelli under the big top to see if I can spot the man in charge."

John lifted a feeble hand.

"Oh, my dear boy," Boz lifted the fence once more. "Was that me?"

John was too busy removing a hunk of mud from his mouth to answer. When he finally had the means to reply, Boz and Page were already halfway across the field, making their way toward the big top.

John followed as fast as he could, but the pale light of the June evening made it difficult to see. He might have tripped over their decapitated forms if he hadn't spotted the light seeping under the tent. Dropping to his stomach next to his sister, he thrust his head under the flap.

A heady scent of popcorn smacked him full in the face. As a stream of soda percolated down his back, John realized they were under a bench set up for spectators. Between a pair of bowed legs, he caught a glimpse of a dirt ring backed by a red curtain.

Btwang. A discordant burst from a ukulele silenced the crowd. The curtain was dragged open to reveal a set of pretty teenage girls, dressed in band uniforms, marching in military fashion and twirling batons.

This wouldn't have been unusual except for the math.

For by John's count, they had two heads, four legs, and only *two* arms. From shoulder to hip, they were fused together.

"The Mimsy Twins," Boz noted.

"John, they're glued," Page whispered. John squeezed her arm to show her that he'd heard.

In spite of their adhesion, the Mimsy Twins were incredibly talented. John watched in awe as they performed an intricate tap dance, their batons crisscrossing high above their heads. A surge of joy rushed through him. So this was what the circus was like!

Up, up went the pinwheels of light . . .

Out went John, yanked backward by his feet.

"Colonel not in attendance," Boz explained. "We'll proceed to the potentate's fire."

There was no time for John to argue. Off they went again, trotting toward the dim flare of a bonfire. Stumbling and bumbling, John felt his left foot sink into a squishy mound and tried not to imagine what it was.

"Remember to let my powers of oratory persuade him," Boz instructed as they drew nearer to the fire. "Oh, and keep your fingers away from the dogs."

"Dogs?" John asked, but the baying of hounds interrupted him. A pair of slavering German shepherds rose up from nowhere and charged. Boz scrambled onto John's back as John tried to thrust Page behind him.

Ruff! Snarfff! Raaarrk! went the dogs. Then they stretched their mouths wide, giving John a glimpse of rows of lethal teeth. He closed his eyes in terror.

"Hello, puppies. It's nice to meet you."

John opened his eyes. Page had stepped out from behind him and was extending her small, delicate fingers toward jaws that could easily devour her arm.

But the dogs didn't swallow her arm. Instead they wagged their tongues, dropped their ears, and rolled over in delight. Page knelt down in the dust to scratch their bellies.

"Heckuva animal trainer you got there, Boz."

CHAPTER 6

THE DREGS OF Colonel Joe's coffee made a sizzling hiss as they landed on the edge of the fire. From behind the flames the old soldier limped, his left leg playing catch-up with his right. He still bore the ramrod posture and handlebar mustache of military service, but his blue uniform had long since faded, and his hair was snowy white. He smiled at Page and frowned at Boz.

"You've got more nerve than a lock-jawed mongoose coming back here, Boz."

Boz clambered down off John's back and bowed.

"Profuse apologies, Colonel, but I was unavoidably detained."

"Where did you dig up the sprouts?" he asked, sniffing suspiciously. At that precise moment, John became aware he had trod in a large patty of horse poo.

"I've brought them to be acrobats," Boz said, pushing the Coggins forward. "Names of John and Page. They're blithe and lithe and full of vim."

With careful deliberation, Colonel Joe rammed his fingers into his ear and pulled out a wad of beeswax. Using a jackknife, he neatly sliced off a section, popped the wax into his mouth, and stuffed the remainder back in its storage space. Then he slowly began to chew.

It took about the same amount of time for him to complete this procedure as it did for John to realize that the Colonel's ear was completely fake.

"Nope, sorry, can't help you," he said finally, pinging a tiny BB of wax at the tip of John's shoe.

Page grabbed John's hand in panic.

"But they're so eager to please," Boz protested. "And think of the appeal to the eight-to-twelve demographic!"

"Nothing doing," Colonel Joe retorted. "Already got a full complement of acts, and I won't need more until next summer. Sorry, kids, but you'll have to go back to your ma and pa, or whoever you've run away from."

He turned back to the fire.

"We can't!" John exclaimed, and a puzzled look appeared in the lee of Colonel Joe's bushy eyebrows.

"What's that?"

"We can't go back." John rummaged desperately in his head for a reason that might convince the Colonel. "If we do, we'll end up like the living dead."

Colonel Joe paused.

"The living dead?" he asked, leaning over the fire to stare long and hard at John. John looked back at him without blinking.

"Yes, sir."

Colonel Joe straightened up and glanced at Boz.

"You prompt him?"

Boz shook his head.

"Explain," Colonel Joe demanded.

John swallowed.

"I guess, it's just . . ." He dug deep and unexpectedly found a memory of his father: *I left Pludgett to follow my dreams. I knew if I stayed, I'd never be able to tell my own stories or explore the world beyond. Trust your heart, John my lad—it's the only compass you have.*

"Well?"

"If we go back to where we came from, we'll be trapped," John told Colonel Joe. "We'll be alive on the outside but dead on the inside."

"So why the circus?"

John thought of the spinning twirls of light.

"Because here you're always free."

"Well, now." Colonel Joe grinned and drummed his fingers on his bum leg. "I don't know if you know it, but you've done gone and saved your rawhide. In the book of Joe, there ain't nothing more important than a life lived free."

"JOHN PEREGRINE COGGIN! Present yourself immediately!"

John blanched. Page blanched. Boz may have blanched, but it was impossible for anyone to tell. He had plunged under a blanket.

"Lie down flat on the ground," Colonel Joe commanded. "Keep your pates cocked sideways."

John and Page obeyed without question.

"Rufus, Rudolphus—to your beds."

John felt a hot, rancid breath on his neck. One of the German shepherds had stretched itself over his entire body and laid its head on his own.

"Johnny," he heard Page whisper.

"Shhh," he answered.

Squelch, squelch, squelch. Though John could see nothing through the suffocating fur of Rudolphus, he knew the sound of Great-Aunt Beauregard's footsteps all too well. She was coming for him. And she was *mad*.

"Where is he?"

Colonel Joe yawned. "Who are you?"

Great-Aunt Beauregard sniffed. "My name is Beauregard Pickett Coggin and I am looking for my great-nephew and -niece. They were kidnapped from Peddington's Practical Hotel by a rogue operative driving a stolen fire engine."

A juicy wad of spit hit the ground near John's eyeball.

"And why do you think they're here?"

Great-Aunt Beauregard erupted. "Because there's a ruddy big fire engine parked outside your two-bit establishment, that's why!"

A hairsbreadth of a moment, then . . .

"Arrived with no one in it."

It was a bad lie extremely well told. On his back, John could feel Rudolphus's massive heart thumping in time with his own. Would Great-Aunt Beauregard believe it?

She would.

To a point.

"That may well be, but the hotel detective suggested that this operative—a ferrety fellow with ginger hair—was also connected with your establishment."

Colonel Joe spat again, to cover Boz's squeak of protest.

"If you're speaking about Boz, he's a huckster and a half. Discovered that last year when he blew up our big top. Came to me yesterday asking for work and I tossed him out on his backside. Just like him to play a practical joke in revenge.

"But I'll have you know, Miss Coggin"—and here Colonel Joe spoke very, very slowly—"when it comes to protecting my troupe from those who want to harm them, I ain't fooling with blanks."

There was a pause.

"Listen." Great-Aunt Beauregard's voice dropped to a conspiratorial whisper. "I don't want to be an inconvenience. You and I are men of the world. If you should happen to run across a golden-haired girl and a chinless boy, you'll let me know, won't you? I'll make it worth your while."

"They that important?"

"Important?" She regained her timpani. "I have trained that boy up in the manner befitting the family business since the day his parents died! I have clothed him, fed him, and imparted to him the secrets of the grave. His destiny is to be the best craftsman of death in Pludgett, and no one"—here John knew she must be priming her lungs for detonation—"I mean *no one* says no to the family business!"

In the warm sauna of Rudolphus's fur, John's skin went cold. Colonel Joe merely chuckled.

"You got an odd idea of family," he said.

"Oh, what would you know about it, you, you . . . Gypsy!"

Squelch, squelch, squelch. Away went the sound of Beauregard's footsteps, back across the field.

"Don't move," Colonel Joe muttered. For a long while John lay under the dog, trying to get the heat back into his body. The murmurs from the big top rose and peaked and faded. Soon there were none.

"Okeydokey, out you come."

From out under Rufus came the frightened face of his sister. From out under the blanket came the bony butt of Boz.

"Look, about Great-Aunt Beauregard—" John began as Page seized hold of his hand.

Colonel Joe lobbed the remainder of his wax into the fire.

"Think I got the gist. You and your sister are more than welcome to join us for a spell."

John's hopes soared.

"But we can't have your names on playbills and such. Not with a poleax like that on the lookout for you. You'll have to earn your keep in other ways than performing. Boz."

Boz snapped to attention.

"You game to work with Betsy again?"

Boz flinched, but only slightly. "I am yours to command."

"Then take our new recruits away and find 'em someplace to sleep." Colonel Joe paused and patted Rufus on the head. "I'll see to it that your great-aunt finds the right road back."

And with a hint of a satisfied smile curling his mustache, he turned and limped off into the night.

"C'mon." Boz tugged at their sleeves. "We'll ensconce you in a nearby barn. Then, when dawn breaks, we shall martial our metabolisms for a new plan of attack."

The two siblings followed Boz away from the fire and toward a tall building under the shadow of a pine tree.

"Boz, who's Betsy?" asked Page.

"Oh, merely my partner in a display of unparalleled skill. Mind the bats," he added, pushing open the barn door.

A symphony of whapping wings greeted them. When John looked up, he glimpsed a swarm of black. The animals appeared to be in a feeding frenzy.

"Don't worry," Boz said, "they're simply dyspeptic. You two can rest over here on these hay bales, and I'll come and retrieve you in the morning." Throwing a jaunty wave, he vanished into the dark.

Petrified, John lay down on a hay bale and listened to the bats circling above him. Page did the same. She had yet to release his hand.

"Johnny," she whispered.

"What is it?"

"I'm scared."

"Me too," John whispered back. "But it will be morning soon, and then we'll be okay. I promise."

"Okay," Page said, but she didn't sound convinced.

John closed his eyes and tried to forget where he was. Page squeezed his hand.

"Johnny," she whispered.

"What?"

"Are we really going to join the circus?"

What other choice did they have? thought John. "Yes."

"What are we going to do if we can't be acrobats?"

John attempted to make his voice sound confident.

"I'm not sure. I bet I can work on fixing the caravans

or building the stage. Colonel Joe will give me some-thing. Don't worry—Great-Aunt Beauregard won't be able to find us."

"Will we be here forever?"

"Maybe." John was having trouble thinking any fur-ther than breakfast. "I guess it depends if we fit in."

"Tell me one of Dad's stories."

"No, it's past midnight. Go to sleep."

There was a fraction of a pause, then . . .

"Johnny?"

"What?"

"I can't sleep."

John took a deep breath. "Try to think of something that makes you happy."

"Like lilies of the valley?"

"Sure, like lilies of the valley."

Page was silent, and John settled back into the prickly hay. He was teetering on the verge of drifting off into his dreams when—

"Johnny?"

"What is it?"

"You stink."

Heaving the biggest sigh known to man, John pried his hand from Page's and stomped over to the door, bump-ing into hay bales all the way. Then, with an enormous heave, he hurled his shoes into the night.

CHAPTER 7

"Up and at 'em, troops! The back of a new day is already broken, and time marches on!"

Boz blew into the barn like a category-five hurricane and came to rest at John's feet. "Where are the foundations of your perambulation?" His baffled face collapsed even farther into itself.

"Where are the what?" John asked blearily. The bright summer sun was making fireflies of the dust around Page's hair.

"Your shoes, young man, your shoes."

"I threw them outside."

"Well, find them! We go, we see, we conquer!"

John found his shoes lodged in a crabapple tree and spent ten minutes running them under the pump. The smell improved somewhat, but Boz insisted that they could not wait another moment.

"Least dallied, soonest rallied. Come along now, come along."

So, with a dead-on imitation of Great-Aunt Beauregard's squelch, John accompanied Page and Boz to the big top.

In the bleached light of morning, the tent had lost what little glamour it had shown the previous night. The stage and curtain had been removed, and in the center stood a peeling pole. Around the pole was a trampled ring of dirt. Around the patch of dirt were ranged the rickety benches.

And on those benches were sprawled, in varying states of consciousness, the Wandering Wayfarers.

There was a wizened elderly lady entwined in a six-foot beard and snoring lustily. There was a scrawny whippet of a man singing lullabies to a pug dog in his arms while a purple pig sulked at his knee. There was a woman striped with the white worms of old facial scars shuffling cards at supersonic speed. There was an olive-skinned man covered in scales from his chest to his waist, curled up with a ukulele.

And then there were the Mimsy Twins. They were tapping out a complicated routine on the benches.

"Come in, come in! All comers welcome!"

An enormously tall man with big bandy legs rose like a balloon and bounded over to them. His hat was pink, his pants were high, and his upside-down pipe was tilted rakishly behind his ear.

"Name's Gentle Giant Georgie. Emcee. And you are . . . ?"

"Wayfarers," said a voice, "meet Dung Boy and Sprout."

The Wandering Wayfarers scrambled to their feet. From the back of the tent came Colonel Joe, trailing a cloud of onion fumes behind him. When he reached the center pole, he looked straight at John and pointed to a place by his side.

"Time to trot," Boz whispered, poking them both in the back.

They trotted. When they reached Colonel Joe, he swiveled his finger. They turned to face the benches.

"Psst!" Boz hissed. "Bow!"

John and Page bowed respectfully.

"Dung Boy and Sprout, meet Mister Missus Hank." The bearded lady scowled. "Porcine Pierre, his dog, Priscilla, and his pig, Frank." Pig and dog nodded. "Tiger Lil." The scarred lady smiled. "Alligator Dan." The scaly man frowned. "And the Mimsy Twins." The girls giggled.

"What will they b-b-be g-g-good for?" Alligator Dan stuttered.

"They're pretty scrawny," Mister Missus Hank chipped in.

"The boy's kinda feral." Porcine Pierre smirked through a set of sharp white teeth. "I could use him as an understudy. Priscilla's got a wicked cough."

"Quiet!" Colonel Joe said. The room fell silent. "Sprout has a knack with animals, so she'll be working to feed and exercise the dogs and horses. Got that, Sprout?"

Colonel Joe looked at Page. She nodded quickly.

"And Boz tells me that Dung Boy here knows his way around a set of tools, so he's on props. We'll sort his induction out later. Questions?"

John had a few hundred. Like why the Colonel had decided to torture him by calling him Dung Boy. Like where Porcine Pierre got off comparing him to Priscilla. Like what an induction meant. But he didn't know which to ask first. The rest of the Wayfarers weren't burdened with same indecision.

"How come we weren't consulted?" Mister Missus Hank huffed. "You know as well as I do that all major decisions must be made by the group."

"Special circumstances," Colonel Joe replied. "Got a situation that needs"—he winked at John—"remedying."

Now John realized why the Colonel was calling him Dung Boy. It meant that the Wayfarers would never be able to reveal his real name.

"How long?" Alligator Dan shot back.

"As long as they're useful. If they're dead weight, you've got my full permission to chuck 'em out. Any objections to that?"

I have one! John wanted to shout. The Wayfarers merely shook their heads.

"Then I'll leave you to get acquainted," Colonel Joe said, and disappeared through the flap.

"Come on over, sweethearts," Gentle Giant Georgie rumbled. "And welcome to the family."

John and Page walked toward the benches and were immediately surrounded.

"Ooooh, what lovely hair you have," Tiger Lil said, stroking Page's head. "Corn silk."

"Won't sweep up much with that," sniffed Mister Missus Hank.

"Let us see! Let us see!" a pair of voices cried out. Up close, John realized that the Mimsy Twins were older than he had first thought, more in their mid-twenties than their mid-teens.

"Hello," the twins uttered in unison, holding out their hands.

"I'm Mabel," said the one on the left.

"And I'm Minny," added the one on the right.

"Hello," John said awkwardly, shaking both hands in turn.

"How do you go to the bathroom?" Page asked.

"When we have to," Mabel replied.

"But what happens when you sit down?"

Mabel and Minny looked at each other and burst into laughter.

"She thinks we're real!" they cried simultaneously. And with mischievous grins, they started to unbutton their coats, squirming to free themselves from their sleeves. When they had finished, two girls now stood in front of John and Page, each with a stump where an arm would be.

"Look, Ma!" Mabel said, shaking her stump. "No hand!"

"But you're really good dancers. Why do you use a disguise?" John asked.

Minny's laugh was tinged with pain.

"Who's going to pay top dollar to see a cripple in a red dress?"

"Besides"—Mabel smiled fiercely—"now you get two for the price of one."

"And where do you come from?" Tiger Lil asked Page.

"We're—"

But John cut her off. The less their new comrades knew about the family business, the better. "We're Boz's cousins."

Alligator Dan snorted, plucked a scale off his chest, and flicked it at Boz.

"You don't look like b-b-bloodsucking leeches."

"I resent that. I come from a distinguished lineage," Boz retorted.

"So do cockroaches." Porcine Pierre snickered.

"Now, now," Gentle Giant Georgie said, silencing the crowd with a wave of his pudgy fingers. "Let's keep our bile to ourselves."

"Have you always wanted to join the circus?" Tiger Lil continued.

"Kind of." John hesitated. "Boz told us about it."

"You'll have to do better than 'kind of' for your induction." Porcine Pierre smirked through his needled teeth.

"What's that?" asked Page.

"It's a test," said Mister Missus Hank. "To see if you're good enough to be a Wayfarer."

"You have to p-p-prove that you can earn money," Alligator Dan corrected. "Using your special talents."

"Like what?"

Dan whipped his ukulele over his shoulder and began playing "Turkey in the Straw." At the first note of music, Priscilla barked twice and reared up on her hind paws. Then she danced an Irish jig.

"Isn't she a beauty?" said Porcine Pierre. "Trained her from a baby."

Jealous of the attention his partner was receiving, Frank head-butted John in the shins.

"Pick a card," Tiger Lil said to Page, holding out a spread deck. Page picked a card—and the rest of the deck vanished into thin air. Gone. John was flabbergasted. He looked at Page's card. She was holding the joker.

"We do our best to please." Tiger Lil smiled, pulling the cards one by one from Mister Missus Hank's beard.

"Don't worry," said Gentle Giant Georgie. "We give everyone a couple of months to get good at their skills.

Then we see if the public is willing to pay."

"It's how we stay independent," Mabel said. "Everyone shares the work, everyone shares the profits."

"All for one and one for all," Minny added.

"So what can you do?" Mister Missus Hank demanded. "Apart from grimace?"

John paused.

"Why, haven't you heard? Dung Boy is an inventor par excellence!" Boz cut in. "The future maker, the schemer of your dreams. This man is the world expert on Hancock's steam engineering. He even has a manual!"

John could have cheerfully kneed Boz in the nether parts. "How do you know about the manual?" he hissed.

"I may have rummaged through your bag," Boz whispered back. "You should probably invest in new socks."

Alligator Dan sniffed.

"I'll b-b-believe you're an engineer when I see it."

"He's good!" Page interjected.

"In the meantime," Tiger Lil intervened, "I know you're going to be very useful."

"If you're working on props," said Mister Missus Hank, stroking her beard, "you can start by making me a better comb. This thing's been knotted up since January."

She shook her head vigorously, and a toy train, a large dead wasp, and an assortment of coins fell from her beard and ricocheted off the floor. Mabel and Minny immediately began fighting over one of the coins.

"Oh, no, you don't," challenged Porcine Pierre. "Frank has been waiting for a hip bath for a year. You know how bad his rheumatics get when he's exposed to salt air."

"Salt him up into a slab of b-b-bacon and you won't have any more trouble with his rheumatics," Alligator Dan quipped.

Porcine Pierre didn't bother to waste a reply. He simply shoved Dan to the ground.

"G-g-get this p-p-pork lover off me!" Dan shrieked as Porcine Pierre bit into Dan's scales with his sharp teeth. Hearing this, Minny and Mabel ceased tugging on the coin and began tugging on Porcine Pierre's arms instead. This had the result of making Pierre look like a demented seagull refusing to let go of a dead fish.

"Children, children!" Gentle Giant Georgie admonished, trying to grab Alligator Dan's collar and pull him away from the melee. Unfortunately, Dan's only reaction was to seize Georgie's leg and refuse to let go. Georgie began to fall, entangling himself in Mister Missus Hank's beard as he went down.

"May I drop a small grain of sand in your shell-like?" Boz whispered into John's ear just after he had jumped to avoid Porcine Pierre's airborne kick. "This may be an appropriate moment to make a well-timed exit."

John looked for Page, but she was already beating a hasty retreat with Tiger Lil.

"Attend to my dorsal fin and follow me!" Boz said,

scooting between Georgie's legs. John followed, crawling on his hands and knees through the thicket of limbs to reemerge in the sunshine.

"There now," Boz said, leaping to his feet and brushing himself off. "Welcome to our happy little tribe."

"Are they going to kill each other?" John asked as a high-pitched shriek from Mister Missus Hank made the tent pole shiver.

"No, no," Boz tutted, "of course not. They'll be right as a fine summer's rain in nanoseconds."

John wasn't sure what a nanosecond was, but he didn't think it would be nearly long enough to turn that fight into a fine summer rain. Especially when he saw Colonel Joe heading toward them with a giant sledgehammer in his hand.

Boz leaned nonchalantly against one of the exterior ropes. It was vibrating.

"Good morning, my lord, liege, and master." Boz did his hybrid curtsy bow to Colonel Joe. "Lovely day to appreciate the constitutional sights."

"Boz, what is going on?"

A massive crash supplied the answer.

"Dung Boy?" Colonel Joe demanded.

John almost wished he was back in the coffin workshop.

"They all wanted me to make props for them. And then Alligator Dan insulted Pierre's pig."

As if in response, Frank came streaking out of the tent, crying and oinking. Colonel Joe watched the purple tail wiggle off into the distance, and then he turned to John.

"Let me give you a tip I picked up in the army." Colonel Joe lowered his voice. "If you value your skull, it's generally best to keep your head off the parapet. Understood?"

John nodded.

"Boz."

Boz sprang forward and knelt at Colonel Joe's feet. "Sire."

Colonel handed Boz the sledgehammer. It hit the ground with a thump. "We're breaking camp. Show Dung Boy how to strike the tents and the caravans. I'll sort out the ruckus."

"I stand and obey." Boz's attempt at saluting with the sledgehammer was thwarted by its weight. Boz went backward. The sledgehammer went nowhere.

Events were happening far too quickly for John. He'd barely said hello, and already people were talking about inductions and dung boys and hip baths. It was a little overwhelming for a boy who'd spent the last six years ensconced in sawdust.

"Wait!" cried John.

Irritated, Colonel Joe paused at the flap of the tent. "What?"

John summoned his meager courage. "Where are we going?"

Colonel Joe looked to Boz. "You want to tell him the route?"

Boz stuck his finger in the air triumphantly. "West! To the land of the free and the home of the brave. South for the winter and north for the spring! We cover the country."

That sounded promising to John. If, that is, he and Page made it that far.

"What about Great-Aunt Beauregard?"

Colonel Joe cocked an eyebrow and chuckled. "Oh, I wouldn't worry 'bout her much. She'll be awfully tied down for the next couple of months."

"So we're safe?" John asked.

Colonel Joe pondered the word.

"Depends on what you mean by safe," he mused. "Despite what you might be thinking, I ain't got much control over the decisions of the Wayfarers. Like me, they all have their reasons for avoiding official interference. Risk their livelihoods, or cross them the wrong way, and they'll feed you to the wolves." He grinned. "Something to bear in mind next time anyone gets to arguing about pigs."

"Huzzah!" cried Boz as Colonel Joe limped off into the big top. "Once more we sail upon the seas of humanity!"

"Would any of them really feed us to the wolves?" John asked.

"Melodramatic twaddle," Boz passed John the handle of the sledgehammer. "The Colonel fancies himself the lead troubadour in the magical mystery tour of life. Pay him no heed."

With every fiber in his muscles protesting, John managed to heave the sledgehammer onto his shoulder.

"What do you think he did to Great-Aunt Beauregard?" panted John.

"I have found through a process of trial and punishment that it is best not to question the ways of Colonel Joe. But enough of the past." Boz blew a raspberry at the rising sun. "Sound the trumpets and strike the drums, look out world, here we come!"

CHAPTER 8

"LADIES AND GENTLEMEN, boys and girls, kings and worms, welcome to the Wandering Wayfarers! Tonight you will be flabbergasted, gobsmacked, gin-cracked, and stupefied by the sights we are about to show. So sit straight, lean back, or lie flat and put your hands together for the one, the only, the Mimsy Twins!"

A burst of spattered applause and a hiccup greeted this announcement.

"You ready, Mabel?"

"Go, go, go!"

John pulled Page against him as the Mimsy Twins rushed past them backstage. The moth-eaten curtain billowed in the sisters' wake.

"John?" whispered Page.

"What?"

"This is even better than stories!"

It certainly was up there, John admitted to himself. How many people got to watch the circus before going to bed?

Not many. Nor were there many, he guessed, whose fortnight had been so jam-packed with activity. While the batons twirled and Priscilla sang, John went over the surprising events of the past two weeks.

To begin with, the Coggins now lived in a caravan. Sure, it was a sway-backed specimen with a creaky floor, a flight of shallow stairs, and dust to kingdom come, but it was *their very own.* There were a couple of bunks for sleeping and a couple of workbenches for props. Page was particularly fond of the ceiling, which was decorated with fading stars and planets, each one encrusted with gold paint.

"It used to belong to a diseased fortune-teller," Boz explained to John. "It's rumored she expired with her last respire in your bunk."

Secondly, John was building something other than coffins. Every morning he sat himself down at a workbench covered in Boz's half-sucked lollipops and waited for the onslaught:

"Dung Boy, we need a new lid on the long drop." This from Mister Missus Hank, who refused to explain where the old one had gone.

"Dung Boy, I'd like you to make me a box where I can

hack myself in two." This from Tiger Lil, who was practicing a new routine.

"Dung Boy, I appear to have ripped a hole in my bottom—could you mend it?" This from Gentle Giant Georgie, who was holding a pair of voluminous striped pants.

John would mend and tend and stitch until his fingers bled. His efforts weren't always a success—Alligator Dan getting wedged in a faulty trapdoor had been an unfortunate episode—but it was excitement beyond belief compared to caskets. All the pent-up streams of his imagination were busting through the dams. John's brain was being flooded with new ideas.

Thirdly, and for the first time in his life, he had a friend. Granted, this friend was about as useful as a fungus-infected cucumber when it came to work, but you can't have everything.

"Here's my theory on manual labor," Boz told John not long after their arrival. He had sprawled himself out on a bunk and was cracking peanuts in his mouth. "It's the one truly noble profession left to mankind. What could be purer of heart than a man raising a roof above his squalling babes? A woman tilling the earth to put a hunk of buggy cabbage on the table? Or a bairn bent over double while he fashions a marionette from a collection of scraps and twigs?"

John, who was attempting to string together a puppet

for Tiger Lil, looked up through sweating eyelids and grimaced. "Then why don't you do it?"

Boz smiled and tossed a peanut at John.

"For the simple reason that I am not worthy. Since you have come, I have learned I am but a hock-fisted hack, a scrap, man's offcut, not fit to touch the tools so hallowed by sacrifice."

To be fair to the speaker, there was some truth in these words. Even Frank was aware that whatever Boz touched turned into an immediate catastrophe. And since John found it easy enough to make mistakes on his own, it was simpler to work when Boz was nowhere to be found.

Which was quite often. Like a demented hummingbird, Boz flitted in and out of camp at every hour of the day, occasionally stumbling in at dawn singing nonsense limericks. If he wasn't doing ecstatic dance moves in his sleep, he might be painting his toenails, stealing cheese sandwiches, or monitoring thunderstorms from the apex of the big top.

He was, in a word, unpredictable.

"Ladies and gentlemen, if you will direct your feet to the side of the enclosure, we have a special surprise for you!"

John was jerked out of his reverie by Page's tug on his arm. Gentle Giant Georgie was back onstage and pointing to the open flap in the tent.

"Quick, John! They're going to do Betsy!" Page whispered.

For days, Colonel Joe had been promising the Coggins they would see Boz and his partner in action. John could hardly believe it was finally going to happen.

Dashing out through the back of the big top, John and Page joined the meager crowd in the field. A U-shaped barrier had been constructed with fence posts and twine. And an ancient cannon lay dormant in the middle of the enclosure.

There was a murmur, a prodding, a flare. Into the center of the U stepped Colonel Joe, a blazing torch in his hand.

"Stand back, now, stand back! Give Betsy some room."

The crowd shuffled closer to the barrier. John got an elbow in his appendix. Page stood on her tiptoes to see. Colonel Joe brushed the tip of the cannon with his torch and—

BOOM!

The firework exploded at the exact same time as Boz began a soaring parabola over the clover. A flaming jet trail pursued him, his hair blown back by the speed of flight. As John watched, Boz overshot the landing net with mathematical precision and disappeared behind a patch of reeds.

"Boz!" John shouted.

"Where'd he go?" asked Page.

A couple of people in the audience clapped. Four of them booed. One man got a broadside for attempting to touch the cannon.

"Nobody lays a finger on Betsy!" barked Colonel Joe.

"C'mon!" John grabbed his sister's hand. "We've got to find Boz."

The siblings took off across the field. In John's head, he was going through all the possible fatal injuries. Broken leg. Fractured skull. Shattered ribs. By the time they'd clambered over a rickety fence, he was bracing himself to build a coffin.

Only to discover Boz emerging from a duck pond, a large frog perched contentedly on his head.

"Are you okay?" John demanded.

"Oh, right as the rain in Coltrane." Boz shooed the frog onto a tree branch. "Merely a miscalculation on my weight-to-height ratio. I shall indulge in pâté de fois gras for a few days, and all will be right with the world."

"What does that mean?" inquired Page.

Boz chuckled.

"It means I get to eat more. Shall we join the others?"

Together, the trio jogged back toward the tent. Colonel Joe was herding the last members of the audience back through the flaps. Some of them appeared to be trying to escape from watching the second half of the show.

"So how come the cannon didn't kill you?" asked Page.

"Kill me?" Boz laughed. "Why, there's no gunpowder left in good old Betsy." He patted the barrel. "The Colonel had her rigged up with coiled springs when he brought her back from the war. The incendiaries and associated works are just for show."

Intrigued, John crouched down to examine the interior. It looked like the springs were hidden behind a metal plate. If he could just get a look at the setup, he might be able to adjust the tension and prevent Boz from overshooting . . .

"Which p-p-part of 'don't touch' did you miss?"

John stood up. At times like this, it was very tempting to tell Alligator Dan exactly where to stick his scales.

"It's coming on ten. You two should b-b-be in b-b-bed."

"But I want to hear Mister Missus Hank's stories about allergic chipmunks," Page protested. "And watch Priscilla dancing the polka and see Tiger Lil make the tent pole disappear—"

"And I want to talk to Pierre about the hip bath," John added.

"Now!"

When it comes to self-determination, there's only so much an eleven-year-old can accomplish. The Coggins went to bed.

CHAPTER 9

IT WAS WELL they did, for the next day the circus was off again.

And the next day.

And the next.

Just as Boz had promised, the Wayfarers headed west with the summer sun. They performed on the outskirts of mill towns and in the middle of cornfields. They squatted near slag heaps from coal mines and at the feet of mountains with snow still icing the peaks. They never stopped.

Which meant that John never stopped. When he wasn't working on props, he was helping Page tear down tents or hitch up horses. Life became a constant round of coming and going.

"Idle hands make for empty bellies," Colonel Joe noted.

For the first month, all this activity was kind of fun. If you didn't like the place you were in, you headed for another. If you couldn't tolerate the snarks of Alligator Dan or Porcine Pierre, you spent the next day learning to read palms with Mabel and Minny. Every hour was a surprise.

Yet as the days wore on, John began to notice the same things on the way out of town. The boys playing baseball. The old dogs on the stoops. The families on Sunday carriage drives. However much Boz babbled about the joys of the open road, John couldn't help but wonder what it would feel like to stay still.

Then there was the little matter of Great-Aunt Beauregard. However many times Colonel Joe reassured him that she was long gone, John remained edgy. He knew that no woman born of her ilk would give up on the family legacy that easily.

In his paranoia, John skulked behind trees to scan the faces of the crowds. He asked Gentle Giant Georgie to watch out for women with dead birds in their hats. He checked over and over that Page was tucked up safe in her bunk.

But three weeks passed, four, and there was still no sign of an avenging aunt. Without meaning to, John began to think that he might have a future with the Wayfarers.

"Johnny, did you hear? I get to take care of *all* the animals now!"

It was a hot afternoon in July, and John was painting roses on a baby carriage for Frank. They were a nauseating shade of pink.

"I'm supposed to brush down the horses every morning." Page was wheezing from her run to the caravan. "And Gentle Giant Georgie says he'll teach me how to ride one. And Mabel and Minny are going to give me some of their dresses, even though they don't have the right number of sleeves, but Mister Missus Hank said that she'd try and make them into something that would fit me.

"Oh, but I haven't told you the best thing! Look what Tiger Lil gave me!"

She dashed to her bunk and returned a minute later holding up a raggedy bear.

"What's that?" John said sarcastically.

"It's a bear, Johnny," Page explained, missing the sneer. "It used to be Tiger Lil's. She said she was keeping it for somebody very special." Without waiting for his reply, Page put the bear down next to him. "I'll be back. I have to go feed Priscilla."

After Page was gone, John wondered why he had snapped at his sister. After all, it was only an old bear. He stared at the black bead of an eye for a minute.

And then he remembered.

It looked like his teddy.

The one his mother used to tuck into his bed at night. The one with the torn ear and the ribbon sewn round its neck. Like most five-year-old boys, John couldn't sleep without his teddy. Wherever it might be—in the garden, under a bureau, hanging from a tree—he needed to have it by his side.

He had been holding his teddy the morning his parents died. He remembered clutching its paw as Great-Aunt Beauregard came barreling down the stairs. A reek of wet wool and turpentine accompanied her.

"Well, they're definitely dead," she said. "Checked twice."

John refused to reply. He was concentrating on the snowflakes scurrying past the window.

"Good thing you're quiet. Don't approve of chatty Cathies. Or Cathcarts."

Still John said nothing.

"Got your sister locked and loaded. You'd better be a deft hand at diapers, young man."

John squeezed his teddy. A fatal mistake.

"Ah. Can't have that endangering the family line," Great-Aunt Beauregard carped, yanking the bear from John's arms. "Germs."

And with a casual flip of her hand, she'd tossed his teddy into the living-room fire.

John put down the pink paintbrush and sighed. Over the years, he'd somehow managed to bury that particular memory. But it was only a bear, he told himself. Only a stupid old bear.

Shutting up shop for the day, John plodded down the steps. The sun was sitting low, tickling the leaves of the trees with a warm yellow. Against the white of the tent, he spotted the silhouettes of a few Wayfarers seated on a couple of benches. Moving closer, he could see Page playing patty-cake with a mother and her baby in the grass.

"Sitcha yourself down, Dung Boy," Colonel Joe called out as John approached. Gentle Giant Georgie was counting the day's take while Alligator Dan retuned his ukulele. "You look like you've got your thinking cap on too tight. What's on your mind?"

Instead of sitting, John kicked at a tent peg. It wouldn't budge. "How come we don't play in bigger towns? There must be lots more people; we could have longer runs. At least they'd pay for their seats."

Gentle Giant Georgie tapped his pipe thoughtfully against his knee. "That's true enough, Colonel. We don't play the big towns."

"Then why not?" John insisted. "We could even find an old place in a city and fix it up as a theater of sorts. Then we wouldn't have to keep moving all the time."

"What's the matter?" Alligator Dan plucked at a string. "Scared of g-g-getting b-b-blisters on your heels?"

"No," John retorted with vigor. "It's just that I don't see the point of working this hard to entertain people if you're always going to be moving on."

A shriek of laughter, that laughter that sounded so much like his father's, rang out. The beautiful bouncing baby had spat up green goo all over Page's shirt.

"Fail your induction, b-b-boyo, and you won't have to worry about moving at all."

The induction! John had completely forgotten about the Wayfarers' test of his moneymaking skills.

"We've just been talking about it." Colonel Joe plucked a wad of beeswax from his false ear and rolled it thoughtfully between his fingers. "I'm looking at the end of September for your public presentation."

John felt the sweat spring to his forehead. September was awfully close. "Can't I keep making props?"

"Like the amazing trapdoor?"

John chewed his bottom lip. Apparently Alligator Dan was still sore about the slippery hinges.

"I can find prop boys in any town." Colonel Joe popped the wax into his mouth. "To be a true Wayfarer, you have to make the most of your talents. Come up with something we've never seen before."

"Like what?" John protested.

"That's for you to figure out."

John didn't know how to respond to this. He was truly doing his best—learning new skills, fixing what was broken. Why wasn't that good enough for Colonel Joe?

"You don't have to do it," said Alligator Dan. "You can p-p-pick up and leave anytime."

"Though we'd hate to lose you," Gentle Giant Georgie soothed.

"Especially," said Colonel Joe, "when we've got a full schedule coming up." He spread his fingers and began to count off. "There's Barnstable and the plow festival. Sissiwhack Junction and the Strawberry Girl parade. The wife and bog races at Chalkton Falls. Guntherville's election for the town cow——"

"And that's only up to the end of July," Alligator Dan noted, yanking at one of his scales and flicking it into the dirt. "So no p-p-pressure on that induction idea." He stood and stretched. "Time for chow. Can't decide whether I want hot dogs or b-b-beef. Tell you what." He grinned, punching John lightly in the arm. "I'll save you some spleen."

And with a jaunty hopping stride, Dan headed for the food wagon.

"You might want to take him up on that offer." Colonel Joe spat out his wax and rose to follow Alligator Dan. "I've got a small job for you after dinner."

John scowled at the retreating backs. "I bet there are lots of better ukulele players in the world."

Gentle Giant Georgie smiled and locked up the takings box. "Never mind Dan—he finds it hard to make friends."

"I can't understand why."

"Well," Georgie said, ignoring John's sarcasm, "I'll tell

you a little secret about Alligator Dan." He dropped his voice into a theatrical whisper. "He'd give his right arm to have what you've got."

By now the sun had sashayed below the horizon, streaking the sky with crimson and gold. As John watched, the mother picked up her burping baby and gave it a kiss on the forehead. Then she helped it wave bye-bye to Page.

"One of these days," John said, "I'm going to make something that lasts. Not something that you have to tear down the moment you put it up. I'm going to build an induction invention that blows the scales off Alligator Dan, and you, and every single kid in Chalkton Falls." He turned to Gentle Giant Georgie. "You think I can do it, don't you?"

But Gentle Giant Georgie had fallen asleep.

CHAPTER 10

"OH . . . UNDERPANTS!"

John plucked up his inkpot and hurled it across the caravan. It smashed into the doorsill right above Boz's head. A scatter spray of black dots peppered the rosy hair.

"Something amiss?"

John scrunched up the list of parts.

"This isn't going to work."

Boz bounded to his side and examined the open manual on the workbench.

"Why, bless my soles! Can it be? Forgive me if I'm misshapen, but you appear to be planning on building a steam carriage with certain similarities to Walter Hancock's patented marvel!"

"Really?" Page charged through the doorway of the caravan and dropped her dog brushes. "Is that what you're going to do for the induction?"

"Maybe," John said cautiously, watching Boz pound out a victory dance with his inky footsteps. "I have the plans. The Wayfarers could use it for rides around the big top and publicity tours before the show. People would pay a lot of money—"

"Miraculous idea!" Boz cried, pirouetting back to his right side. Page was already hugging his hip on the left. "So how does this fabulous steam-powered vehicle"—he squinted his eyes to examine the title—"aptly called the Autopsy, work?"

"You see here?" John stuck the tip of his screwdriver on the diagram of the carriage. "This is the engine compartment. First, you feed coal through this feed pipe into a furnace under the boiler. The fire heats up the water in the boiler to make steam. The steam goes through this

MAIN BODY

other pipe"—he traced a line that went across the top of the compartment—"and gets put under pressure. That pressure pushes the piston back and forth"—he pointed to something that looked like a toilet plunger—"which cranks the crankshaft"—he moved the screwdriver down to a setup of rods and chains and circles—"which rotates the axle that turns the wheels!"

He glanced up. Page looked dazed. Boz's face was as blank as a white page.

"You don't get it, do you?"

Boz shook his head. "Not a pitwit. But that doesn't matter," he added, thumping the bench with his fist, "because you do!"

John bit his lip.

"Well, I know how it works in theory. But I've never built anything like this before."

"But you're smart," Page said. "Look at the box you made for Tiger Lil. You can do anything!"

John appreciated his sister's enthusiasm, even if he didn't quite believe in her judgment.

"And we'll be the magician's assistants! The procurers of pipes. The collectors of crankshafts." Boz yanked the curtain from the window above them and waved it over the manual. "Abracadabra, let there be steam!"

John reached over and slid the manual out from underneath the fabric.

"It's not going to be that easy."

"But you remember what happens to the heroes in Dad's stories," Page prodded him. "It's never easy."

"Leap, my dear boy, leap! Look not at the cliff below you but at the sky above."

John reexamined the diagram. It would be incredibly satisfying to show Colonel Joe what he was capable of. He tried to imagine the faces of the audience when a steam-driven carriage came chugging across the field. Maybe he could have all the Wayfarers standing on the platform.

"Okay," he said, putting up his palm to shut Boz's mouth, "but we're going to start small. Do what the diagram says. I don't want things exploding in my face."

"Of course," said Boz, seizing hold of the manual. "It will be simple as huckleberry pie!"

But by early September, John had learned one very important lesson:

When it came to Boz, nothing was ever simple as huckleberry pie.

No sooner had John decided to build the Autopsy than Boz had trumpeted the news to the Wayfarers.

Reactions were mixed. Tiger Lil thought he was brave, the Mimsy Twins thought he was optimistic, and Alligator Dan thought he was delusional. Colonel Joe said nothing—and gave him a starter loan.

Yet eventually, as John and Boz and Page started to assemble the engine compartment, opinions swung around.

Now that the Wayfarers could see a rudimentary boiler and crankshaft taking shape in front of their eyes, some of them began to believe in the Autopsy's possibilities.

Unfortunately, that meant they also wanted to be part of it.

"You should divert some of the steam and stick a pipe organ right here!" Minny pointed to an area on the diagram in front of the engine compartment. "And we can play duets."

"Add a springboard on the top," said Porcine Pierre, "and I'll teach Frank and Priscilla to do a high dive."

"If you can figure out how to harness the smoke from the furnace," Gentle Giant Georgie noted, "we can have special effects for Tiger Lil's magic show."

John's response was typical of a new inventor—he attempted to please everyone. But the more he adjusted and fiddled and tweaked, the worse things became. One day the boiler would work, the next night it split. One hour the crankshaft would hum, the next minute it broke. The chains got tangled, the pipes slid sideways, and the piston went *phfft*. The bills for parts were astronomical.

Most galling of all, John knew he could do better. With patience, time, and a finer grasp of engineering, he was confident he could make it work. Yet he had none of those things.

Page did her best to be encouraging, saying how proud Mom and Dad would be, but her praise only made him feel worse. Every time she helped him rebuild the faltering crankshaft, John remembered Great-Aunt Beauregard's comments about his father's nitwilliness. What if the Autopsy never worked? Wouldn't it be safer to be back at the coffin workshop, doing what he knew best?

After two months of hard labor, John had a nonfunctioning steam engine, a six-year-old shadow, and an induction ceremony that was right around the corner.

On this September day of reckoning he found himself explaining to the Mimsy Twins—again—why the pipe organ wasn't possible. Mabel and Minny were having none of it.

"You're supposed to be creative," Mabel said. "Why can't you make it up?"

"Because I don't know anything about musical instruments," John retorted. "Besides, I'd need something like a hundred and one pipes to get started."

"Then scrounge for some," Minny said.

"I would," replied John heatedly, "if we ever went near a city where there were places to scrounge!"

"I don't care what your excuse is," Mabel said, her eyes filling with stage tears. "I know it's because you don't really want to be a Wayfarer."

They had barely finished flouncing out of the caravan when Boz hurtled through the entrance, hair sparkling like a constellation, a cloth sack in hand.

"Tally ho, Johnny Jump-Up. The sheep are in the manger, the cows are being born, and all is right with the world."

"No, it's not," John said, fiddling with the axle chain.

"Alas, what's bothering the brain of our resident genius? Moan a little my way and I'll do my best to appease ya."

"Nothing."

"Now that's not a very original response."

"All right, fine." John threw the chain into a box. "You want to know what's bothering me? I'm tired of trying to make everyone happy! Page keeps telling me I'm a genius and the Wayfarers are breathing down my neck about the induction and the stupid steam engine WILL NOT WORK. It's exactly like making coffins. Only harder."

Boz grinned.

"You, my fine fellow, may be suffering from a galloping case of the responsibles," he said gravely, seizing John's wrist and cocking his own head sideways. "It begins with an almost invisible twinge to the conscience and results in an insidious rash of the shouldn'ts."

He dropped John's wrist and peered into John's left ear.

"Yes, there's no doubt about it!" he yelled. "A galloping case of the responsibles."

"What does that mean in English?" John snarled.

"It means, my dear boy, that you need to stop worrying about other people for a moment and enjoy yourself.

92

Rest is just what the doctor of enlightenment orders." Boz shook his head. "A case of the responsibles in a boy of eleven is particularly serious—I'm extremely glad we've caught it in time."

"So what am I supposed to do? Take a pill?"

Boz grinned again and tossed his sack over his shoulder. "Might I suggest a little field trip instead?"

He bolted out the door. John paused for a fraction of a second, then threw back his stool and followed Boz down the steps.

"Where are we going?"

"Top secret research! Mime's the word!"

Ducking and diving, Boz wove his way between the caravans, flattening himself against walls and skittering under wheels.

If these maneuvers were meant to evade detection, they failed miserably.

"Hey, where are you going?"

Page came running up beside them as they were scaling the fence that marked the boundary of their camp. Tiger Lil's bear came with her.

"Is it for the Autopsy? I wanna come!" She tugged at John's trousers with her free hand.

"We're busy, Page," John replied roughly, shaking his leg.

"Please, Johnny, please let me come."

"My dear girl," said Boz—he was doing an arabesque

on one of the fence poles—"whither we flither is no fit place for a lady."

"Go play with your bear," John sniped. "Maybe you two can have a tea party with your horsies."

Page's cheeks mottled with fury. She slapped John hard on the ankle and sprinted back toward the caravans.

Boz shrugged and backflipped into the adjoining corn field.

"Thin epidermi you Coggins have."

John refused to respond. There was no law that said he had to do everything with his sister.

A bare ten minutes later, a small hillock appeared in front of them. Unlike the feathery tops of unharvested corn that surrounded it, the area had been mown. This, John assumed, was to accommodate the shed that stood on the top. A set of double doors, bound tight with a padlock, marked the entrance.

And in front of that entrance stood a decidedly disgruntled Alligator Dan.

"What's he guarding?" John whispered.

"An adventure."

"How do we get in?"

"Elementary, my dear flotsam. I took the liberty of loosening a few boards yesterday. We need only slip our svelte selves between them."

"But what about Alligator Dan?"

Boz held the sack up against his ear.

"Do you happen to know the one paradoxical point about our reptilian friend?"

"No."

"He's ophidiophobic."

"He's what?" John asked.

"He's afraid of snakes," Boz said, untying the top of the sack and letting a ginormous garter snake slither out over his shoulder.

For a moment, the snake looked bored. Then, suddenly, it raised its head and flicked its tongue in the air. With a quick shimmering spiral, it wound itself down Boz's arm and into the grass. Faster than you can say jackrabbit, it headed straight for Alligator Dan.

"It's almost as if it knows exactly where to go," John marveled, watching the snake slither closer and closer.

"Naturally," Boz said. "I tell you . . ." He sighed. "It's not easy hiding six bird eggs and a live newt in a man's pockets."

By this time, the snake was at Alligator Dan's feet. And Alligator Dan was just beginning to get a vague inkling that something wasn't quite right. Unfortunately for him, he didn't discover what that something was until the snake had made it halfway up the inside of his trousers.

With an almighty screech, Dan launched himself farther than Boz from Betsy. When he finally descended, he came down sprinting. Through the grass he bounded, his legs and arms whirling like windmills and his chest scales flapping in the breeze.

John was finding it difficult to breathe from laughing, but Boz was all business.

"No time to waste, dear boy, no time to waste."

Slithering in his predecessor's path, Boz crossed the field and inserted himself between the boards. John quickly followed.

After squeezing through this six-inch space, it would have been smart to exhale. But on seeing what was within, John's breath got lodged somewhere around his larynx.

"Isn't she a beauty?" said Boz. "The mayor of Hayseed's brand-new bundle of joy. Alligator Dan has been hired to see that she's not disturbed before the town celebrations tomorrow. But I thought you might be interested in examining her parts."

John couldn't speak for joy. He had heard rumors of automobiles when they'd lived in Pludgett, but this was the first time he had seen one in the flesh.

From stem to stern, it was a vehicle built for speed. It had two large wheels at the back and one squat specimen at the front. A buggy seat was provided to hold the driver and passenger, with a large space for luggage between the top of the chassis and the back of the seat. A thin metal rod crowned with a wheel served for the steering.

But, for John, the brightest wonder of all was the engine.

"Enlighten me as to how this functions," said Boz, lifting up the hood. "Is it steam?"

"No, I read about this! It's called internal combustion," John said excitedly, peering under the chassis. "It works through a little series of explosions. A spark hits the gasoline, that fires a reaction, that pushes the piston, that turns the crankshaft, that moves the wheels. You start her up by winding that handle and . . ."

Bwwurrpp! A cloud of greasy smoke enveloped John's face.

"Ah, now I see."

Boz leaped into the buggy seat and bounced a few times on the leather.

"I'm not sure if we should be doing this," John said.

"Merely testing your theory," Boz rejoined. He patted the hood. "Shall we determine if it runs?"

John was in agony. The juicy apple of temptation was dangling right there in front of him.

"What if they catch us?"

"Then we are caught." Boz smiled. "But then again, what if they don't?"

That was enough for John. He scrambled into the buggy seat. Boz reached for the brake.

"Wait!" John grabbed his arm. "We're locked in, remember?"

"Immaterial, my dear boy." Boz released the brake and the car lurched forward. "While loosening the boards, I also took the liberty of emancipating the door hinges."

BANG! went the shed doors onto the ground. *Bumpety, bump* went the vehicle as they steamrollered over them. Down the hill they sped, faster and faster, picking up momentum with every push of the pistons.

Until they slid to a halt in a slippery patch of grass. The engine spluttered and died.

"Hmmm," murmured Boz, jumping onto the ground and scratching his hair into stiff meringuelike peaks. "Perhaps a little less forward propulsion on initial expulsion."

John scrambled into the driver's seat. Forget the risk. The initial run had made him the happiest he had been in weeks. He wasn't going to let a few bumps stand in the way of that.

"Death or glory, Boz! Crank her up!" he yelled, turning the wheels hard over right.

Boz cranked and, miraculously, the engine puttered to life again.

"Get in!"

In climbed Boz. Up came the brakes.

"We're free, Boz!" John cried. "We're free!"

CHAPTER 11

It was the best of days; it was the best of engines.

Under the friendly heavens, the horizon was evenly divided into wispy corn and endless sky. Where the corn ended, the stubby bronze of wheat fields began. On those hard-packed farm roads, the mayor's baby galloped along with glee.

And John was in the driver's seat. It was as if he and the automobile spoke a secret language. He could hear the motor talking to him, chortling as it puttered down hills, whining a little on the tight bends. He pictured the crankshafts huffing and puffing, running around and around the cylinder like the frantic legs of Alligator Dan.

And that got him thinking. "Hey, Boz?"

Boz was leaning out over the road, plucking dandelions from the ditches.

"Boz!"

Boz placed half of his body in the vicinity of a seat.

"How did you find this?"

"Happenstance, my dear boy. Our comrade's shiny new ukulele alerted my suspicions to a game afoot. Now where, I asked myself, would a bottom-dwelling creature of limited imagination find the funds for such an instrument? I took it upon myself to discover the answer. Which, as you have observed, lay in some light security work."

John stroked the leather cushion.

"She must be worth a fortune."

"Tittle-tattle around town says that the mayor will unveil her at the Festival of the Future on the morrow. Show a little wheel, flash her pearly brights."

On any other day, this information might have caused John to turn around and head straight back for the shed. But not today, not in a dream like this. Today he didn't give a flying patootie about the mayor or the festival or the ending of things. Today he was conqueror of the skies.

Right up until the point when he noticed the crimson leaves dangling from the trees and the starlings wheeling in gusts of black wings.

"'Nothing gold can stay.'"

The memory of his father's voice pierced him to the marrow. Where had they been when his dad had said this? In a room? At a window?

No . . . John remembered. They'd been sitting by the side of the old yellow house on the edge of the sky-blue sea. John must have been five. Five years old and gazing at the autumn storm.

"But you know what, John? It's mighty pretty while it lasts."

For one brief moment, the sun had broken through the thickening clouds and a shaft of light had touched their faces. Then it was gone.

Like his house, like his sea, like his parents. Gone.

John turned to Boz, who was once again hanging off the side, his tongue panting like a golden retriever's.

"Boz!"

"Mmmm?"

"Boz. Could you please sit in one place?"

"But of course," Boz tucked his feet up behind his head. "How can I be of assistance?"

"Where do you come from?"

"Like all mammalians, I come from the dust of the stars and the dregs of the ocean."

"No, I mean, where were you born?"

Boz yanked on his hair. "'Fraid I can't remember."

"You can't remember?"

"Well, I was very young at the time."

"Have you always traveled?"

"Always! For I'll take the highway, and skip down the

byway, and I'll be a roamer forever."

"Don't you get tired of moving?"

"Never." Boz paused. "Thinking of your own peculiar and particular circumstances, are we?"

John nodded.

"Ah, the ancestral dilemma. The striver versus the hiver, the rover versus the drover. It is a pretty pickle." He patted John on the shoulder. "May I recommend that you save the worry for your next existence? Let life take the wheel for a while."

Boz tipped his toe to his ear and jauntily began whistling "Turkey in the Straw." John couldn't help but smile.

"Turkey in the straw, turkey in the hay," replied the engine. Boz stopped whistling. John stopped smiling.

"Ahem, you didn't, by any propitious chance, sing?" asked Boz.

"No," John replied, scanning the few deserted shacks alongside the fields. Nothing.

"Ah," Boz said. "A figment of my imagination."

He began to whistle again.

"Turkey in the straw, turkey in the hay," twittered the engine. That did it. John jammed on the brakes and leaned over the back of the buggy seat.

"Page! You get out of there!" he shouted. Page crawled out of the luggage rack and stood on the road looking up at her brother. Her skin was flushed, but her eyes held no apology.

"Hello, Johnny."

"What were you doing in there?"

"I wanted to come."

"You're too little to be here."

"I am not. I've grown two inches this summer. Lil measured me."

"We're doing boy stuff!"

"Then pretend I'm a boy."

"You're not a boy!"

A cough sounded from behind them. "Ahem. I don't wish to interrupt this blissful family reunion, but it appears we may have a more urgent matter on our metacarpi."

Boz pointed to the road behind them. In the far-off distance, a pair of men on horses were approaching at pace.

"Who are they?"

"The identification of the portside gentleman escapes me, but I am rather afeared that the personage riding the bay mare and attired in the fetching white hat is the sheriff."

"What?"

"So if I might suggest we continue our journey apace?"

John needed no further encouragement.

"Get in, Page!"

Page scrambled into the seat, the engine roared, and away they raced along the long unending road.

"Boz, where does this go?" shouted John.

"To market, to market," Boz replied between the juddering of the wheels. The mayor's baby wasn't quite accustomed to being whipped into speeds of thirty-five miles per hour. "Into the belly of the beast. In, through, and out the other end."

"Isn't there a side road we can take, somewhere with trees where we can get out and hide?"

Boz shook his head as the rest of the vehicle shook him.

"Not until we're past the town. But *nil desperandum*, my dear boy, we've got the jump on our eager bloodhounds."

Jump was the right word for it, John thought desperately. The entire automobile was jittering and jabbering with the pace. Every hole and hoofprint registered as an electric jolt up the spine. The engine wailed in protest.

The outlines of Hayseed were rising rapidly in front of them. A barn, a house, a church. Toddlers stood in their front doors and gawked as the mayor's baby went clattering by. John held on to the wheel like grim death and kept his eyes fixed on the road. They just needed to make it past the town.

That was going to be easier said than done. The street was packed with preparations for the Festival of the Future. Wagons and horses and crates littered the road; men with bunting crowded the sidewalks.

"Vacate the viaducts!" Boz shouted as they shuddered

toward a trio of men laden with a wreath of orange chrysanthemums. *Squish* went the flowers under the wheel of the mayor's baby.

"Hang on to your boutonnieres, me hearties, takeoff is imminent!"

Up a ramp they went, onto the festival's temporary stage. Through a banner reading

Welcome to Hayseed, Town of the Future!

they tore. Down the steps they came, shuddering and groaning, but by the grace of the gods, still moving.

"By gimcrackedy gee!" laughed Boz, yanking the banner from his neck. "The mayor's got a corker on his hands! I'd lay you ten to one we'd give a two-ton hippopotamus a run for his money!"

John ignored him. He crouched low over the wheel, concentrating on the gap ahead. There was the end of the town, there was the giant grove of trees that would shield their escape. They could hide forever in that wood.

We're gonna make it, John thought. We're gonna make it.

"Johnny!" Page screamed.

"Quiet, Page!" he barked. "We're almost there!"

"But Johnny! It's Great-Aunt Beauregard!"

CHAPTER 12

CRASH! WENT THE mayor's baby into an elaborate edible sculpture in the entrance of Hayseed's Fruit and Vegetable Emporium. A rainbow of zucchini and squash, green peppers and eggplant soared into the air. For a split second, a large, plump, glistening tomato hovered like Mars above John's head. Then . . . **SPLAT!** It exploded on his nose.

John plucked the seeds from his eyes and eyebrows. By some miracle of machinery, he'd managed to plow the vehicle into the deserted shop without damaging the passengers. His sister scrambled out of her seat.

"Quick, Johnny, behind the counter!"

Over the bench they flew. Boz was already there, his hair crowned with a ring of garlic.

"Have you noticed, my dear boy, that we seem to

spend a disproportionate amount of our leisure time in sequestration?"

"Shhh!"

"I don't give a flying fig for your piddly festival!" blared a depressingly familiar voice. "I want my property back!"

There was an odd creaking noise, like the gasp of a dehydrated water wheel. On his hands and knees, John crawled to the far end of the counter and peeked around.

There was his Great-Aunt Beauregard, in all her vole-coated, slab-faced glory. Her dress was irreproachable, her posture impeccable, and her expression one of righteous fury. Thanks to a grisly hawk perched on the edge of her sunbonnet, she towered over the man in the white cowboy hat beside her.

Overall, she looked pretty good for a woman strapped to an upright gurney.

John dropped behind the counter in panic.

And there was Page, disappearing into the floor.

Boz put his left finger to his lips and pointed with his right finger toward the hole. Then he too vanished.

Swift and silent, John followed, grabbing hold of the rope handle and pulling the trapdoor shut as he went.

The root cellar smelled of rat urine, but it was relatively safe. For the moment.

"Johnny." Page's voice tickled his ear. "What are we going to do?"

John pinched her to be quiet.

Clomp, rumble, clomp, rumble. The vibrations from above sent a shower of dirt trickling through a knothole in the floorboards. Cautiously, John peered through it.

The man in the white hat had pushed Great-Aunt Beauregard farther into the room and was now down on his knees, fishing turnips out from the wheels of the mayor's baby.

"They're not in there, you dolt-headed dimwit! They're not anywhere in this room!"

Great-Aunt Beauregard's eyes roamed toward the floor. John ducked reflexively.

"Look, lady," a voice drawled. "If you hadn't insisted on holding me up, I would've had your kids safely in hand. As it is, I've got a guard posted on the front door and my men on the alert. We got 'em locked up tight. It'd be a lot easier if you weren't here to help."

John risked another glance through the knothole. The two figures had faced off like heavyweight boxers.

"It's not my fault some fool of a surveyor didn't know how to orient a road sign!" his great-aunt rejoined. "As it is, I'm in remarkable condition for a woman who fell into a bog and disconnected my peritonia! Do you realize I was forced to spend three months in traction before I was able to leave Pludgett and trace that thing they call Boz? You're lucky that I have the strength to address you."

The sheriff didn't look like he thought himself particularly lucky.

"Okay, then *I'll* search the store," he countered. "And you stay with the guard outside."

"Fine!" Great-Aunt Beauregard replied. "But remember, my great-niece and -nephew are unwilling accessories in this automotive debacle. Your job is to release the Coggins into my custody and prosecute their carrot-topped kidnapper to the full extent of the law."

"Don't tell me my job, lady!"

"And don't think I won't be reporting your insolence to the mayor!"

Another burst of dirt exploded through the knothole. The stomp and rumble faded into silence.

"Johnny!" Page hissed, yanking at his shirt. "They're going to find us!"

John shook her off.

"I know!" he hissed back. "Boz?"

A comet of red flashed amid the gloom at the back of the cellar.

"Boz, wait!"

The two siblings chased the comet to a flight of stairs, emerging in a passageway between the store and an outbuilding.

"Boz!"

Boz paused halfway up a fence.

"Where are you going?" John demanded.

"I'm afraid the time has come, the optimist said, to wish you a fond farewell. I have an appointment in Lombardo with a chiropodist, and it may require a thorough reconfiguration of the kidneys. Do look me up if you're ever in the area."

And with that, he was off along the rooftops.

"Where's he going?" asked Page.

"He's running away."

"He's leaving us?"

"Seems so." John watched the last of Boz's locks vanish over an outhouse. Somehow he wasn't particularly surprised.

"What do we do?"

A piercing whistle filled the air.

"It's the acrobat from the circus! The kidnapper!"

"After him!"

"Now, Page!"

Grabbing his sister by the hand, John streaked to the end of the passageway and, once again, cautiously peered around the corner.

Like a spring river in flood, the entire town appeared to be surging past the sunlit gap. Tightening his grip even further, John dragged Page up the side street and toward the crowd.

The town was a maelstrom. Drunks, dogs, and teens were seeping out of every door, swelling the wave of pursuers. There was a rush of hooves and barks and shouts and feet, all concentrated toward the end of town. Apparently Boz's stealthy escape hadn't gone exactly as planned.

"Quick!" John said to his sister. Fighting against the tide of pursuers, he headed for the closest hitching post. Seizing the only horse left available—a bay mare—he pushed Page onto the saddle and jumped up behind her. With a yank of the reins, he charged down the road from which they had come.

When he looked back at Hayseed, the town had been drained of every drop of human life save one. A lone, lonely figure standing stiff as a palace guard outside the vegetable emporium. His practically apoplectic and completely immobile great-aunt.

CHAPTER 13

DUSK WAS FALLING over the fluttering flag of the big top as John drew the bay mare to a halt. While he tied up the horse, Page sprinted ahead to the Wayfarers, her shoes flapping against the soles of her feet. John knew they had to get straight out of town. His great-aunt wasn't going to stay stationary for long.

"Evening, Dung Boy."

John jumped. Colonel Joe was sitting on the ground, leaning against a tree, a bucket by his side. A large lump of honeycomb lay in his right hand, his jackknife in his left. In the blue light, he was easy to miss.

"Had yourself a little adventure?" The Colonel dug his knife into the comb and dropped a hunk into the bucket.

John's throat felt too dry to form words. He tried to

swallow. He gagged instead.

"I may have the wrong end of the horse, but that looks a heckuva lot like the sheriff's bay mare."

"Ack, ack" was John's reply.

Colonel Joe chewed thoughtfully on a piece of wax and gazed out at the swaying stalks of grass. From far off in the distance, John heard an owl shriek as it dove upon a field mouse. The soft breeze smelled of sleep.

"The Wayfarers want to see you. You ready to face the music?"

"Ack, ack." John tried again.

Colonel Joe stood, shut his knife, and spat into the grass.

"Here," he said, handing John the jackknife. "I got an inkling you may be needing this."

The din inside the big top was deafening.

"Where's Boz?"

"I can't believe you took the girl!"

"This is no time for hijinks!"

"We have a b-b-bone to p-p-pick with you!"

The Wayfarers' admonishments grew louder and louder, drowning John's ears in a swarm of furious buzzing.

"Stop!" Page yelled. "He can't hear!"

Her voice calmed the crowd. They retreated, leaving Colonel Joe in the middle of the circle.

"We had a visit from our neighbor." He tilted his head

in the direction of the cornfield. "Seems someone stole the mayor's automobile. There's a whole pack of people out looking for Boz. Where is he?"

"Gone," John croaked.

Colonel Joe nodded.

"That would be about right. And you?"

"Me?"

"You gonna tell us where you've been?"

John threw his shoulders back and found his saliva.

"I was with him. We crashed it into a store. In Hayseed."

"Because we saw Great-Aunt Beauregard!" Page exclaimed.

Colonel Joe glanced at John. He nodded.

"She's here looking for us. And the sheriff knows where Boz has been. You need to protect us!" He took an appealing step closer to the Colonel. "Please!"

Colonel Joe stuck his finger in his ear and jiggled it around.

"Told you once before, Dung Boy, I ain't got the last say." He sighed. "'Fraid this one's going to have to go to a majority vote. You and your sister better sit on the bench while we make up our minds."

John spent the next few minutes chewing his nails to bleeding beds. The Wayfarers had huddled themselves into a circle, giving him nothing to analyze but their backs. There were whispers, exclamations, and grunts, but no identifiable words. Finally, excruciatingly slowly, they broke apart and turned.

John examined the group. Mister Missus Hank was inspecting her beard for nits. Tiger Lil was tying her shoe. Gentle Giant Georgie was priming his pipe. Porcine Pierre was rolling Priscilla's ball in his hand. And Mabel and Minny were fiddling with their hem. Only Alligator Dan and Colonel Joe met him eye to eye. They didn't look happy.

"We've decided you can't stay," said Colonel Joe.

For a moment, John couldn't answer.

"Why?" he finally gasped.

"We're not harboring thieves and fugitives," Alligator Dan retorted. "We g-g-got our own scales to think about."

John suddenly remembered Colonel Joe's caution. So this was what it felt like to be fed to the wolves.

"They'll shut us down if they find you here," Colonel Joe explained. "In the eyes of the law, we're kidnappers."

"But you're not kidnappers," John shouted. "We want to be here!"

"Tough chewy cookies!" Mister Missus Hank replied.

"It was a tight vote," said Gentle Giant Georgie sadly. "Nothing we can do."

"You can hide us!"

"You're not staying in our caravan," the Mimsy Twins rejoined. "You smell."

"But what about the Autopsy?"

"The one that's dead on arrival?" snarked Porcine Pierre. "Yeah, we're really banking on that."

"It's special!" Page exclaimed.

"It doesn't work," Alligator Dan said flatly.

It doesn't work. Those words hit John like a cannonball to the solar plexus. Alligator Dan was right. The Autopsy was a dud. *He* was a dud. Even if he could stay, he'd be wasting Colonel Joe's money and time. This was the real world of coffins and contracts and cash. It was time to face facts.

"You're right."

"Porcine Pierre can take you as far as Littlemere," Tiger Lil said. "There's a big flour mill where they're always hiring new hands. We'll send the sheriff's mare south to provide a diversion."

"What about Page?" asked John.

"I'm willing to risk hiding the girl," piped up Mister Missus Hank. "She may get lucky with a goatee."

"No." Page crossed her arms. "I'm going."

"You don't have to," said Tiger Lil. "Georgie and I will keep you safe."

Gentle Giant Georgie smiled.

"Glad to. Never had a daughter."

Page shook her head. "No." She walked over and stood facing John. "You're my brother. I'll never leave you, Johnny. I promise."

"But Page," John replied, "I don't know how I'm going to take care of you."

"I was the one who made you crash. I go where you go."

She looked so funny and brave, standing there with her mud-streaked nose and her frayed overalls, that John had an irresistible urge to smile.

Tiger Lil opened her mouth to protest, but Gentle Giant Georgie cut her off. "Better do as the girl says."

John held on tight to Page's hand and turned to face Colonel Joe.

"We can't be found," he insisted.

Colonel Joe nodded. "It's a three-day journey to Littlemere. We'll give you a good head start."

John curtly returned the nod. "Thanks." He turned his attention to his sister. She was studying the ground with keen intent. "Are you sure, Page?" he asked.

Page raised her head and grinned.

"I'll bring my bear."

CHAPTER 14

THE LONELIEST FEELING in the world is to be on the outside looking in.

John stood in the middle of the road staring forlornly at the patches of lamplight in the farmhouse windows. His stomach was growling.

It had been a long haul with Porcine Pierre to Littlemere. By night, John and Page had slept along the road, rolled up in blankets too thin to beat back the cold. By day, they huddled under a tarp in the cart and discussed the future.

"I can work at the mills too," Page offered.

"No," said John. "Once I've got a job, we'll look for a room to rent in the city. And you can go back to school. But we can't be us anymore," John instructed his sister. "You'll need to change your name."

"I want to be Gardenia."

"You can't be Gardenia, that's not a real name."

"Okay, then I want to be Nora."

John nodded. That was their mother's name.

"Then I'll be Harry." That was their father's name. Just right for a no-good failure, John thought sadly.

Names were the easy part. Figuring out what story John was going to tell the mill owners was trickier. Whichever direction she went after Hayseed, Great-Aunt Beauregard would be searching for runaways and homeless siblings. What they really needed, John realized, was a fake family.

The challenge of coming up with one didn't settle his insides any. By the time they reached the outskirts of Littlemere, John felt about as optimistic as a slab of cold meat.

"Well, this is it," Porcine Pierre griped. He'd been decidedly annoyed about abandoning his pets for a fool's errand. "Never thought I'd see the day when I'd have to play nursemaid."

"Where are the flour mills?"

Porcine Pierre pointed in the vague direction of the city.

"Over thataway. Better get a move on if you want to find a place to bunk down. I have to give Priscilla her weekly worm medication." He wheeled the cart around. "Good luck!" he called out as he trundled off into the night.

John took a deep breath. The money that Colonel Joe had given them wouldn't go very far. He was going to need to find work fast.

Page came up and laid her hand in his. It was chapped from the dry wind that was kicking up the leaves around them.

Then all of a sudden, from atop the dark jagged line of the spruces, up popped the moon. It was round and full and big enough to swim in, and it seemed to be saying to John, "Lamps may live and lamps may die, but I go on forever."

John squared his shoulders and tried to suppress a yawn.

"C'mon, Page. We'll see if we can find something to eat."

And so they began their weary walk. John was at least encouraged to see that Littlemere was quite unlike Pludgett. Instead of swampy marshes and sinking foundations, there were narrow streets and gingerbread roofs. In lieu of iron grills and sooty ashes, there were secret squares and gurgling fountains.

The houses were oddest of all, with second stories that sighed and sagged like the bosoms of fat old ladies. The overhangs were broad enough to shield a walker from the weather without shutting out the sky above. As John and Page trudged along the deserted cobblestones, petals from the window boxes drifted onto their shoulders.

But not one light was on, not one door was open. When they reached the center of Littlemere, the clock in the city hall read half past one. Slumped together in a corner of a large doorway, the siblings fell into an uneasy sleep.

It didn't last long. John was awakened by the clock tolling four and the eerie sensation of something climbing up his nose. He brushed it off and rose to his feet. The ladybug flitted away.

"Page, get up. We can't stay here."

At the next corner, the Coggins ran into a blizzard of hanging signs. The boards creaked in chorus, whispering of their wares—"Luigi the Kosher Butcher," "Pepe's Boots and Saddles," "Gustaf Lingold, Dentist & Chiropractor."

But by far the noisiest signs were for one profession that made John's mouth water. Littlemere, it seems, was a city of bakers.

Bread bakers, pastry bakers, cake bakers, cookie bakers, scone bakers, doughnut bakers, pizza bakers, muffin bakers, pie bakers—John could have made a wish for any of them, and the word would have miraculously appeared.

Even more torturous were the window displays of desserts. There were glossy golden piecrusts with geysers of cherry juice erupting from the slits. There were plump creams oozing out of their pastry shells. Worst of all, there were cakes. White cakes and orange cakes and cakes berimmed with curls of shaved chocolate.

This sight, framed in the window of the bakery at the end of the street, was the last straw. Page moaned. John groaned.

"Are you ill?" came a concerned voice from above. It was a deep, warm voice, like custard itself. Page moaned again.

"Oh, my!" said the lemon custard, and a shutter slammed. John could hear the pitter-patter of footsteps on a wooden flight of stairs. The door to the shop was flung open. A floured pair of hands reached into the darkness. The heavy door swung closed behind them.

After John had recovered his equilibrium, he found himself in a room of shadows, with only a faint light from the street bouncing off the polished countertops.

"This way, this way," the lemon custard urged.

They stumbled through a small passage and into a back kitchen. In the corner, a mighty stove sat grunting and grumbling and belching out gusts of heat. Fat circles of dough lay piled in bowls on a wooden table.

"There now," the lemon custard said, depositing them on stools next to the table, "have a rest while I get the breakfast loaves out."

John opened his eyes wide to get a good look at their mysterious benefactor and almost crushed Page's hand. The custard woman wasn't lemony at all, but a beautiful milky tea color, swathed in a red poppy dress and blue apron. Everything about her was buffed of edges, from her sloped shoulders to her round-toed clogs.

"I was closing my bedroom window when I heard your voices," she said, taking up a flat wooden paddle and opening the oven. "And I thought, who could that be at this time of night? But if there's one sound I know, it's the sound of hunger."

Out from the oven came a glistening loaf, as brown as a walnut, which the woman placed in front of them. Steam erupted as she cut two slices. Then she spread a creamy slab of butter on each and handed them to John and Page.

"Careful! Very hot!"

John didn't care. He'd set fire to his stomach if it meant he could get more of that delicious melting crust. Page was matching him mouthful for mouthful.

"Slowly! You'll hurt yourselves if you're not careful." The woman laughed. "You must have walked from the ends of the earth."

"We have," John said dreamily, his eyes closing of their own accord.

"We do a lot of walking," Page added before her head slumped to the table.

And then the world went black. When John finally awoke, it was to the sound of whistling wind. He sat up and examined his surroundings. Page was fast asleep in the trundle bed beside him, tucked between starched white sheets. They appeared to be in an attic. Apart from the beds, there was only a large bureau and a window to the sky.

John rose, wincing a little at the chilly boards beneath his feet, and crossed to the window. Chimneys upon chimneys greeted him. Smoke tendrils twisted in the breeze. From this height, he could see clear across the city to the spruce forests and the hills beyond.

"Page! Look at this!" he exclaimed, but Page was already beside him, her chin resting on the sill.

"Well, good afternoon, sleepyheads!" said the voice from the night before. John and Page turned to see the woman poke her head in the door. "Feeling better? I'm Maria Persimmons. Come and be welcome."

The Coggins followed her down the stairs to the kitchen.

"I'm finishing up some apple-and-fennel tarts for the dinner crowd." She flicked a towel over the floury stools. "Pull up a pew."

John shot at a glance at his sister as he sat down. "Why did you say that?"

Maria appeared puzzled.

"Pull up a pew? I learned it from my grandmother." She pulled a pan from the oven. "This is her recipe," she added, placing a gigantic tart in front of them. An aroma of crisp sunshine rose from the pastry.

"Now, then." Maria sat down with a thump on her

chair and began to carve the tart. "I'd like to ask you a few questions, if I might."

John twitched. Boz was much better at the lying game. "Okay."

"First of all, what do I call you?"

"Harry," replied John quickly. "And this is Nora," he said, before Page could speak.

"Excellent," Maria said, handing John a piece of tart. "How do you do, Harry?" She handed Page another. "And how do you do, Nora?"

"I'm thirsty."

Maria laughed and stood up to fetch Page a glass of water from the sink.

"And where do you come from?" she asked with her back to the table.

John looked at Page and Page looked at John. Maria turned in time to catch the end of the exchange. "Are you runaways?"

John shook his head. "Not exactly."

Maria sat down at the table. "Are you in any kind of trouble?"

John shook his head again. "Not really."

"Do you have any family?"

John paused. "Not precisely."

"I seem to be asking all the wrong questions, don't I?" Maria rubbed a bit of flour from her nose. "Well, then, let me try again. Do you have anywhere to go?"

John laid down his fork reluctantly. The tart was delicious.

"I'm headed to the mills to find work."

Maria gasped. "But you must be only nine!"

"I'm eleven." John raised his chin. "I'm short for my age."

"And are you going to work in the mills too?" she asked Page.

Page shook her head. "I'm going back to kindergarten."

Maria scratched a bit of dried dough from her arm. "I'm not sure I understand this. . . ."

"Look, sorry we bothered you," said John, pushing back his stool. The sooner they got going to the mills, the sooner Maria's interrogation would be over. "Thanks for the food and the beds and stuff. We'll be leaving." He took Page's arm. "Let's go, Nora."

"No," Page said firmly, holding on to the edge of the table with a grip of steel. "I don't want to."

"We're bothering the kind lady." John tugged harder. "I DON'T WANT TO GO!"

Maria coughed politely. John and Page looked up.

"Could I make a proposal?" asked Maria. "My cousin Leslie is away for the next few months, and I always have room in the attic. What if you two stayed here?"

She turned to John and smoothed her hands over her apron.

"I'm not going to stop you from trying the mills, but

I *will* say that I'm currently short of help in the bakery. You could work for your room and board, and I could have some company. It's not a great job offer, but I hope you'll consider it."

John didn't have to ask Page what she thought of this idea. She was hopping up and down on her stool like one of Mister Missus Hank's fleas.

But John's mind was in turmoil. Should they stay? It seemed like the ideal choice now, but what if Maria kept asking questions? What if she started blabbing about her new boarders all over town? What if Great-Aunt Beauregard tracked them down?

"I should have added," Maria said, watching John's expression, "that this arrangement has to be completely under the table. The Littlemere police would have a hissy fit if they knew I had children working in my shop."

John nipped at his thumbnail. If the arrangement was under the table, then . . .

"Okay!" shouted Page. "We'll stay!"

CHAPTER 15

THE WORLD, JOHN soon discovered, looked mighty different when you worked in a bakery.

Gone were the splinters and the saws and the planks.

In were the chickens.

Every morning John followed the same routine. First he would rise early, far earlier than Page, and run downstairs to the kitchen.

"Hello, Maria!" he'd cry.

Hard at work by the oven, Maria would usually pretend to be startled and throw her oven mitts up in the air.

"Harry, Harry, quite contrary," she'd say with a broad smile that put the lie to her complaint. "You ought to be in the army with a cannonade like that."

"Reporting for egg duty!"

Maria would laugh and hand him an old willow basket.

"Well, then, Captain Harry, I expect a full complement."

"Yes, sir!"

"Wait," Maria never failed to say. "You'll take something for the road?"

Then she might present him with a piping hot roll or a cup of oatmeal. John would use them to warm his belly as he walked down the narrow backyard to the chicken coop. There, in an incubator of feathers and nests, he collected the eggs from Maria's special breed of Henrietta hens.

By the time he got back, Page would be opening up the front door of the Rise and Shine Bakery and Maria would be calling out to the street: "It's a beautiful brandnew day. Come and be welcome!"

Come and be welcome.

If there was one phrase that summed up a human being, this was the moral, motto, and fluttering flag of Miss Maria Persimmons.

John and Page could not believe their luck. Their new landlady never ceased to smell of cinnamon and warm dough, nor lose the flour from her nose, no matter how hard she scrubbed. She was as delectable as the food she made—and the food she made was the best in Littlemere.

Which, of course, meant customers. Lots of them. During those first few hours of the morning, the Coggins ran marathons behind the bakery counters. John fetched and Page bagged. Page took the orders and John distributed change. They soon became popular fixtures.

"Why, if it isn't the muffin man!" puffed the limping butcher.

"Show me that sunny smile!" cooed the cross-eyed seamstress.

"Hop to it, stubby, I'm starved!" cried the Roman-esque matron.

There were questions, to be sure. Who were these unusual newcomers, the customers asked Maria, the girl with the golden hair and the undersized boy with the quivery lip? Why were they here?

But Maria had a story to beat back the most inquisi-tive residents.

"This is Harry and this is Nora. They're Patsy's kids—did you never meet my friend Patsy? She's having a rough time of it. Had to go overseas for . . . treatment." Maria wiped away a false tear. "Seems I've been blessed where others have been cursed."

John always smiled when he heard this tale. Great-Aunt Beauregard would never be posting a "Wanted!" notice for poor Patsy's kids.

After the breakfast rush, the day relaxed into a more regular routine. While Maria cleaned and prepared her bread for the dinner crowd, the Coggins went through Maria's old lesson books at the kitchen table. John found himself reciting facts and figures to the rhythmic creaking of the rolling pin. Six and a quarter, igneous rock, king of the gods. The world rolled on, and John rolled with it.

One morning in early October, John discovered a thin, green book among his pile of lessons.

"What's this?" he asked Maria.

"Have a look," Maria said, kicking the door of the oven, a door that permanently refused to close. "My father wrote it."

John opened the book. It was called *The Theory of Energy*. Maria's father had apparently been obsessed with the subject, since he'd scribbled handwritten notes alongside his printed text and illustrations.

"I thought it might be fun to look at," Maria noted.

John paused for a long moment . . . and pushed the book away.

"No, thanks."

Maria glanced at Page. Page crossed her eyes.

"Okay." Maria shrugged. "If you change your mind, I'll stick it on the shelf next to the cookbooks. You can take it out anytime."

It was a torment for John to watch his new employer close the book. There, right in front of him(!), were the secrets of steam and oil and fire. There, perhaps(!), lay the answers to his problems with the malfunctioning Autopsy.

But after the disastrous ending with the Wayfarers,

John was bound and determined to be practical. His old dreams had gotten him into exceedingly hot water. No, the smartest thing to do, he told himself, was to learn a craft that wasn't so potentially hazardous.

Fortunately Maria was happy to oblige. Her lessons in cooking took place, without fail, in the late afternoon, after John and Page had run themselves ragged making deliveries.

"Now, you know," Maria warned them at the beginning, "this is secret family stuff I'm showing you. If my competitors get their hands on this"—she drew her finger across her throat—"I'm a cooked goose."

"We won't tell anybody," John promised.

"You wouldn't look very nice cooked," Page added.

"Well, then," Maria said, "let's get started."

So all through the autumn, as lace frosted on the windows and the wind howled in the chimneys, John and Page baked. Maria taught them how to make cherry doughnuts and raisin rolls, buttery croissants and blueberry muffins. Day after day, they sweated sugar and spice and everything nice, and left trails of vanilla on the floor.

Life would have been grand if it hadn't been for one thing. John kept thinking of his mother. How could he not? She was always there—in the tilt of Maria's head, in the hand on his shoulder, in the wry corner of a grin.

Yet, in a few very important ways, she wasn't. For

example, Maria liked to wear pink. John's mother said pink made her look like a flamingo. Maria was sad when the rain fell. His mother used to run outside to stomp in the puddles. Maria adored cats, but his mother had always sneezed twice when she met one, one quick snort and then an almighty *ACHOO!*

Most telling of all, his mother had been a terrible cook.

This was the one memory that constantly tortured John: a day not long before his parents had become sick, a gunmetal morning in early winter.

Wandering into the kitchen of the old yellow house had been like stumbling into a bomb site. There was chocolate on windows, chocolate on the floor, chocolate lodged in the cracks above the sink. To make her soufflé, his mother had managed to use every dish in the cupboard, plus a couple of pots from the garden shed. It had taken four hours, but finally, she was ready to take her masterpiece out of the oven.

"It rose, John love, it rose!"

John watched her hold the soufflé high up in the air as she strutted toward the table.

Then, the fatal flaw. A nail, a board, a divot? Whatever it was, it snatched at her foot halfway across the floor.

Down she went in a tumble of elbows and knees.

Scrunch! went the soufflé under her chest.

For one horrible moment, John thought he might

actually witness his mother bawl.

Then she saw her son's face and burst out laughing.

"Not to worry, John love. All you have to do when you fall over is pick yourself up and brush yourself off," and she brushed her hands down her dress. This didn't help the soufflé any.

"You've got chocolate on your tummy," John said.

His mother slapped her hands to her cheeks in dismay.

"Now it's on your face," John added, starting to giggle.

She grabbed her hair in despair.

"Now it's in your hair!"

"Oh, yeah?" his mother replied, taking up a chunk of gooey crumbs and spreading it through John's locks. "Now it's in yours!"

It had been a day to remember. And yet, like his father's golden ray of sun, snuffed out in an instant.

No wonder, then, that John grew increasingly morose as the year dimmed. He snipped at Page and snarled at the spruces. He retreated from his duties and stopped taking baking lessons in the afternoon. Eventually, on a cold December day, Maria braved the silence.

"Harry, what's wrong?" she asked, placing a vase of holly on the attic bureau.

John refused to answer her. He was going over and over a dull mathematical problem from one of his lesson books.

Maria sat down next to him on the bed, smoothing

the corner of his bedspread as she did. For a few minutes she said nothing. Then she took a deep breath and spoke.

"You know, you remind me a lot of my dad."

Still John refused to reply.

"Sometimes it even hurts to look at you."

John lifted his head.

"I don't usually talk about him," Maria continued. Her fingers were fretting at a snarl of threads on the bedspread's hem. "He was killed in an accident when I was eighteen. But he was wonderful. Smarter than a serpent, could fix anything on the planet, never said three words when one would do. And gentle! Oh, Harry, he was a gentle man. He always promised to take care of me." She tried to yank the knot from the hem. It wouldn't budge. "I miss him."

This time, John knew the tears in the corners of Maria's eyes weren't fake. Not knowing what to say to help, he studied the page in front of him until the figures blurred.

Maria sniffed and pushed the knot away from her. "I guess that's why it hurts. You make me remember."

Slowly John pulled out Colonel Joe's jackknife and severed the threads on the knot. Then . . .

"You make me remember too," he said.

A watery smile replaced Maria's frown.

"You can't bring him back, Harry, but I'm awfully glad you're here."

From that moment forward, John decided he would try to be more gracious. Though it was still difficult for him to contemplate chocolate soufflés, his awkwardness with Maria began to ease. She had her memories; he had his. You lived with them, or you twisted yourself into knots.

Besides, winter in a bakery could be awfully hard to resist. Especially when New Year's Day was spent in a warm kitchen with a pack of gold-rimmed playing cards.

"Guess what, you two?" said Maria, removing a tray of muffins and kicking at the oven door. "I have a surprise."

"Is it a new recipe?" Page asked eagerly.

"Nope," Maria said, "it's a new inmate. Leslie is returning next week."

"That's your cousin, right?"

"That's right, Nora. My late aunt's only son."

"He's been gone a long time," John noted.

"Yes," answered Maria. "But he's eager to be back. I'm sure you'll like him, Harry. He's very smart and very nice."

Nice, as John well knew, was a word that adults used when they didn't know what else to say. He studied his cards. Leslie was an unknown commodity, a person who might or might not have questions about Maria's new employees. A seed of uneasiness began to form in John's stomach.

"What are you going to tell him about us?"

"I've already written to him about Patsy being away. He said he didn't mind. But, please, both of you, please try to make him feel at home."

There was a strange undercurrent flowing beneath this conversation. All the time she was talking, Maria kept trying to push her hair behind her ears or scratch her elbows. John knew the signs. Maria was worried.

"What's wrong, Johnny?" Page whispered as Maria dashed out to the shop to tend to a customer.

"Nothing," John said, squeezing his cards tight in his hands. He wasn't sure he was going to like Leslie at all.

CHAPTER
16

"Never fear, my dears, Leslie is here!"

Two enormous duffel bags came flying through the air and hit John square in the chest.

"Cousin Maria, you're looking positively peachy. If I were ten years older and unrelated, I'd carry you off to church." Leslie slobbered a kiss on Maria's hand.

"That's very kind of you to say." Maria wiped her fingers on her apron. "Leslie, this is Harry and Nora, Patsy's kids. Harry and Nora, this is Leslie."

Leslie smiled a syrupy smile.

"Pleased to meetcha."

It was incredible, John thought, but Leslie really did look like a tall, sixteen-year-old version of Frank.

It wasn't just the flaring nostrils and the wires that dangled from the interior of his nose that did it. Nor was it the coarse hair on his head or the straggly fringe that fluttered on his upper lip. It was the whole of him, from his sharp, pointed ears to his thick, stocky body to his thin, stubbly legs. Yes, there was no doubt about it. Leslie looked like a pig.

Still, John reminded himself, even pigs have their good points.

"Harry, do you mind helping Leslie to his room?" Maria said. "I want to get Nora to bed."

John nodded and picked up a bag. It appeared to be weighted with rocks. Large ones. "You've got clean sheets," he managed to gasp out as he dragged Leslie's bag up the stairs.

"Good-o," Leslie said, pausing a moment when they reached the landing. "I'd give you a hand, but I've strained my back." He brought out an embroidered handkerchief and delicately wiped it across his forehead. "So you won't object to bringing up the other one? There's a good chap."

"Actually—*owwww!*"

In dropping the bag on the floor of the spare room, John had dropped it right on his toe.

"Whoops! Clumsy wumsy." Leslie giggled as he removed his jacket. "I see I'll have to be careful with you in the kitchen. Wouldn't want you to set yourself on fire."

John's toe was throbbing too intensely for him to be able to answer.

"But you should know, Harry Hornblower, that I run

a tight ship." Leslie sucked in his stomach so he could admire his profile in the full-length mirror. His man breasts stuck out proudly from his chest. "I know what little boys are like. Remember—there'll be no stealing of sweets when I'm in charge."

He wagged a teasing finger at John in the mirror.

"Understand?"

Oh, I understand, John thought. I understand you completely.

Unfortunately for John, Maria did not. For the very next morning, Leslie was in front of the counter greeting customers.

"Mrs. Potts, how does your husband resist you in that sinfully becoming dress?"

This to a woman wearing a potato sack.

"Miss Templeton, I do declare you are getting younger by the moment. A girl of fourteen could not hope to compete with such dewiness." This to a woman who was pushing sixty well past its limits.

"Madame Lacoste, I did not expect to be touched by an angel from heaven today!"

This to a woman who had about as much warmth as a hunk of frozen quartz.

"He's terrible!" John whispered to Page during the morning rush.

"And he's a liar," she whispered back. "He told Gappy Preese that he could weave a curtain for the gods from her hair." Gabby Preese was practically bald. "We should tell Maria!" Page insisted.

After Leslie had retreated to his morning bath, the Coggins took their observations to their benefactress. But Maria would hear nothing against her cousin.

"It's nice to give someone a compliment."

"But what if the compliment isn't true?" John demanded. "Doesn't that mean that he's being a suck-up?"

Maria sighed and hung the pot she was drying on a hook above her head.

"Life is not all black and white, I'm afraid, chickadees. Sometimes people don't say what they mean or mean what they say. But that doesn't always make them bad.

"Please," she said, "please try to get to know him."

So John marshaled his patience and did his best at lunch to make friends. "Maria said you were traveling. Did you have a good trip?"

Leslie patted his mustache with his napkin and winked at Maria. "Most excellent."

"Where did you go?" asked Page.

"Ooooh, all over! I was doing a tour of real estate possibilities in the south of the country." He leaned back. "In fact, I was telling Maria about the oodles of opportunities along the Pludgett to Riverton railway line."

"Pludgett?" asked Page. John grabbed at her elbow under the table. She made a squeak like a rusty hinge.

"Yes," said Leslie, peering quizzically at Page. "Do you know it?"

John held his breath.

"All right, everybody, back to work!" Maria stood up and whipped a tea towel across the crumbs. "Leslie, could you help me change the sign for specials to anadama bread?"

"Of course," Leslie cooed. "Anything for my pretty cousin."

With a bow and a flourish, he plucked up the last roll and shepherded Maria into the shop.

"Sorry, Johnny," muttered Page.

"It's okay," John muttered back. "I don't think he noticed. Still, let's try to act as normal as possible."

But, alas for John, normal was not to be. For the arrival of Leslie spelled doom to everyday life. Leslie disrupted everything—from the first moment the Coggins woke up, when he gargled his mouthwash, to the last moment before they went to sleep, when he could be heard warbling off-key arias through the floor.

He interrupted their baking lessons and curtailed their playtime. He wore pants two sizes too small and curled his hair with Vaseline. He insisted on cooking dinner, serving up meatloaf so hard and dry that Maria broke a steak knife trying to saw through it.

Even worse, after three days he decided that John and Page needed a tutor.

"You're a busy lady, Miss Maria. You shouldn't have to worry your pretty head over algebra and acronyms. Leave it to me, I'll fill these young minds with the wisdom of the ages."

The wisdom of the ages, John was to learn, consisted of Leslie's stories about his achievements. How he scored the winning goal in a decisive hockey match. How he shamed his teacher by telling her how the Battle of Killimanjay was *really* won. How he astounded the citizens of Howst by purchasing their castle.

"It was built by the owner of the Riverton railway to look like the fortifications of the conquistadors. Naturally, I'm thinking of resurrecting it as a time-share rental for golfers. There's a silver mine operator in Barramesh who's simply gagging at the prospect."

John was gagging too. At the smell of Leslie's cologne.

The situation became so dire that Page took to barricading herself in their attic room in the afternoons and talking nonstop to her bear. John's solution was to hang out with the chickens in the chicken coop. They might smell funny, but at least their conversation didn't make him want to pull his fingernails off and jab them into his ears.

The only thing stopping John from going completely around the bend was Maria. He knew she was putting up with Leslie for reasons other than family, but for the life of him, he couldn't fathom her motives. Though he didn't understand why, he realized it was important for him and his sister to keep their tempers.

One bitterly cold night at the beginning of February, John woke to hear familiar footsteps trotting down the stairs. Being careful not to wake Page, he pulled on his sweater and followed.

When he reached the kitchen, he peeked in the door. A large leather tome was spread out on the table. With a pencil in her left hand, Maria was making forlorn stabs at the page.

"Are you okay, Maria?" John whispered.

Maria looked up from her book. Poppy seeds freckled her cheeks.

"Harry! You gave me a fright. What are you doing up so late?"

"I couldn't sleep. Are you okay?"

"I'm fine."

"Your eyes are red."

"Are they?" Maria laughed ruefully. "I guess all this fun is keeping me up too late."

John sat down opposite her.

"What is it?"

Maria smiled.

"Never lose your persistence, Harry, no matter what. I love that about you."

He waited. She sighed and turned the accounting book toward him.

"I'm worried about the spring. Coal keeps getting more expensive, and that old oven is going to bake its last cookie any day now."

"And we're costing you money," John said.

Maria wrinkled her forehead.

"Oh, no, that's not what I meant. I love having you and Nora here. You're the best thing that's happened to me since sourdough starter. I can't imagine what this winter would have been like without you."

"But we're still costing you money."

Maria sighed and closed the tome.

"Money, schmoney. Let's not think about it anymore. Something wonderful and unexpected will happen. It always does, if you wait long enough."

THUMP! THUMP! THUMP! THUMP! THUMP!

They both sprang to their feet.

"Who could that be?" Maria was clutching her accounting book to her chest.

"Someone who doesn't know how to use the bell," John replied. But he didn't fancy seeing who that might be. Especially if their visitor happened to be sporting a taxidermied bluebird in her hat.

Holding John's hand tight in hers, Maria crept into the shop and up to the window. With the moonlight bouncing off the cobblestones, they could glimpse a figure shrouded in a high-collared cloak. A figure no taller than John himself. With blazing red hair.

"It's Boz!" John shouted, throwing open the door.

Boz—for that was who it was—did a graceful somer-sault into the shop and emerged, only slightly flustered, from the interior of his cloak.

"*Ave Caesar.* We who were about to die salute you." Boz rose and bowed to John and Maria in turn.

"Hello." Maria laughed. "You must be nearly frozen. Here, come and be welcome."

As Boz entered the kitchen, and the light of the table lamp fell upon his face, John realized his erstwhile friend must have been through the wars. He was sporting a torn coat, a pair of pukey-green long johns tied with a rope, and two enormous black eyes. He looked exactly like a ginger raccoon.

"What happened to you?"

Boz twisted his feral face toward John. "Life, my dear boy. The vicissitudes of vicarious living."

There was a mute appeal in those odd blue eyes that John was forced to acknowledge. Yes, he was still furi-ous at Boz for ditching them in Hayseed. Yes, there were things that Boz did that drove him six ways to insanity. But beneath the bravado, John could see, his friend was very, very hungry. And maybe, just maybe, a little afraid.

A makeshift truce, it seemed, was called for.

"Maria, this is my friend, Boz. Boz, this is Maria. My sister *Nora* and I are staying with her," he added, giving Boz a meaningful look that said, "Work with me."

Boz nodded and swept his hair to the floor.

"Charmed, milady."

"Where have you been? Since we met in Hayseed?" John added hastily.

"I have been where angels fear to tread. Though I rush to reassure you"—he winked at John—"far, far from the madding crowd." He turned to Maria. "Would you, by any propitious happenstance, have a more suitable wardrobe available for a vertically challenged visitor? I appear to have left my trousers somewhere in last week."

"I'm afraid you'll have to wear an old pair of Harry's trousers for the present. Until we can find a way to fix you up properly," Maria said, choking back her laugh. "Harry, why don't I give Boz something to eat while you go upstairs to fetch him some clothes?"

So off John went, treading softly on the stairs. He was almost at the top when he heard "Huff, puff, huff, puff, huff," coming from behind Leslie's door. Quietly, oh so quietly, John pushed it open.

Leslie was standing in the middle of the floor with his hands stretched to the ceiling. John saw his right eye slide to one side to examine the intruder.

"You're up late," Leslie puffed.

"What are you doing?"

"Evening calisthenics," Leslie huffed, leaning over and wriggling his fat bottom in the air. "Mustn't neglect my figure."

John began to retreat.

"And what are you doing?" puffed Leslie, attempting a push-up and failing miserably.

John stopped.

"My friend Boz arrived. He needs some clothes."

Leslie huffed. He was having trouble returning himself to an upright position.

"Is he planning to be here long?"

"I don't know," John retorted.

"Does he eat much?"

"Not really."

"Well, then, I suppose he can stay." Leslie wobbled into a stand. "Only for a few days, though. I don't want my future assets being eaten away by every tomcat that starts scratching at the door."

The seed of uneasiness that had been growing inside John now swelled to something the size of a watermelon. "What do you mean, your future assets?"

Leslie flexed his right arm and poked the nonexistent muscle beneath the flesh.

"Didn't Maria tell you?"

"What?"

"If she can't pay back the money my mother loaned her, the business reverts to my ownership." Leslie crouched into a squat and bounced his elbows up and down. "Judging by her account books, I'd give it till sometime in the spring."

He stood and began touching his toes.

"One, two, one, two. Selling a working bakery like this should give me exactly the capital I need to convert my castle at Howst into a showpiece for investors." He threw back his shoulders and pounded his chest for emphasis. "Harry, you may not know it yet, but you are looking at the next real estate king of this country."

Then, as a fitting finale, Leslie farted.

CHAPTER
17

THOUGH LESLIE'S FART faded—slowly—from the house, the memory of his words did not. All through the next day, as Boz was introduced to the workings of the bakery and a temporary room in a closet off the back kitchen, John inwardly panicked.

Nor did his worries end with bed. He lay awake that night going over and over Leslie's revelation, his thoughts tumbling around and around on creaking gears.

They were living with Maria. Which meant that Maria didn't have enough money to pay back Leslie. Which meant that the Pig would sell the bakery. Which meant that Maria would be miserable. And the Coggins would be left homeless, with Great-Aunt Beauregard looking for them and nowhere to go. Again.

John sighed, and Page stirred restlessly in her sleep.

Facts, John, facts, he reprimanded himself. *Worries don't solve problems.* He smacked himself on the forehead to drive the point home to his brain.

Why doesn't Maria have enough money? Because her oven is dying and she can't afford to pay for fuel. So she should buy a new oven with which she could bake and sell twice as much. But she doesn't have the money to buy a new one. So maybe I could try to fix the old one. But then she would still have to buy the coal. Unless . . .

He sat up.

If I can find a way to build a new oven that runs on something other than coal, he thought, yanking up his socks. *If I can devise an oven that runs on something everyone wants to get rid of, like vegetable scraps, then Maria won't have to spend anything on fuel. Then she could bake as much as she wants!*

The blood in John's head was pumping now, the gears beginning to whirr with excitement. But he made no sound, pausing only to grab a piece of paper and a pencil from the top of the bureau.

Down the stairs he crept to the kitchen, holding his breath all the way. Very carefully, very quietly, he shut the door and lit the candle. The tiny flame flickered over the cookbook shelf as he pulled down the volume that Maria had put there. He laid out his pencil and paper and opened the book to the page on principles of convection. Finally, John began to draw.

He was so immersed in his task that he didn't hear

the door creak open again, nor the *swish swish* of a creature dragging itself across the floor. It was not until the wizened face popped up from under the table that he noticed. And it was all he could do not to yell.

"Whatcha doing?" Boz whispered through a mouthful of crumbs.

"Go away, Boz." John gave him a not-so-friendly push.

"Now is that any way to treat a *verus amicus*?"

"Why should I tell you? You left me and Page. By ourselves. With my great-aunt Beauregard and a crowd of angry townspeople out to kill us for ruining their festival."

"Nonsense. Maim, perhaps, but not kill."

"Go away, Boz!"

"I can see that you're perturbed." In a moment, Boz had slid past the stool and vaulted onto the table, smushing John's drawings under his butt. "But I had hoped my heroics at Peddington's Practical Hotel would have gone some way toward remedying my remissness."

John's silence was pardon enough for Boz. He wiggled his torso cheerfully and clapped his hands together. "So what might you be up to?"

"I'm working," John retorted.

"On what, pray tell? A cure for halitosis? A resurrected Autopsy?"

"No!"

"Then what?" Boz lifted a buttock high in the air and peered at the sheets under it. "You know what comes of thwarting a cat's instinct for curiousness."

"Fewer furballs," John said, snatching for the paper.

Boz whipped out a drawing and placed his hand on John's forehead to prevent John from reaching it. "It can't get no satisfaction."

Boz raised his prize toward the light. Seeing the hopelessness of the situation, John sat back on his stool with a thump. They were silent for a moment as Boz examined the drawing. Then—

"You know, my wee wriggler, this is very interesting."

John said nothing.

"In fact, if my ocular powers don't deceive me, I'd say that this was a design for a new oven. A new brick oven fueled not by coal, but by some alternative means. A new, supremely efficient oven that will allow Maria Persimmons to blast her bitterest rivals somewhere into the next century."

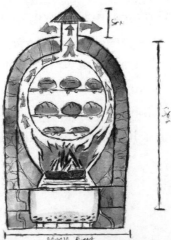

"I know it might not work," John grunted as Boz returned the drawings to him. "But I want to do something more for her."

"Aha! Do I detect the budding bloom of the genus *crushus cinnamonius?*"

"What are you talking about, Boz?"

"He's saying you're sweet on Maria," said Leslie from the open door. "Understandable emotion for little boys experiencing the change. Trying your hand at love poetry?" he inquired, swaggering into the room and reaching for the drawings. Boz snatched them from his fingers.

"Yes, he has. Would you like to hear what he wrote?"

Leslie snorted in joy. "Go on, Boz, I haven't had a good laugh in a long while."

"Oh, Maria, mamma mia, your luscious heels are hairy.
Your songs are sweet as milk, I do not want for dairy.
Your hair's like grass and tarnished brass; it's you I want
to marry."

"Let me see that," Leslie said suspiciously, reaching again for the paper. But Boz had a different thought in mind. He chomped down, hard, on Leslie's index finger. Leslie howled in pain.

"Oh, I am sorry," Boz said as Leslie danced round the room, blood spattering his plum-colored nightshirt. "Did I hurt you? Instinct, you know. I always like to have a bite before breakfast. You ought to put a plaster on that," Boz advised as Leslie jammed his finger in his mouth to stop the bleeding. "It might become septic."

In agony, Leslie stumbled out of the kitchen.

John frowned. "Boz, that was a bit much."

"My profuse apologies, my dear boy, but there was not much else I could do."

"You tried to eat his finger."

"A mere flesh wound. He'll soon recover." Boz flapped his arm dismissively. "In the meantime, I have saved your plans." He handed them back to John. "And as a sincere token of my esteem, I would like to offer my assistance."

Boz knelt like a knight of old.

"I, Boz the Malodorous Mendicant, do solemnly swear to help Prince John the Delusional build the most magnificent cooking oven that the world has hitherto seen."

"No."

"No?"

"Remember what happened the last time you tried to help me? We ended up facefirst in a vegetable emporium."

"But this is different!" Boz exclaimed. "We are dealing with things of a stationary bent. There is little risk of adventures in motoring."

John sighed. It *would* be useful to have another pair of hands.

"Okay. But only if you *promise on your life* to let me be in charge."

"Right, then, to work!" Boz leaped to his feet. "First things last! Have you decided upon a combustible?"

"A what?"

"Fuel, my dear boy, fuel."

"I don't know. It needs to be cheap. I was thinking vegetable scraps—"

Boz cut him off.

"While I admire your ecological evangelism, might I suggest a more potent alternative?"

"Like what?"

Boz opened the door to the stove, reached into his pocket, and threw an object into the flames.

A miniature fireball shot past John's nose.

"What was that?"

Boz uncurled his stunted fingers. In his palm lay a dried poo pellet from Maria's Henrietta hens.

"Chicken poo?"

"Chicken poo," Boz said sternly. "Particularly powerful chicken poo. Of course, it won't be of much assistance in Maria's current configuration, but your new oven should put paid to that particular conundrum."

John considered the situation. Boz was right. If he could find a way to tap into that energy, Maria would never have to pay for coal again. Seeing his interest, Boz solemnly handed him the pellet.

"Your poo, sir. Now naturally, I am acting under the assumption that you intend to keep this project strictly on the subterranean QT."

"What?"

"You want to keep it a secret from Maria."

"Yes," John said. "And Page." He couldn't bear to see a look of disappointment on his sister's face. If he failed again, he would have no one to blame but himself.

"As you wish," Boz said, rubbing his hands together and pacing round the table. "But we will need a suitable cover story for our nefarious activities. And to keep the warbling warthog from sniffing out the truth. The small vestiges of cells in his cerebrum may have already made him suspicious."

John was certain of that. Leslie might be dumb, but he wasn't blind. He was going to know something was up if they started building an oven in the backyard.

"'Wunderbar,' he shouted, in his most eloquent Egyptian, 'I have it!'" Boz twirled on his toes.

"Shhh!" John clamped a hand over Boz's mouth. "You're going to wake up the whole street!"

Boz crossed his eyes.

"Do you promise to keep your voice down?"

Boz nodded.

"Fine," John said, removing his hand. "What's your idea?"

Boz leaned in and twirled the imaginary end of an imaginary mustache. "Rubbish."

"Rubbish?" asked John.

"Rubbish," answered Boz. "The disintegrating dreck of modern civilization, the garbage of garçons, the picks of literati's litter."

"I know what trash is," John interrupted, "but what does that have to do with ovens?"

"Simple, my dear Simon. We pretend we are building an incinerator to burn rubbish!" Boz trumpeted, his voice bouncing off the rafters. "It is square, sturdy, and made like a brick pit house. It will send up a smokescreen wide enough to hide a colossus. And for the coup de pue, it is stinky enough to deflect even the most persistent inquisitors. Masked in this sheep's clothing, our wolf will emerge in the spring with its bellyful of chicken excrement and its throat full of fresh-baked bread."

John picked at the knife scar on the table. The idea wasn't completely crazy. A trash incinerator would explain the bricks they would need, and the smoke. If it worked, Maria could build an extension onto the back of the bakery and have a whole new kitchen, twice the size of her old one.

But what if it was a bust? What if things went splat all over the kitchen floor? Would he be able to live with himself if his new invention didn't work? Then John remembered. He wouldn't be able to live here at all unless it did.

He took a deep breath.

"Okay. Let's go for it."

CHAPTER
18

THAT WAS ALL the encouragement Boz needed. Within a day, there was a pile of bricks stacked in the backyard near the chicken coop. Within two, there was enough mortar to patch a volcano.

"Where did you get all this stuff?" asked John, dancing a little to keep himself from shearing apart in the February wind.

Boz waved his palm vaguely in the direction of the street.

"Oh, here and there, here and there," he offered. "When it comes to acquisition, I am of the firm belief that ethical field posts have always been built on the shifting sands of time. Or, to put it another way . . ." He tossed a brick at John. "Ask me no questions and I'll tell you no lies."

John only wished that Page had the same idea. While Maria was more than happy to let them experiment in the backyard, Page was deeply suspicious of their activities.

"Why do you have to build an incinernator?"

"Incinerator," he corrected.

"Why?"

"Because I want to see if I can."

"It doesn't make any sense," she said perceptively. Too perceptively for John's liking.

"You'll understand when you're older."

That was a red flag to a china bull. Having already gone through feast and famine with her brother, Page was not impressed with being compared to a baby in diapers. For the next twenty-four hours, she hardly spoke to him.

But Page was a doddle compared to the Pig. After a couple of days of observation, and just before the actual construction began, Leslie elected to supervise the project.

"This is one of my future assets you're building," he told a protesting John. "Bungling boys should not be left in charge."

"What are we going to do?" hissed John as Leslie started examining each brick in the brick pile. "We can't work with him sniffing around!"

"What we need is a diversionary ally," Boz replied.

"Someone to distract our bumptious observer during key hours of the afternoon."

"Like who?"

Boz cast a meaningful glance at the attic window.

"But she'll tell Maria!" John protested. "Or be disappointed when it doesn't work. Or get in my way."

Boz shook his kaleidoscopic locks and sighed. "You underestimate your sister, my dear boy. You always have."

That was a hard truth for John to hear. He had been there when Page took her first step and said her first word. Now Boz was telling him that he didn't know his own family? John's thoughts were stormy as he climbed the stairs to the attic.

"Page?"

Page put down Tiger Lil's bear and gazed at her brother with a stern expression. At that precise moment, she looked very much like Colonel Joe. John gulped. This was going to be harder than he had anticipated.

"I think I need your help."

Without hesitation, Page barrel rolled her brother into a hug. "Took you long enough!"

And so began the great chicken poo conspiracy. The plan was simple: Page would endure two hideous hours of lessons in real estate sales while John and Boz worked like blazes to construct the oven. Whenever Leslie felt the need to inspect the rate of progress, Page would block him from getting too close, and John would be there to explain away the odder aspects of the incinerator.

But it was at midnight in the attic that the real developments took place. It was then that John honed the details, using Page as his sounding board.

Although his domed oven was based on simple methods of convection—the idea that cooled air could be drawn into a top oven, heated hot by the fire pit below, used to bake bread, and then pulled out through the flue—John had a lot of practical "hows" to consider. How much air should he let in? How big should the fire pit be? How good would the bricks be at radiating heat? The Coggins stayed awake by arguing.

"If you put the flue in this place, then the air can go this way."

"But hot air rises, Page. It's a simple law of physics."

"Physics is dumb."

It was a good thing they had Boz. Perhaps as an act of penance for running away in Hayseed, their friend worked harder than ever before. He helped the Coggins set up experiments to test their ideas; he fetched any materials they needed; he even went sploshing out in a rainstorm to erect a tent over the drying mortar. He returned two hours later looking like a beaver in a mud wrap.

With Page and Boz as John's assistants, the work went quickly. By late March, John had a fully functional, rather handsome brick baking oven.

The only problem was, it didn't work.

At least, not in the way John had hoped it would. The main difficulty was heat. Starting the fire pit with a small amount of wood and dried poo pellets didn't generate nearly enough energy to warm the entire interior of the oven. Somehow, the pellets weren't exploding as they had when Boz had thrown them into Maria's stove.

To combat this problem, John resorted to adding more wood and pellets, then more, then more, until finally, on a weekend when Leslie was scouting for housing opportunities north of the city, John had added enough fuel to cook a loaf of bread.

It took eight hours to bake.

Still, it looked nice enough when it emerged.

"Here's to your first teetering step on the road to immortality!" Boz shouted.

The sky was porcelain blue and the sun was warm enough to seep through John's coat as the trio took their first bites of bread. Boz munched his crust thoughtfully.

"Nutty, with a hint of maple and malt, followed by a crisp and crunchy finish. Though I sense a top note of flavor, something that I can't quite put my taste buds on. . . ."

"It tastes like chicken poo," Page said.

Boz took another bite.

"Yes, now that you mention it, there is a certain avian chew."

"This is foul," said John, throwing his bread on the ground.

Boz tutted.

"Now, now, save the hysterics for the poultry."

But John was not to be comforted. The bread tasted awful, and even if it didn't, Maria's chickens could never create enough poo to feed the fire day after day.

What was worse, John also had to deal with the fact that the grown-ups now thought he had built an incinerator. Maria began leaving him buckets of trash to take out and burn—buckets that Boz mysteriously disposed of—and Leslie was eager to examine his new asset.

When John protested that it wasn't finished, Leslie became mistrustful about the whole project. One morning, he sneaked out to have a look under the tarp, and it took an "accidental" tackle from Boz to prevent him from discovering their endeavors. Leslie emerged from the scrum with a busted lip and bruised earlobes. Boz emerged minus a large hunk of hair.

The bruised earlobes bought John a few more days without supervision. After an agony of experimentation with Page, he decided that the overall size of the fire pit was the issue. In the cavernous space, the pellets required lots of wood to ignite. Even worse, they soon lost their effectiveness in the frigid air. He had to find a more efficient way to burn fewer pellets.

By Friday night, he was back at his task. The city clock

was tolling one as John quenched the flames from his sixteenth attempt of the evening. He'd sent Page to bed after the tenth. It was cold out in the yard and warm by the bricks. Despite the smell of the chicken poo, John couldn't help himself. He slumped down on the side of the oven and fell asleep.

He dreamed of ladybugs being chased by tomatoes and woke, four hours later, sweating with excitement.

"Boz!" he cried.

"Good morning, my dear boy." Boz was busy sweeping out the remains of John's experiments.

"I've solved the pellet problem!"

Boz clapped his hands, sending a plume of poo ash flying into the air.

"Do tell."

"The mayor's baby."

If a squashed cabbage face can ever look wistful, Boz looked wistful. "Ah, yes. The finale of our bucolic summer sojourn together."

"You remember how I was telling you that the engine worked by sparking a series of little explosions in a small space—the smaller the space, the bigger the explosion?"

Boz's blue eyes glinted briefly. "Ah. Light is beginning to dawn on marble head."

"If we start with a really strong explosion from one pellet in a tiny area . . . ," John said, taking a stick and drawing his idea in the mud. "If we keep the pellets right next to each other in a kind of generator, then that explosion should make enough heat to explode two more pellets, then four more pellets, and then—"

"And then you will have the most powerful oven in our hyperkinetic universe!"

"We're going to have to find a way to let the heat off gradually, so it can surround a closed-off section where the food will be cooked, but I think if we can spark the first explosion, we've got it!"

"Leave that to me, my dear boy!" cried Boz, snatching his wool cap from his pocket and plonking it on his head. "I know the whereabouts of every overachieving accelerant ever to offend an actuarial heart. I will be back faster than you can say flash flood insurance!"

And before anyone could protest, he did a flying somersault over the fence.

Since John had absolutely no idea what Boz meant, he returned to the problem at hand. By the late afternoon he had built a miniature generator where he could begin the explosions.

The primary materials were mortar, bricks, and metal vents. Once he had a few pellets going, he could open the vents and close the door to the bottom section. That would give the oven more than enough heat to bake the bread in an enclosed top section. Plus, with only a few pellets as fuel, the food wouldn't taste like chicken poo.

It was enough to bring back hope. John was so cheerful at dinner that Maria thought he was sick. Though she was due to help a neighbor with a new baby that night, she looked unhappy at leaving him.

"You haven't been this happy in days. Are you running a fever?" she asked.

"Nope," said John, handing Leslie the last brownie. Boz had yet to return.

Maria put a cool hand on his forehead.

"A little warm, but not burning," she muttered.

"I feel fine," said John. He gave Page a mysterious smile. He had decided not to tell her about the generator until he was absolutely sure it worked.

"You'd tell me if anything was wrong?"

"Sure," John said, eager for the hour when he could return to his experiments.

"I could stay home tonight." Maria hesitated.

"I'm fine!" John insisted. And he was.

Nevertheless, it was past eleven before Page succumbed to fatigue and Leslie stopped huffing and puffing in his room. When he was certain everyone was asleep, John crept down the stairs and laid out his drawings on the kitchen table.

His main concern was what kind of fuel he would use to kick-start the pellets in the generator. Perhaps he could coat one pellet in an accelerant and then throw a match through a special vent. But would the generator be strong enough to contain the force of the reaction?

"I have returned! By the grace of the almighty sod, my coursers now ride again on this hallowed soil—"

"Shhh!"

"Ooops." Boz clapped his hand to his mouth. "My apologies," he squeaked through his fingers. "What are you doing?"

"I'm trying to find a way to light the first pellet without burning out the generator," said John, sketching in the new vent.

"Can I assist?"

"No."

"But, my dear boy—"

"Not now, Boz, I need to concentrate. If I can't figure out how to manage the heat, then I won't be able to use any accelerant at all."

"Fine." Boz sulked. "I know when I'm not wanted."

Dragging his feet noisily along the floor, he disappeared out the back door.

Only to return five minutes later.

"Ahem."

"Go away, Boz."

"There is something I want to show you."

"Go away, Boz!"

"But if I could only point out—"

John sighed and threw his pencil down on the table.

"Boz, until I've finished this drawing, don't talk to me unless your pants are on fire, do you understand?"

Surly silence was Boz's reply.

"Why don't you go outside and restock the pellets?" John suggested. "I'll come out when I'm done."

Boz gave John a brusque nod and stomped outside.

Only to return again five minutes later.

"Ahem."

John ignored him.

"Ahem. AHEM!"

"What *is* it, Boz?"

"My pants are on fire."

CHAPTER 19

John looked at Boz's pants. A bright and merry flame was tickling his left hem. But that wasn't all. A thin and whispering trail of fire had followed Boz up to the back door.

"Boz!" John shrieked. "You're on fire!"

"That appears to be the case."

"Then put yourself out!" John yelled, grabbing a bowl and rushing to the sink. But Boz was already rolling around on the floor.

"Stop, drop, and revolve. Repeat until extinguished."

"What's going on?" Page was standing at the foot of the stairs in her pajamas and slippers. She held her bear in one hand while she fretfully rubbed the sleep from her eyes with the other.

Boz explained while John doused the flame that had

come in through the back door. "Well, you see, as I was fetching various inflammatory substances to try in the oven, I seem to have dripped some on the ground and, it appears, on my trousers. I imagine this happened in the transit of materials. Naturally, when I accidentally dropped a match, this had the effect of lighting both the trail and the hem."

John gulped. "Boz, you didn't drip any near the oven, did you?"

Boz considered this for a minute.

"Boz!"

"My dear boy, my profuse apologies, but I'm rather afraid that I did."

John rushed out the back door with Page close on his heels. The tongue of fire that had followed Boz into the house had died out. But a sinuous flicker was now making its way toward the oven. And a nearby pile of cans.

"Boz, are those gasoline cans?" asked Page.

"Not all of them," Boz said. "Some of them are much more powerful."

The tongue was beginning to lick at the bottom part of the oven.

"Boz, you didn't put accelerants on any pellets, did you?" demanded John.

Boz tugged at his hair. "It is difficult to remember such things in times of imminent crisis, but if I were to put my hand over my heart and take the oath of office—"

"Boz!" the Coggins both shouted.

"I may have placed some coated pellets inside the oven. Naturally, I wasn't planning to light them without your consent."

The flame was crawling up to the mouth of the generator.

"But I'm sure you have nothing to worry about," Boz said. "That bottom compartment is built like a rock—it can easily withstand a diminutive explosion. Once the pellets have blown, we'll have a nice little fire generating heat for Maria's morning loaf. I can almost taste the honeyed notes of—"

BOOOOOOM!

In all his life, John had never heard such a noise. The blast knocked a hole right through the top of the bake oven, sending a volcano of smoke and flame into the sky. An enormous shock wave slammed into the chicken coop, causing the wall to crumple slowly inward. Plumes of white feathers rose up into the air as the chickens fled through the windows to safety.

John, Page, and Boz were thrown onto their backs. When John looked up, he could see that most of the backyard was being engulfed in a bonfire. It looked almost festive.

"I knew it!" cried a voice from above them. "Criminals! Hooligans! I'll have you arrested!"

It was Leslie, leaning out of his window. His face flashed orange in the flames, making him resemble a hog with a suntan.

John would have responded, but at that precise moment his mouth was full of chicken wings. The frantic birds were streaming past the back door of the house, clucking and squawking in terror.

"What's happening?"' screamed Page.

"Can he really have us arrested?" John shouted to Boz, who was wrestling with not one but four chickens.

Boz removed a beak from his pinky finger and nodded.

"Afraid so!" he yelled back. "Malicious destruction of property, arson, not to mention an unlicensed bake oven. I'd say ten to twelve years' hard labor or an identification parade for the benefit of the Hayseed constabulary. It may not be opportune for us to linger."

There was a slam as Leslie banged his window down.

"What's he saying?" Page cried.

There was no way John was going to wait around for his great-aunt to pluck him out of a lineup. He bolted for the side of the house, where a narrow lane led into the street. Boz and Page followed—Boz skipping and Page clinging to John's sweater. Away in the distance, fire-engine sirens began to wail.

"I have to run, Page."

"Where are we going?"

John pulled his hand from hers. "Not you. You stay with Maria."

"No!" Page yelled. The sirens were growing louder and louder with each step up the lane.

"You didn't have anything to do with this," John insisted. "You need to stay here."

"No!" she said as the fire engines came roaring around the corner. "I'm going!"

"May I recommend a little expediency?" Boz interrupted. "We appear to be facing a crisis of exothermic proportions."

Fire engines were pulling up to the bakery, men leaping from the side with ladders and hoses in hand. A crowd was coagulating, attracted by the sirens. With remarkable grace, Boz sprinted across the road, zipping and nipping between the engines, and vanished down a street.

"Let's go, Johnny, let's go!" urged Page. The smoke from the explosions was beginning to sear John's eyes, making it almost impossible for him to see. He had no choice but to give his sister the lead.

Through the chaos they flew, over hoses and under rearing horses. When they reached the entrance of the opposite street, John paused long enough to look at the bakery. Leslie was near the front doorway, pointing wildly toward the backyard, and the firemen were already storming down the lane.

From up above the chimneys rose a cloud of white birds singed black by the smoke. One chicken's tail was on fire, and it seemed to rise higher and higher into the night. Until, quite suddenly, it plummeted to the earth.

"C'mon, Johnny!" Page yanked him hard. They caught up with Boz at the end of the street, where it forked into two dark and dismal ends.

"Where should we go?" John gasped as they paused to catch their breath.

Boz ran his fingers through his hair, leaving a trail of soot in the red.

"I am always amused at the role that coincidence plays in our manifest destinies. Who would have thought a fire engine would be both the source of our salvation and the cause of our downfall? Thus does the wheel of fortune turn, leaving us but a prey to time—"

"Boz!!"

"Left," he said, startled. "It's almost a straight shot to the depot."

"The depot?"

"We have a freight train to catch."

It was a sprint of Olympic proportions. In three beats, the trio was there, on the edge of a scrubby wasteland covered in rusting carriages. A square building lay to their right and fields of early crops to their left.

"What do we do now?"

"Attend here and keep your head down," chirped Boz,

his eyes glinting as he hopped from side to side. "The railway guards are distantly related to Accipitridae. I'll proceed to divert their attention. When you hear the whistle, begin your hundred-yard dash to the depot. I will await your company in the black boxcar!"

And with that, he was off again, a firefly of volatility blinking in the night.

For a time, John and Page said nothing. With all the excitement, John had not been aware of the cold, but he knew it now. He could feel Page shivering next to him.

Then, through the dark, he heard a mewling, whimpering sound. He looked around, expecting to see a wounded animal. Instead, he saw water glistening on Page's cheeks.

"Why are you crying?"

"Because I'm hungry!" Page spat at him. "Because I'm scared. And because you took me away from the one person who felt like home."

John reached out his hand but she batted it away. "Don't touch me!"

"But Page, I didn't make you come."

"Yes, you did! You're my brother. I told you, Johnny. I will never leave you. Not even if they chop my head off."

John felt the tears prickling in his eyes, and he swallowed hard to hold them back. "I'm sorry, Page. I'm very, very sorry."

"I don't care."

John had no energy left to protest. The air was so sharp that he could feel the pores in his skin freezing, one by one. Soon they'd be able to break little pieces off each other—noses and fingers and toes. This was the second time he'd led Page into a calamity, and it looked like it might be their last.

"Johnny, what's that?"

John listened for a moment. From far, far away he caught the faint whiff of a sound.

Shuguwugahshuguwugahshuguwugah.

The sound swished across the wasteland. It was a sound he had heard before. If only he weren't so cold, he might be able to remember . . .

Woooooiwiwiwiwooooooiwiw!

"It sounds like one of your dragons," Page said, clutching his coat. "Do you think it will eat us?"

Suddenly an icicle melted in his brain.

"That's not a dragon, Page! That's a freight train!"

John grabbed Page's hand and started running toward the depot. He could see the outline of the building growing larger and larger, but he could also feel Page tiring, her steps shortening as they drew closer.

A billowing cloud of white, a huge belch of steam, rose from the flatlands, and the dragon screamed again.

Woooooiwiwiwiwooooooiwiw!

"Hurry, Page! It's almost there!"

They tore through the scrub as the iron creature

came charging up to the depot, looking as if it would blast straight through. But at the last moment, the beast groaned to a walk, then a crawl, and then, letting out a deep and weary sigh, a complete stop.

Their shins bruised and scraped, John and Page hurtled toward the boxcars. It was not nearly fast enough. The goods had been unloaded. The dragon was already stirring back to life.

"What color was it?" John cried as the whistle blew a shrill warning.

"Black!" Page pointed her finger. "Look!"

There was a rumble of a door being rolled back, and there was Boz, grinning maniacally. "Greetings! *Hic sunt dragones*—time and mail wait for no man. Upsy-daisy, my little floret."

He threw down a frayed bit of rope, and Page grabbed it. The train was on the move now, the wheels cranking slowly round and round as it picked up momentum. Boz pulled and John pushed and up Page scrambled.

"Why did you climb the monster?" Boz asked as he chucked the rope to John. "Why, because it was there!"

With one huge tug from Boz, John went flying into the boxcar, landing with an almighty thud on the floor. A stupendous cloud of dry dirt rose around him as the freight train raced into the darkness. They were safe.

But they were not alone.

CHAPTER 20

"CLOSE THE DOOR! Air's cold enough to skate on!"

Swaying merrily with the motion of the car, Boz bumbled shut the door, casting the inhabitants into further gloom.

A small flame burst into being. John watched a match arc through the air and land in a metal box. A welcoming surge of heat soon followed.

"Never seen a brazier light so quickly." A tall, penitent-looking man materialized from the murk. "You young 'uns must be good luck with fire."

"Good luck, hah!" A broad-shouldered gorilla lumbered into view. Thick hair burst from the cuffs of his shirt and the collar of his worn coat. "That's half a bottle of Holler's private supply."

"I'm Tom," the penitent man said. "And this is Cal.

Feel free to warm yourselves up."

John took Page's hand and cautiously approached the brazier.

"Why, you're nothing but babes!" wheezed Tom as the glow caught the undersides of their cheeks.

"Babes in arms," Boz said, throwing his arm around John's shoulder. "My little family."

"What are you doing with this reprobate?" asked Tom. "You should be at home, tucked up safe in bed."

"We would have been," Page grumped, holding her fingers before the brazier, "if John hadn't messed everything up by—"

"Well," Boz interrupted, his grin showing the gums of his missing teeth, "now that we're all snug as bugs in a Tyrolean rug, why don't we let these lice—I mean nice"—he corrected, as Cal glowered—"men talk among themselves?"

"Oh, no." Cal seized hold of Boz's hair. "You don't leave us dying with malaria and get away with it."

"Malaria?" queried John.

"Yes, well," Boz ahemmed. "The unfortunate upshot of my salad days. I'm afraid these gentlemen and I made our acquaintance during the excavation of a canal." He scratched at his cheek. "I was recruiting a few good men and true for digging."

"You said it was the next gold rush. You said there'd be beer and women and dancing bands! And what did we get?" Cal yanked Boz three times in the air for emphasis. "Jaguars and skeeters and dysentery."

"My dear sir," Boz replied. "If you choose to lead a rootless existence, you must be prepared to forgo fertilizer."

A curious lump appeared in John's throat. He looked over at Page. She was shivering uncontrollably. "A rootless existence," he repeated to himself.

"Leave him be, Cal." Tom took a stick and nudged a few of the coals to the side of the brazier. "He was just doing his job."

Cal dropped Boz to the floor of the train car and stomped off back into the black.

"I hate to bring it up," Tom said to John, "but you two look done in." He clamped the lid on the brazier. "And we need to save on fuel."

"O-k-k-kay," chattered Page. Tiny rays of light were still shooting from aeration holes near the coals.

"Here now." Tom shrugged off his coat and handed it to John. "Wrap your sister in that."

But Page would have nothing to do with her sibling.

"Go away!" She lay down next to the brazier and curled her body into a spiral around her bear. "I'm fine."

"You don't want one of Dad's stories?" John asked.

"No!"

John peered into the corners. Tom and Cal were bedding down on the floor. Boz had found a perch on top of a crate. The world felt cold and dark and rank.

When he could endure the silence no longer, John draped the coat over as much of his sister as possible, lay down next to her, and closed his eyes.

He awoke five hours later to a raw reality. Page was missing. And Boz, sound asleep, was sucking his thumb.

"Page?" he yelled over the *click clank clunk* of the train wheels. "Page!"

"Shaddup your face!" Cal gargled, and a cold lump of coal whizzed over John's head.

"I'm over here," Page said quietly. She was sitting by the edge of the boxcar, the doors flung wide open to the clammy dawn.

"Get back, Page," scolded John. "You might fall out."

Page gave him a look that would kill spiders dead. "I don't fall out of things."

John hung his head. His tongue felt like sandpaper and his body was aching. With considerable pain, he sat down next to his sister.

They appeared to be racing beside an endless river of fog. It lapped around John's ankles and knees, numbing his legs.

Then, very slowly, a glimmer of peach-colored light began to seep through. As John and Page watched, the light rose higher, growing stronger by the moment. Rocks began to emerge in the river. Only they weren't rocks, John realized, but the outlines of budding trees and flowering bushes. A bed of green grass could suddenly be seen, the blades still flecked with white.

Finally the round ball of the sun emerged, riding high above the misty river, turning the fog from peach to gold. The gray retreated into the crevices of the trees, and a world of gentle hills stretched out before them.

Phhhheeeeeeewww went the train whistle, to greet the day.

"That was good," Page said, and John knew he was forgiven, at least for the moment.

"Shaddup your face!"

Another piece of coal went zinging over their heads and bounced off into the grass.

"Johnny," Page said softly. "What are we going to do now?"

John shrugged.

"I don't know."

"We could go back to Maria's—"

"We can never go back, Page. Do you understand? I blew our cover. Great-Aunt Beauregard *and* the Littlemere police will both be looking for us now. We're fugitives."

Page hung her head.

John glanced away. He hadn't meant to snap at his sister, but her words had brought every vivid detail of the nightmare back to life. Not only had he failed at his inventions, he had destroyed the dreams of the only adult who had given them love. Maria must despise him.

"Salutations, my little pipettes! And how do you fare

on this fine frosty morning?"

A fastball of coal whanged Boz in the ear. He shook his skull a couple of times and proceeded in a slightly lower voice. "Wonder of wonder, miracle of miracles—the glory of creation in all her finest linen. But I repeat myself. Did you sleep well?"

"I have to go to the bathroom," Page said.

Boz coughed.

"Well, I'm afraid the facilities here aren't quite what you're used to. There is however, a tin receptacle . . ."

"A what?"

Boz coughed again.

"A bucket. Behind those boxes. We empty it every ten miles or so."

Page wrinkled her nose, squared her shoulders, and went in search of the bucket. Boz sat down beside John. "And how about you? Feeling chip, chip, chippety, eh?"

"No."

"Come now, don't be downhearted, my boy. The light at the end of the tunnel—"

"—is an oncoming engine," John finished as the freight train yawned a whistle.

"You're sad."

"I blew up the bakery!"

"Well, I admit, that is a bird's nest in the gears."

"And now we're on a train bound for nowhere . . ."

"Actually, southwest, to be precise."

"With nothing but a tin bucket. And I've let everyone down. Again!"

Boz appeared to have no answer to this. It was hard for John to tell whether his expression meant that he was sorry or that he had simply resolved not to make a bad situation worse. It was a relief when they both heard the clang of a coffee pot.

"Ah, breakfast," said Boz, hastily retreating into the interior.

The scent of coffee couldn't quite mask the fumes that came from men who hadn't brushed their teeth or washed their clothes in several weeks. Page, still in her pajamas, was finding it hard to chew through the stale crackers that Cal had handed to her.

Eating wasn't a problem for John. All he could think about was the burned-out wreck of a business that Maria would currently be surveying. Being hungry didn't enter into the equation.

Since nobody wished to talk, it was left to Boz to try and make conversation.

"Fine morning," he began.

Only the coffee spurting on the side of the pot answered him.

"Excellent pneumatic pressure being exerted in the upper strata of the hemispheric regions."

Tom cracked his knuckles.

"And which golden vista of opportunity are you approaching?"

"Would someone stuff a stick in that catbird and have done?" Cal griped.

Surprisingly, it was Page who jumped to Boz's defense.

"He's only being nice," she said, chucking her food on the ground. "You could try it."

John tried hard not to laugh at the face of a hard-bitten man silenced by a girl wearing sooty pink slippers.

"Sorry, lass," Cal said finally. "We're not what you'd call morning people."

"Hummph," she answered. "I'm tired. I'm going back to bed." She clomped off into the shadows.

"So where be ye bound?" repeated Boz, once he had assured himself that Cal was not within range of any coal.

"We're going south." Tom's voice was quiet and sad.

"Like everything else in this world," Cal chipped in.

"Good laboring jobs, we've heard," Tom added, rubbing his fingers along his stubble. "In the copper mines."

John leaned his back against a packing case near the open door, closed his eyes, and tried not to let the stench choke his lungs. Up until now, he hadn't had the courage to think about their destination. What if his only option at the end of the ride was a job in the mines?

He attempted to imagine what it would be like working underground. Never to see sunshine, always to be picking away at rock. A world without vision.

"Got the jiggers?"

John opened his eyes. Tom had sat down opposite him.

"I'm thinking about the future."

Tom nodded. "Do that sometimes myself."

John picked at a piece of ash on his sweater. He wondered what Page could do while he was stuck below the crust of the earth. He certainly didn't want her with him.

"Do you have any family, Tom?"

Tom paused. "I did. A brother. A mother."

"What happened?"

"They died." He struggled to make his tongue shape the words. "When I was in prison."

"I'm sorry."

"Me too."

"What were you in prison for?"

Tom sighed and tugged on his cap. The stink from his armpit as he lifted his hand was gag inducing, but John made no comment.

"They call it breaking and entering. Getting in where I wasn't supposed to. Picking locks with knives and slicing windows open." He sniffed. "Don't get yourself arrested, kid. God's creatures were never meant to live in cages."

There was something in the twitch of Tom's jaw that reminded John of his father. So this was the flip side of a life of freedom, he thought. The worry and the uncertainty and the fear. This was what happened to men who decided to follow their dreams.

John pulled out Colonel Joe's jackknife. "Tom?"

"Yep?"

"Will you teach me how to pick a lock?"

Tom paused. "You going to steal?"

"Maybe." John sneaked a sideways glance at his sister. "If I have to."

"Well, if that's what you want." Shaking his head a little, Tom slipped his hand into his coat pocket and took out a padlock. "You can practice on my good-luck charm."

"May I join your merry band?" Boz interrupted, plopping himself down between their legs. "I do so enjoy improving my dexterity."

Thus it was that John learned how to twiddle a lock with a jackknife. It was a remarkably smooth introduction to a life of crime. Boz was passable at the task, but John was a true engineer. Within a couple of hours, he could jimmy the gears open in ten seconds.

Even Cal was impressed. "That's a neat trick you've got there. Should've had you with me on the Simmons job."

John almost found the courage to smile. Then he noticed that the men were snapping their suspenders and tying their shoes. The train was slowing, the *clickety-clack* turning into a *cl-ick-e-ty-cl-ack*.

"What's happening?"

"Engineers changing over in Riverton. We got about a quarter of an hour to scrounge for food."

"I'll go," John said, scrambling to his feet.

"No," Tom said, laying a paw on his shoulder. "You stick to your sister. Hide behind the crates in case someone comes around. I'll get enough for the three of us."

The train slowed to a chug, and Cal and Tom leaped out the door. John saw a flash of red streak past him . . .

Then a bolt of gold.

"Page! Where are you going?"

"To help!"

She hared off after Boz before John could protest. He was bracing himself to follow when he heard a dog bark, far too close for comfort. This was followed by a shout. John scrambled behind a crate.

Tromp went the boots on the gravel. John held his hand over his mouth and tried to breathe through his eyelids. There was a *crinch* and *crunch* near the door of the boxcar. A man belched.

"All clear, Billy!" a jolly voice finally rang out. "Rats must have abandoned the ship. Give Sally a kiss for me!"

John couldn't catch the response from the engineer up at the front, but it was evidently funny, for the jolly voice chuckled. The boots shuffled away.

"Luck of the ladybug," John muttered to himself. When he was certain the guard was gone, he scurried out from behind the crates and poked his head into the sunshine.

"JOHN PEREGRINE COGGIN!"

CHAPTER 21

THIS TIME, JOHN knew, there would be no amazing escape.

"How dare you shame the family name with your antics! Remove yourself from that contraption!" John felt his feet fly out behind him as he landed with a thud on his great-aunt's shoulder.

"Where is your sister?" she demanded, dumping him like a sack of nails on the ground.

Oh, no, Page! thought John. She might return at any moment. He had to warn everyone. Quick as a blink, he said very loudly, "I asked Boz to take her back to the Wayfarers."

Would it work?

It would.

"First sensible thought you've ever had," Great-Aunt Beauregard grunted. "I will have to collect her later. You, on the other hand"—she hauled him up by the scruff of his neck—"are coming with me."

Please, Page, please keep yourself hidden, John prayed as he was pushed and prodded and pinched toward the station.

"Are we going back to Pludgett on a train?" he yelled. If nothing else, at least Boz and the others might realize where he was headed.

"Did you lose your hearing as well as your wits?" his great-aunt snapped. "YES, WE ARE GOING BACK TO PLUDGETT!" she bellowed. "IMMEDIATELY!"

She wasn't joking. The Riverton to Pludgett train was sounding its final whistle as she lugged John into a weather-beaten carriage and plonked him on a stained leather seat.

"Now," Great-Aunt Beauregard said, removing a hat festooned with a catatonic cardinal and a trio of yellow finches. "We have a couple of days before we reach Pludgett. So you and I are going to have a little talk."

John darted a glance toward the window. Had Boz returned yet? Catching his look by the tail, his great-aunt reached over and jammed the blind down.

"Answer me, boy!"

"Yes, Great-Aunt Beauregard."

She thrust out her jaw and nodded. "Better."

"Riverton to Pludgett Express!" the conductor trumpeted. "Making scheduled stops at Weekeg, Oilston,

Mummer, Howst, and Pludgett. All aboard!"

Thug, thug, thug went the colossal wheels along the iron tracks. John knew that, unlike the mayor's baby, this vehicle could only take one road—and that road dead-ended in a coffin.

"I'm not sure if I impressed upon you the magnitude of our contract," his great-aunt began. "You, John Peregrine Coggin, are the eldest living descendant of our line. As the heir apparent, it is your moral duty to contribute to the family business."

John bristled.

"Says who?"

If it was possible for an impenetrable slab of granite to look puzzled, Great-Aunt Beauregard looked puzzled. Bravado, apparently, had not been what she was expecting. She shifted tack.

"Consider, boy, what I have been through to locate you after Hayseed. First, I had to establish your coordinates. The sheriff searched the Wayfarers' camp from top to bottom but could find no trace of your existence. It was equal odds you had run away on the mayor's horse or fled with your ginger-nut companion.

"Laid up with my discombobulated peritonia, I sent word to every police station within a hundred-mile radius to be on the alert. And think! Think what a reception I was given from some of our so-called protectors of life and property!"

John could well imagine what the police had said after receiving a communiqué from Great-Aunt Beauregard. No doubt she had informed them that they were all a bunch of lily-livered, saw-kneed, crackpot constables who didn't know their tasks from their hacksaws.

"Faced with rank incompetence, I was forced to turn to my colleagues for help. From an embalmer in Herriot, I discovered that a figure answering the description of your scarlet confederate had been spotted in the north. It took me six months—"

Here she dropped any pretense at civility and discharged a full round.

"SIX MONTHS! To track that fox to Littlemere. And even then I didn't know where you were holed up."

Much as he fought against it, John had to respect his great-aunt's dedication. It was not every woman who could follow the trail of Boz.

"So how did you find us?"

His great-aunt's attempt at a smirk cracked a minuscule line in her top lip.

"You should stay away from fire."

John sighed a heavy sigh. This was rapidly becoming a theme in his life.

"At the epicenter of your ill-timed eruption, I spoke to a sensible fellow named Leslie who reported you fleeing in the direction of the depot."

"Did you meet Maria?"

The words flew out of John's mouth before he could stop them.

His great-aunt tilted her head.

"I encountered a person of that name," she said slowly.

"What did she say?"

The crack in her lip widened.

"She said she never wanted to see you again."

The universe exploded. It was confirmed, then. Maria hated his guts. John had had one shot—one shot—at saving her business, and he'd manage to destroy it with a heap of dried poo. He didn't blame her for hating him. He hated himself.

Great-Aunt Beauregard was oblivious to his distress.

". . . then I found out from the stationmaster where the hobos usually stopped for food, took a fast passenger service to Riverton, and there, as you are no doubt aware, I discovered you."

The finches shimmied and shook as she opened her handbag and laid the contract on the seat beside her.

"And now let us proceed to the matter of the partnership. . . ."

John was barely paying attention. Memories of his disasters were flooding fast and furious through his mind. The sputters of his broke-backed Autopsy. The glistening ripe tomato hovering above the mayor's baby. The panicked squawk of the Henrietta hens.

". . . furthermore, I have decided to allow you to begin working on the shredder thingymabob."

This yanked him back to reality.

"What?"

Great-Aunt Beauregard leaned back and folded her arms across her remarkable bosom. "As much as it pains me to say it, I have decided to give you one half day on Sundays to model improvements. Congratulations, John. Your imagination is going to make us very rich."

Although you wouldn't have believed it to look at him, there was a desperate war being waged inside John.

On the one side was his brain.

Go back to Pludgett, it demanded. You're finished being a boy. Sign the contract, ask the police to find Page, and give up on impossibilities.

On the other side was his heart. It didn't have anything to say. It simply fought like a hero.

For several agonizing minutes, the two warriors remained locked in battle. The brain thrust, and the heart parried. The heart charged, and the brain blocked.

Finally, with a stunning blow, the brain cleaved John's heart in two. And there, inside, was the one feeling that common sense could never defeat.

Hope.

"No!" John shouted.

He was almost loud enough to wake the catatonic cardinal.

"No?" Great-Aunt Beauregard repeated.

"No! I won't do it." John had reached the end of the line. "I won't let you get ahold of Page and I won't become a partner in the family business. I'm not a train you can push down a track—I'll take my own road! I'll run away and run away and run away again. *You can't make me sign that contract!*"

"YOU!" bawled his great-aunt, tearing off a finch and hurling it at his head. "You are just like your father! Your pie-in-the-sky, gim-whacked, used tea bag of a father!"

John was not going to take that sitting down. "My father was not a used tea bag!"

His great-aunt snorted. "Really? The scribbling story-teller? The so-called writer? I remember the day he said he was getting married and leaving Pludgett. I told him the same thing I'm telling you now: the only certainty in life is death. Your father and mother lived on air and dreams, boy, and look where that got them. Six feet under and food for worms."

John lashed out with a kick, but his Great-Aunt Beauregard caught him by the ankle and tossed him back on the seat.

"You, at least, have some vestiges of the family's cranial capacity. Wake up to the world! I have a sturdy, steady business that will keep you and your sister occupied for the rest of your existence. And you wish to give up this security to chase after Page's rainbows? If you think that kind of life will make you happy, you've got mush for brains."

John refused to be defeated.

"Well, you know what? You're just like me! You dream too, Great-Aunt Beauregard! Only you dream about death and money. At least Page and I believe in rainbows!"

"Tickets, tickets."

John didn't hesitate. Head down and heart pounding, he bashed past the conductor and out into the corridor. Down to the end of the carriage he ran, lurching sideways into the walls as the train jerked and swayed.

A strong shove of his shoulder sent the door flying open. And now he was standing on the metal platform between the cars, wind rushing through his hair, white water churning in the gaps below his feet. Over the bridge the locomotive charged, full steam ahead.

It's now or never, John thought as he stared at the frothing fury of the river. "Now or never," he repeated over and over, more to gird his loins than anything else. His great-aunt's caterwaul was growing louder. She'd be here in a couple of seconds.

You know, he told himself, I might die. He stood on the last step of the train and looked up at the cotton-candy clouds. It was almost a relief to know that he didn't have to fight any longer.

If this is it, he thought, then I will miss Colonel Joe.

I will miss Maria and the chickens. John paused with his foot extended over the raging surge. I might even miss Boz. Even though he's insane.

But most of all, he thought as he closed his eyes and stepped into the abyss, I will miss Page.

CHAPTER
22

"YOU'RE NOT DEAD, are you?"

A whisper, like the angry protest of a gnat, zipped through his ear.

"Because if you are, not to put too fine a point upon a convoluted conundrum, it would be most inconvenient."

The gnat sputtered, coughed, then ROARED:

"I don't think he's dead! Merely a case of the catawampus, brought on by a mixture of iodine deficiency and a lack of subcutaneous nitrogen."

"Johnny! Johnny! Wake up!"

John felt a pair of hands grasp his shoulders.

"Don't shake him, girl—you'll send his brain rattling," a deep, unfamiliar voice said.

"Johnny," Page told him quietly, "open your eyes."

Slowly, painfully, John cracked one eye open. He was

lying in what appeared to be an ancient chamber, with a stone slab for a ceiling and only a small square of light. It cast a nimbus of white around Page's hair. She looked like an angel. A very worried angel.

"I thought you'd never wake up."

"But it didn't take you long to bury me," John joked, trying to rise. His head was thundering. "This place feels like a tomb."

"That's because it is," cried the deep voice, the clipped consonants bouncing around the stone.

A new figure stepped into the square of light. From what John could make out, it was a female figure, though a somewhat lean and lizardy one. She was very tall and had a miniature umbrella strapped to her head.

"The tomb of the Medapandac peoples of the subwestern deserts. Safest place for you."

John tried to process this information but could only be grateful for the feeling of Page's hand on his back.

"You've got a concussion, boy," the woman said. "Wanted to get you out of the midday heat. We'll take you into camp when you're feeling more chipper. Here— drink some of this. Slowly."

She thrust a canteen into his hands. Raising his arm, John realized that his whole body had been bruised and battered. Large blue circles tattooed his limbs.

"The girl will see that you take it easy. In the meantime, you"—the lizard lady pointed to Boz with one hand and gestured to the back of the tomb with the other—"need to stand watch while I excavate the outhouses."

Boz began to demur.

"Tell it to the Marines," the woman said briskly. "We're wasting time." Seizing Boz by his forelocks, she clambered out of the tomb.

"Are you okay?" Page asked, after Boz's screams of protest had dissipated.

"Everything hurts," John said.

"Poor Johnny," Page cooed, patting his back gingerly. "You look like a floppy fish."

"Thanks. Who found me?"

"Miss Doyle," said Page. "The lady with the umbrella. A woman of uncommon talents."

"A what?" John asked.

"That's what she calls herself. A woman of uncommon talents. What does it mean?"

"It means she thinks she's the bees knees."

"That's a funny thing to believe," Page said thoughtfully. "I think she's really smart."

"What happened?"

"You fell off a train."

John remembered that part. Or at least, he remembered falling, falling, falling, and then . . .

SMACK!

Hitting the water. Things were considerably fuzzier after that.

"How did you find me?"

"I heard you yelling to Great-Aunt Beauregard. And I didn't know what to do. So I asked Boz and he didn't know either. Then the boxcar left and Tom left and we were by ourselves. Boz said he was going to find out if the barometer was falling, and that's when we met Miss Doyle and her mule and I told her what was happening. She said it was lucky we met her. She only comes into Riverton once a year for supplies."

"So how did *she* find me?"

Page grinned.

"The stationmaster came running out saying that they'd received a telegram about a dark-haired boy falling off the train into the Chimchi River. Wanted a search party organized. Miss Doyle said, 'Very secret, come with me.' And she picked up Boz and led us right to the place where you were!"

"How did she know that?"

"She used a funny word for it. Sounds like de-moosed."

"Deduced?"

"That's it. She said she deduced it."

"I want to get up," John said, trying to swing his legs over the side of the tomb. Waves of nausea sloshed through his chest. He grimaced.

"Are you going to be okay?"

John looked at his little sister. She was wearing what must have been an old shirt of Miss Doyle's, tucked into a pair of cutoff trousers. Her hair was a nest of knots and her cheeks were buffed pink by the sun.

"Yes." He smiled.

Using Page's shoulder as a support, John climbed up the ladder of the tomb and stepped onto the surface of the moon.

Miles and miles of rocks lay embedded in a skin of dried mud. In the foreground of this barren planet stood a huddle of tents and one obstinate mule. The mule, Page told him, was called Heraclitus. And the huddle, John was soon to learn, represented the home base for the scientific expedition of the redoubtable Patricia M. Doyle.

"I am an archeologist," she informed him over lunch. "Subspecies *insatiabilex curiousitix*. My goal is to find evidence on the Medapandac, a tribe that disappeared ten thousand years ago in mysterious circumstances."

"There's a whole city buried under the ground!" Page said.

"Filled with temples and amphitheaters and tombs and stone dwellings," Miss Doyle noted.

"But they're invisible," Page added. "Eaten by dirt."

"One moment they're here"—Miss Doyle snapped her fingers—"and the next, *phhhhft!* Gone."

Like Maria's bakery, John thought.

"What do you always say about civilizations?" asked Page.

"All things change, nothing abides." Miss Doyle smiled. "Except me."

Her strategy, Miss Doyle made clear to John, was to excavate the entire area, top to bottom, end to end. So far she had unearthed a couple of tombs, and she was now concentrating her attention on where the outhouses had been.

"For nine months of the year, this is my life's work. I have six weeks to go before the desert grows too hot. Then I pack up and head overseas for the summer."

John chewed on his raisins for a minute. "Can I ask you a question?"

"You've already asked it," Miss Doyle replied. "But you may ask another."

"How did you know where to find me?"

"Simple law of probability. Having studied the alluvial patterns of the Chimchi River for my research, I know all the twists and turns of its currents. There was only one spot where an eleven-year-old boy would fetch up onto dry land. Assuming he wasn't dead and having his face sucked off by leeches, of course."

"And you found me there?"

"In the precise spot I predicted. It appears you have a remarkable will to survive."

"So you saved my life."

"Of course I did. I'm a woman of uncommon talents." Miss Doyle threw her napkin onto the rickety card table. "Now, since your sister has explained your circumstances to me—"

John leaped in his skin.

"Your great-aunt is still alive?" Miss Doyle demanded. "You didn't try anything immoral?"

He shook his head in wonder.

"Then she's unlikely to find you here," she mused. "This site is unknown to the scientific world, and until I publish my results, I intend to keep it that way. No one saw your sister leave with me at the station, and no one followed us to the camp. I made sure of that."

John was pleased to hear it. Thankfully, they'd have plenty of advance warning if his great-aunt did unearth their whereabouts. You couldn't hide an emaciated rabbit in this landscape.

"If your relative cannot find you in the river," Miss Doyle continued, "she will assume you are either drowned— probable—or left to wander the wilderness—improbable. I took the precaution of stripping you of your outer shirt and leaving it to the current. It's possible that she'll send out scouts, but I have plenty of secret places . . . places much more comfortable than under circus dogs . . . to stow you if she does.

"Your friend here"—she tapped Boz on the head—"I have enlisted as an all-purpose lookout."

Behind cheeks stuffed with beans, Boz grimaced.

"Thank you," said John. "You're being very kind."

"Yes, I am." Miss Doyle yawned and stretched her leathery arms over her head. "But I'm sure it will pass. In the meantime, you and your sister will make yourselves useful at the dig site. Once the coast is clear and I am overseas, you can decide on your next move. Do we have a deal?"

John nodded. An embryo of a plan was beginning to form in his head. Overseas sounded like a good, long way from everything. A place where John Coggin, inventor, fugitive, and failure, could easily disappear. A place where he and Page would be safe forever from family responsibilities. It was the perfect solution to his problems. He simply needed to find a way to make himself indispensable.

"Good. Then I think that's enough eating for one afternoon. You, John, are on sick leave until tomorrow. Rest in the main tent and mind the scorpions. Page and Boz will do the dishes while I continue my investigations into the gastrointestinal evidence of early man. You'll start work tomorrow morning."

CHAPTER 23

BLLLWWWHAATTTT!

John awoke to the sound of a constipated elephant in its death throes.

"What is that?" he moaned.

"Reveille," Page said as she rolled out of her cot and landed with a bump on the ground. "Miss Doyle likes to play her trumpet in the morning."

She may like it, John thought as he crept out of the tent, but I don't think anyone else does.

And he was right—even the rattlesnakes hid in terror when Miss Doyle sounded her daily yawp. Still, apart from the initial cacophony, John couldn't really complain. Anything was better than copper mines and coffins.

It was a strange feeling to be getting dressed and eating breakfast and brushing one's teeth in the desert. John had seen many landscapes on his travels with the Wayfarers, but none as alien as this. Walking with Page to the dig site was like walking across a lunar crater.

"Chip chop!" Miss Doyle called out. The sheen on her umbrella was shimmering like a mirage.

While Page clambered into the pit, John examined his new place of work. Though the sun was already scorching cracks into the ground, a sturdy canvas tarp had been strung up on poles to protect anyone working below. A very bored Boz was lounging under the edge, keeping an eye on the horizon.

"I want to get this outhouse cataloged before I go." Miss Doyle pivoted and began climbing down a ladder. "Rich stuff to be found in people's old poo," she noted.

"Like what?" John asked, following her into an earthen room.

"Seeds, bones, bits, and bobs. What they ate, what they drank, what was crawling around inside them and eating their intestines . . ."

John looked over at Page. She was happily labeling what appeared to be a piece of stone dung.

"What they threw up and what they threw out," Miss Doyle finished, handing John a box covered with a screen. "See this? This shard tells me that the Medapandac enjoyed a glass of goat's blood with their evening meal."

John examined the shard with care. No matter which

way he turned it, he couldn't understand what Miss Doyle was talking about. He chewed on his bottom lip. Making himself indispensable was going to be more complicated than he had imagined.

Then again, everything was complicated when you worked for Miss Doyle. His new employer, he decided, had more than one screw missing. She might spend hours removing the dirt from a femur, then suddenly seize a pickax and go at the ground with the fury of a hurricane. When she wasn't instructing John about the eighty-two varieties of grain in the area, she was using Boz to explain how the Medapandac disemboweled their cattle.

She certainly didn't sleep like any normal person. Every afternoon, bang on the dot of one, she'd curl up in the most convenient dig site—sometimes right next to a skeleton—and stay like that for an hour without moving. John almost fell on top of her one day. She simply flicked her long, reptilian tongue to the side of her mouth.

In spite of her idiosyncrasies, John did his best to be of service. Whatever the task might be, from counting stone flakes to sorting kneecaps, he was the first to volunteer. He asked intelligent questions and listened patiently to Miss Doyle's three-hour answers. He squished scorpions with the air of a man who cared nothing for death.

But that wasn't all. To sweeten the honey, he began to devise little improvements to Miss Doyle's excavation.

With a rope, his jackknife, and the heel of a bucket, he cobbled together a basic pulley system for shifting dirt. He fixed the axle on her wheelbarrow. He mended the ribs on her umbrella.

The goal was simple. He needed to persuade Miss Doyle that both Coggins were worth taking overseas. Like many in this world, John had finally reached the point where he no longer cared to imagine what *could* be. His only purpose was to survive what *was*.

There was one major stumbling block to his plan: Miss Doyle's pride and pleasure in working alone. Three weeks into his labors, as John was cleaning cattle ribs near the tomb, he judged the time was ripe to ask her why.

"Never took much to live humans," Miss Doyle told him matter-of-factly. "And they never took much to me," she continued, picking a beetle out of her hair and popping it into her mouth. "It's a hard cross to bear, being a woman of uncommon talents."

She sniffed and resumed her analysis of the artifacts. As she had explained in great depth to John, her theory was that the cattle bones formed part of a ritual feast. Boz had labeled it the barbeque pit.

"*I* like living with you," John hazarded. "And I *love* being an archeologist."

Miss Doyle did not reply. John dug his knuckles into his thigh. Had he played his cards too early?

"In fact, I thought Page and I could come with you. To work. Overseas." Where we can disappear forever, he added in his head.

Miss Doyle cackled. A very sere cackle.

"What's so funny?"

She squatted back on her haunches and tilted her umbrella off her eyes.

"Look, I'm not the kind to spread mustard on a rotten cabbage, so I'll be frank. You're a terrible liar." The force of her gaze compelled John to look to the ground. "You don't want to be an archeologist. I've been observing you during your time here—you'd be much better off making things that people will dig up later."

Sure, thought John, if they weren't all blown to smithereens.

"I tried that."

"You mean the chicken poo debacle?"

John reared his head. He was going to have Boz's vocal chords for guitar strings. "Who told you about that?"

"Your sister. Now don't scowl," she said sternly. "I asked, and she answered. It's an excellent and efficient way to get through the world."

So Boz hadn't told Miss Doyle. Well, that made him a little less of a pathological liar.

"Yes, I tried to make an oven run on chicken poo," John admitted.

"Well, why not give it another go?"

"It won't work. My inventions never work. It's no use."

"Then you're just like your great-aunt wants you to be."

"Really?" challenged John. "How?"

"Dead on the inside."

"Am not!" John yelled, bouncing to his feet and hurling his brush to the ground.

"Are so!" Miss Doyle stood and barked back. "If you're not out there learning, you've given up. Great lives are built on risk, John. You must accept the perils of existence."

John was so angry, his hands were shaking and tiny red spots were obscuring his vision. "I'm not dead!"

"Not yet," Miss Doyle said, squinting at the crinkles in John's forehead. "But if you keep on reacting like that to an honest opinion, you might as well be. Breathe, boy, breathe."

John took a deep breath, and the red spots began to fade.

"Are you okay?"

John nodded.

"Right," Miss Doyle said, "then this conversation is closed. Back to work."

CHAPTER
24

"HELP ME! SOMEBODY help me!" John screamed.

A huge serpent of fire was slinking through the desert, engulfing fleeing geckos and swallowing rocks whole. In the black of night, its crimson skin flickered and shivered. Through the camp it came, each razor-sharp scale tinged with flame. It was at the tarps, it was at the tomb, it was at the tent! It reared its head, opened its horrible fanged mouth wide, and—

"Johnny, wake up! Wake up!"

Page shook her brother so hard she pushed him off his cot. On the dry-packed ground he lay shivering in his own sweat.

"You had a dream," she said, wrapping her blanket around him. "It's okay."

John ducked his head. Dawn was seeping through the slit in the tent flap.

"It's okay," Page repeated, patting the blanket.

"Anything wrong?" Miss Doyle shouted from outside the tent.

"I'm fine," John finally managed to say.

But he wasn't fine.

A month had passed with them living on top of the buried city of the Medapandac, and his dreams were getting worse. If it wasn't fire and floods, it was Maria and his mother. Sometimes they were apart—Maria weeping tears of blood into the smoking rubble of her bakery, his mother tripping and falling into a pit full of bones—and sometimes they were together, both reaching out their hands to him from a fast-moving freight car. Regardless of how hard he ran, he could never catch up.

And then there was the one with his father. They'd be sitting on the stone bench in the sunshine, and a cloud would drift by. Then another. Then more and more, until the whole sky was a mass of roiling thunder. It always ended with a lightning bolt severing the bench in two.

John was smart enough to know that these dreams weren't appearing out of nowhere. In fourteen days, Miss Doyle would be moving on. And he had no idea what to do.

"Where are you going when you head overseas?" he asked her at the end of breakfast. His veins were still icy with leftover fear.

"Mandalina," Miss Doyle replied, using her long

tongue to put a final lick on the rim of her plate. "For work on a contract dig. Have to raise enough funds to finance the next stage of operations."

"We need to come."

Miss Doyle peered at him over her nose.

"I thought we'd discussed this."

John put down his spoon.

"Not for archeology," he clarified. "Just on the ship. Page is awfully good with animals, and I can find work with the crew. Please, Miss Doyle, please. We have nothing left here."

Miss Doyle placed her fingers together in a contemplative steeple.

"And what about Boz?"

Boz. John had forgotten Boz. Boz the magnificent, Boz the ridiculous, Boz the danger to any person standing within twenty feet. What was he going to do with Boz?

"I don't know," John answered.

"Well, that's honest, at least."

Miss Doyle stared at her bowl for a long moment. Then she nodded.

"Okay. I'll find you two passage on the ship. The captain has a wife with sticky kisses—maybe she can find someplace to stow you. But there'll be no sentimental twaddle from me, do you understand?" She handed her spoon to John for washing. "Think of it as payment for a job well done."

John smiled. No one could accuse Miss Doyle of being sentimental.

But if John was hoping that the new plan would bury his nightmares, he was sorely mistaken. If anything, his visions became more convoluted.

Now he dreamed of standing with Page on the deck of an ocean liner while Maria and their mother called to them from the pier at Pludgett. They'd be laughing and waving handkerchiefs and happy as birds—right up to the point when a hideous vulture swooped down and pinioned them with its claws.

Great-Aunt Beauregard was still out there, John knew. Still waiting to entrap them in the family business. Until the Coggins were on the other side of the world, he couldn't sleep easy.

Miss Doyle appeared to be thinking along similar lines. Soon after the vulture dream, she summoned him from the pit.

"John, come here."

"What's wrong?" he said, scrambling up the ladder. "Did you see someone?"

Miss Doyle was standing in a sandy patch near the tents. In lieu of her umbrella, there was a cowboy's hat. In place of her pursed lips, a frown.

"I was examining the knife marks on the scapula of a thirteen-year-old this morning when it occurred to me that every boy should know how to knee someone in the groin. Especially boys that are blessed with great-aunts off their rockers. So, let's have it—come at me."

Miss Doyle tossed her hat to the side, squatted in the dust, and lowered her brow menacingly. John sniggered.

"What?" she barked.

"You look really, really stu—"

He never finished his sentence. Before he knew what was happening, he found himself somersaulting through the air and landing on his back in a gigantic puff of sand. He tried to stand up, but his eyes met only the buffed tip of Miss Doyle's boot.

"First rule of self-defense. Never underestimate your enemy. Especially if she's a woman."

She reached down and lent John her hand. As soon as he had a good grasp on it, she let go. The sand had traveled halfway up John's nostrils before he had the sense to breathe out again.

"Second rule of self-defense," she said. "Never trust your enemy. Unless, of course," Miss Doyle added, "she happens to be a woman of uncommon talents."

John coughed and spluttered and attempted to get to his feet. She pinned him down with her boot.

"Do you understand what I've been telling you? You've got to be on your guard at all times."

John nodded.

"Good, then on your feet." She lifted her boot, and John brought his left foot around in a long sweeping motion. It caught Miss Doyle on the ankle and sent her tumbling to the ground beside him. She lay motionless and facedown in the dirt.

Then, with a gush of sand, she flipped over onto her back and laughed. It was a thundering, sonorous laugh that rolled across the dig site. It sounded remarkably like her trumpet.

"Excellent work, John. Excellent. We'll make a thinker out of you yet."

It was the first, and most important, of Miss Doyle's lessons in the art of self-defense. For the next week, one hour a day was devoted to the finer points of disarmament. Of course, Miss Doyle also insisted that Page be instructed.

"If I'm going to teach you the ways of the world, your sister learns too. You look out for each other. You're the only family you've got."

As for Boz, he appointed himself honorary referee. Every afternoon, he would sit in a folding chair on the side of the patch, a straw hat firmly planted on his scarlet hair, and award points and penalties.

"This is the life, is it not, my lovelies?" he would say, typically at the precise moment when John's arm was being twisted into a figure eight by his little sister. Apparently, Page still hadn't quite forgiven him for the bakery.

"The primal pull of the animal instincts, the blood and guts and glory of the testosteronal urge!"

"Ugggh," replied John.

A few days into the tutorial, Boz made the mistake of chipping in a suggestion.

"Ahem. Forgive me for being forward, Mademoiselle Doyle, but I have noticed that you are neglecting a certain cruciate element in your instruction."

"Which is?" demanded Miss Doyle, drawing herself up to her full six feet.

"You aren't teaching your dilatory pupils the art of combat. You aren't teaching them how to fight with their fists."

"Correct," Miss Doyle said.

"But why not?" Boz jumped to his feet and began to shadowbox around her riding pants. "If you should need some pugilistic assistance, I'd be willing to lend a glove. In my time, I was known to my fellow featherweights as the Prancing Pony of Principessa."

He danced the first few steps of the cancan and threw a series of wild punches at a cactus.

"If you value your reproductive organs, you will stop that immediately," Miss Doyle growled.

Boz stopped.

Miss Doyle pointed to the seat, and Boz shuffled back to his position. Page was trying hard not to laugh.

Miss Doyle turned to address John. "Above all, remember that you are small insects in a world of clumsy mammals. If you attempt to do what Boz did, you will either be sat on or squashed." She planted her hands on her hips. "The reason I am not teaching you how to fight with your fists is because I fully expect you and your sister to fight with your brains."

"Forgive me for interrupting," Boz chimed in. His every muscle was straining from the effort of staying in his seat. "But I don't see how a surplus of cerebra is going to aid our young heroes in the pursuit of happiness."

Miss Doyle picked up her hat and brushed the dust from the brim. "Then come with me." She strode off in the direction of a distant cluster of rocks, leaving John and Page and Boz to catch up.

By the time they reached the outcrop, John's lungs were on fire. Miss Doyle was waiting for them beside a heap of whitish stone.

"Tell me what you see," she said.

John looked. It appeared to be precisely what it was.

"A heap of stone," he answered.

"Wrong! Assemble your facts before theorizing. Look again—look closely," she instructed.

John crouched down next to the rocks. He saw only a mass of crumbling limestone. He sat there for a minute, waiting for a brilliant idea to come to his brain. Page stood behind him, her hand resting on his shoulder.

"Remember where you are, remember what you have learned, and use your imagination. Think, boy, think!" Miss Doyle urged.

John stared again. Then he saw it. A knob sticking out of a stone—a knob that was like nothing he had seen before in nature.

"This stone has been shaped," he said, pointing to his discovery.

Miss Doyle smiled.

"Excellent. Why?"

John chewed on his lower lip.

"To hold something?" Page offered tentatively.

"In a way," Miss Doyle answered. "I will give you both a clue. All of these stones, at one time, were shaped."

There was a cry like a throttled sheep from behind them.

"By gosh, oh golly, oh Jehoshaphat, it's a pyramid!" Boz yelled.

Much as it pained her, Miss Doyle had to concede the point. "Quite right. This is the Temple of Froom."

"How marvelous!" Boz clapped his hands together.

"Do you know anything about the Temple of Froom?" Miss Doyle challenged.

"No. But how marvelous that I should not." Boz grinned.

"The Temple of Froom," Miss Doyle said, directing her remarks at John and Page, "was the largest temple of the Medapandac. They built it at the height of their power, when this place was a lush and fertile valley. That knob that you saw sticking out was a way to transport the stone. They would tie a rope around each block and have their cattle pull it on rolling logs. This was one they forgot to chisel off afterward."

"Why did they build it?" asked Page.

"To honor Hom, their god of creation. According to the myth, Hom breathed his magic into every living thing at the time of birth. The Medapandac people believed that this was what helped them grow and prosper. They called it the divine gift of Hom. We might call it imagination."

"I like that," John said. "The gift of Hom."

"But what happened to the temple?" insisted Page.

"Marauders!" Boz exclaimed. "Cutthroats, brigands, the attack of enemy tribes. Mighty are the men who wield the swords."

"Wrong. They destroyed it themselves."

"Come again?" Boz asked.

Miss Doyle crushed the dust between her fingers. "In the process of building the temple, the Medapandac discovered that this kind of limestone makes for a particularly effective plaster. So they began to use it to reinforce their housing. But they didn't know that this kind of limestone plaster also reacts badly to water. Almost as soon as they had applied the first coat, it started to crumble."

"But why did they tear the temple down?" Page insisted.

"Because they didn't fight with their brains!" Miss

Doyle yelled. John had never seen her look so angry. "Any smart person would have said, 'Maybe we should be doing something different. Maybe we need to try another material.' But not the Medapandac. They kept on cutting down more and more trees to heat the lime plaster. Without the trees, there was no shade for their cattle, their farms began to erode into the rivers, and the mud made the water undrinkable. In time, all that was left was a ruined landscape."

"And they blamed Hom for giving them the idea," John concluded.

"They did. They thought he was cruel and malicious. So right before they started their great migration, they tore down his temple in a fit of spite." Miss Doyle was patting the stone in the same way Page might pat a frightened dog. "Leaving only this to tell us the tale."

"O loathsome ignorance!" Boz bawled, wiping his eyes with the edge of his sock. "How sad the sagas of ancestors can be."

"Twaddle," Miss Doyle said, giving the temple one last pat. "If they'd done a little experimentation, they would have discovered that they only needed to add some of the sand they were standing on to stabilize the limestone." She brushed her hands off vigorously, spraying Boz with a fine layer of sediment. "Gods, my foot."

By now the sun was sinking and the cracks in the earth were snapping with the drop in temperature. Miss Doyle rubbed her stomach.

"Gravy, that's what I need." She pointed at John. "You and your sister can get the meal ready."

"They shouldn't have blamed Hom," John said, picturing a whirling flurry of stones and statues crashing down. "He probably would have showed them the solution, if they had asked."

Miss Doyle gave him what might have been a smile, or might have been a pang of hunger.

"Fight with your brains, boy, and you won't go wrong."

And off she went.

CHAPTER 25

FOR REASONS HE couldn't quite decipher, the story of Hom made John as testy as a bear with an ulcerated molar. He found himself thinking about the way the Medapandac might have cut the stone, or how they might have harnessed the oxen, or what kinds of wood they used to reduce the plaster.

Page was the first to notice the change.

"You look funny." It was the day before their departure, and Page was helping him harness Heraclitus to the water wagon. They were headed down to an outlet of the Chimchi River to wash their laundry. Or at least, three of them were. Security duty had finally proved too much of a strain on Boz's limbic capacity. He had disappeared on the night after the discussion of the temple. Miss Doyle had taught John and Page a few new words for "ruddy flipping fool" that day.

"How do you mean, funny?"

"You've got that thinking look on."

John heaved a bucket into the back of the wagon. "And what does that mean?"

"I don't know," Page said, scratching Heraclitus between the ears. "It's this look you get. You had it a lot when we were in the caravan."

John heaved another bucket. Page watched him carefully.

"You're not building something new, are you?" she demanded.

"No."

"Because if you are, it better not blow up."

John scowled and climbed into the wagon. "I'm not going to build anything ever again. So why don't you leave me alone?"

Page stuck out her tongue at him.

"Stop your squawking," Miss Doyle warned, appearing at John's side and twiddling the angle of her umbrella to block the sun. "We've got a lot to do."

On the long drive that followed, John kept harping on the idea of the temple. There was something important in what Miss Doyle had told them, something he needed to acknowledge. But what?

It wasn't until they had reached the riverbed and John was rinsing his socks away from the others that he finally understood. And when he did, he let out a small, but thoroughly heartfelt, war whoop.

A red head popped up over the opposite embankment.

"'Allo," Boz shouted, sending John sprawling backward with surprise into the water.

"My dear boy, my most profuse apologies," Boz jabbered, climbing down the embankment and wading across the shallows as John stumbled to his feet. "Here, let me assist you."

This effort, of course, resulted in both of them tumbling facefirst into the river.

John shook him off. "I'm fine, Boz, really. I *don't* need any help."

"Well, if you insist. I was only attempting to be of some service."

"Where have you been?" John asked, pouring silt out of his shoe.

"Reconnaissance," Boz replied.

"You mean you skived off because you hated having to work."

Boz smiled. "Well, that too." He sat down on the bank and fished a fish out from his pocket. "And what was the cause of your gaseous bellow of a *casus belli?*"

"What?"

"Your whooping, my dear boy."

John hesitated. "Do you promise not to tell anyone?"

Boz stood up and raised his hand. "I solemnly swear—"

John pulled him back down. "No, don't do that again. Just be quiet and listen."

Boz said nothing but tilted his ear suggestively.

"Well," John said, his excitement getting the better of him, "I think I've discovered how to keep the generator in the chicken poo oven from exploding."

Boz made a motion to leap to his feet in joy but caught himself by the top of his trousers and returned to a seated position.

"I figured it out while I was thinking about the Temple of Froom. It wasn't the pellets that were the problem with the oven," John continued eagerly. "Well, apart from the cans of gasoline next to them. It was what was holding the generator together. We were using the wrong mortar!"

"Euripides!" Boz blasted. "By George, I think you've got it!"

John grinned, happiness rising in him like yeasty bubbles.

"If we had built the oven with the mortar that people use to make fireplaces, then the generator might have been strong enough to contain the heat of the first reaction. It wouldn't have spread to the other accelerants."

Boz clapped his hands in glee.

But John had forgotten. They were leaving the country tomorrow. The bakery was destroyed. And, as his great-aunt had so helpfully pointed out, Maria never wanted to see him again. He could build eighteen new ovens, and it wouldn't matter. Their life here was over.

"Never mind." John sank down. "Forget I even told you about it."

"Only listen to what I have been attempting to convey to your cochlea, my dear boy! In my perambulations I happened to poke my head in at the station and . . ." Boz reached into his jacket pocket and pulled out a wad of paper. With a flourish, he flipped it open.

In big bold letters, it read:

MISSING!
HARRY *and* NORA
PERSIMMONS

Eleven-year-old boy and six-year-old girl last seen near Riverton Station.

Boy in red sweater. Girl in pajamas and carrying a bear.

May be in the custody of a cunning businesswoman with birds in her hat.

Will be in Riverton Station on May 15 at 3 p.m. to investigate leads.

LARGE REWARD FOR
ANY KNOWLEDGE OF
WHEREABOUTS!

Maria Persimmons

John's hands began to shake as he reread the notice. "She gave us her last name."

Boz grinned. "Seems your sweetness of nature made quite an impression on the taste buds of our culinary goddess. And today, it appears, the gods have seen fit to grant her prayers."

The faint jingle of a warning bell rang in John's head. What had Miss Doyle said? Fight with your brains? Those phrases—"cunning businesswoman," "investigate leads"—had a weirdly ominous tone.

"I want to show this to Miss Doyle."

"My dear boy, do you think that wise? She might object to losing the inestimable joy of your company, and I—"

John cut him off. "I'm telling Page and I'm telling Miss Doyle."

Unfortunately, Miss Doyle was of John's opinion.

"Quite right," she said, inspecting the notice. "It's obvious bait."

"But it's signed by Maria!" protested Page.

"It could be signed by the president, for all I care," Miss Doyle countered. "We're not walking into a trap. Besides, how do you know that Maria isn't being compensated by your great-aunt to lure you back?"

That hit home for John. "She would never do that!"

"You'd be surprised at how low human nature can stoop. You destroyed her business, John. She may be in need of the cash."

It was too much. Believing that Maria would betray

them was tantamount to saying that stars were made of coconuts or the tides were governed by the decrees of houseflies.

Unless, thought John, she hates me even more than I realized.

"That's why we should go," insisted Page. "So you can explain things to her!"

John squeezed the notice in his fist and shook his head. "Miss Doyle's right, Page. It's too dangerous."

"But if we don't go now, we'll never see her again. This is the only chance we'll get to have a family! I don't want to keep running away. I'm tired of running. I've done everything you told me to do, Johnny. Now it's your turn. Listen to me!"

It was the most passionate speech John had ever heard his sister give. She stood as tall as her spine could stretch, eyes straight and head lifted, demanding an equal share of the adventure.

And, oh, how he wanted to give in. How he wanted to tell her that words were true and people were honest and the clear, straight soul of a six-year-old girl could conquer the world.

Yet he knew life wasn't like that. Even in fairy tales, he realized, queens morph into witches and vows turn into traps. Yes, Page deserved to be happy. But no, he could not run the risk of destroying of what little safety she had left.

"No, Page. I won't let you go."

Page stomped her foot. "You know what your problem is? You're scared!"

She picked up a laundry basket and huffed off over the bank.

"Let her be," Miss Doyle advised. "She needs to simmer down."

John tightened his grip on the notice. In a way, Page was right. He was scared. But what about caution? And common sense? Wasn't that the lesson of the Autopsy and the oven of poo? How *do* you lead a life of risk without leaping into the abyss?

His thoughts were interrupted by a tap on his shoulder.

"Ahem, I hate to disturb your introspection, but I am having some difficulty establishing the coordinates of your sister."

"What?"

Boz pointed to the north. "I think she may have scarpered to the station."

All his nightmares burst into fresh life. John scurried over the embankment, dirt slipping and slopping beneath his feet. There was the wagon, precisely where they had left it.

But there was no Heraclitus the mule.

And there was no Page.

"Page! Come back!" John bellowed to the wind. The wind did not deign to answer.

Out of the clear blue sky, his companions sprang down beside him. Miss Doyle's umbrella was blown upward with the force of her landing.

"Does she know how to get to the station?" demanded John.

"'Twas the way we came on the day we rescued you," moped Boz.

Miss Doyle glanced at the sun.

"She's only been gone ten minutes. We may catch her if we run."

"How far is it to the station?"

There was little mistaking Miss Doyle's grimace. "Miles."

CHAPTER
26

THERE MAY BE more beautiful things than a spring afternoon by the side of the Chimchi River, but they are few and far between. The birches were breezing, the waters were gossiping, and an unseen bird was singing the "Hallelujah Chorus."

If John hadn't been pursuing his misguided sister up the switchbacks of a trail, the vista would have been splendid.

Then, unexpectedly, disaster struck. Attempting to vault over a root, Miss Doyle fumbled her landing. Her foot twisted sideways, and her body cartwheeled over the edge of the path. Both she and her torqued umbrella came to rest in a puddle of mud.

"Miss Doyle!"

"I'm okay." Miss Doyle's attempt to stand was punished with what appeared to be a poker of red-hot pain. "I'm not okay. I've twisted my ankle."

"We can come down——" began John.

"You don't have time!" Miss Doyle rejoined, using her hands to push herself onto her knobbly knees. "Get to your sister——I'll follow as soon as I can."

John hesitated. What if he didn't make it back? He had visions of lions and tigers and unspeakable things done to injured prey.

"I'm fine!" Miss Doyle yelled, reading his thoughts. "Look!" She gingerly put her weight on her feet. "Not broken, just twisted. I'll use a stick and limp. And if you don't get after your sister," she said, starting to struggle up the bank, "I'll get after the pair of you!"

On John ran, with Boz hard on his heels. In an uncertain world, you had to respect the oaths of a woman of uncommon talents.

It was funny, but as he ran, John could feel his blood shifting from his head to his heart. For months he had lived with the fear of his old world reclaiming Page. Now that the moment had arrived, he found, to his surprise, that he wasn't afraid. He was *mad*.

Finally, just as John was thinking his body might burst into flecks of rubbery flesh, Boz jerked his arm.

"Over there!" he whispered. "The station is through those trees!"

John slowed to a stealthy shuffle. As he crept closer

and closer, wading through a carpet of pine needles, his adrenaline began to surge. Whoever was waiting for him at the station, be it Great-Aunt Beauregard or the entire subwestern police force, he was ready.

At the edge of the pines, he paused to assess the situation. There were a couple of antiquated geezers sitting outside the front, drinking beer and playing dice on an upturned barrel. There was a freight train hissing and sighing on a sidetrack. There was a plump chestnut of a woman making her way out of the building. It all looked ridiculously normal.

"Now what?" John murmured to himself.

"One might suggest a two-pronged assault with a feint to the starboard . . ."

"Boz, let me think."

"Mum's the word. From henceforth, I'll be as garrulous as a stone, as talkative as a tomb, as loquacious as a mock turtle . . ."

"Boz, shut up!"

Boz shut up.

John examined the front door once more and came to a decision.

"I'll go ahead," he said, "and see who's in there. You check the freight train. If I don't come back out, fetch Miss Doyle as quick as you can."

Boz nodded.

"Boz, whatever you do, find Page. If something should

happen to me, your job is to make sure she's safe. Got it?"

Boz nodded. "Be of cautious action, my dear boy."

John didn't need to be told twice. Shadowing the shadows, he hugged the far corner of the building and peeked through a window. Nothing. No Great-Aunt Beauregard. No Page. No police. Only a trimly manufactured stationmaster, checking his watch.

Clenching his fists, John boldly walked toward the door, braced for flight if the men with the dice should happen to morph into his great-aunt's henchmen. They ignored him.

"Afternoon, son. If you're 'specting to meet someone, the next train to Pludgett arrives at quarter past." The stationmaster placed his watch back in his waistcoat.

"Excuse me," said John, taking a deep breath, "but have you seen a large lady wearing a hat with dead birds?"

The stationmaster regarded John with a stare of considerable skepticism.

"No."

A fillip of hope propelled John into the waiting room. Could it be that Maria had written the notice after all? Could it be that Page was right?

"How about a woman named Maria Persimmons? She put up a sign that she said she would be here at three p.m."

"Oh, that," the stationmaster said. "Private room— over there."

He pointed to an innocuous door under a sign that read "No Spitting or Gratuitous Swearing."

John paused. As much as he wanted to believe in the possibility of redemption, he knew too well what lengths his great-aunt would go to. This could still be an ambush.

Clenching his fists again, John strode over to the private room, turned the knob, opened the door, and—

"If I was going to arrest you, Hornblower, I would have done it a lot sooner."

Leslie crossed his pimpled ankles on the edge of the desk and crammed a cream puff into his mouth.

What was the Pig doing here? Keeping himself planted in the doorway, John inspected the room. There was only one other door—presumably leading to the platform— and an odor of oily dust. Bar the desk, two chairs, and Leslie's pink and perspiring presence, it was empty.

"Where's Maria?"

"Coming. She sent me on ahead to make sure we didn't miss you." Leslie licked his fingers one by one. A gobbet of cream clung to the wiry strands of his mustache.

"You hate me," John spat out. "Why would Maria send you?"

Leslie burped.

"Paperwork. I can't get ahold of what's left of the property without Maria's sign-off. And she wouldn't sign off until I promised to help her find you."

"So *you're* the one who posted the notice?"

Leslie nodded.

"Don't mistake me," he said, helping himself to another cream puff. "I'd much rather have you thrown in jail, but apparently baking accidents aren't an arrestable offense."

John's ribs expanded a hairbreadth.

"Where's Page?"

"Bathroom. She said something about putting flowers in her hair before Maria arrived." Leslie sniffed. "And cleaning her fingernails."

John's ribs expanded another inch. Leslie's rudeness was reassuringly familiar.

"So when is Maria coming?"

"Next train from Littlemere. She's taking the pair of you back today."

John would have leaped on the desk for joy if he hadn't been afraid of squishing the box of assorted plain and chocolate cream puffs. For a boy who had been surviving for six weeks on a diet of canned beans, they looked mighty appealing.

"Did she make those for us?"

Leslie licked his lips. "She might have."

Quick as a skink, John darted forward, seized a chocolate-covered puff, and returned to the open door. Leslie merely snorted. Tentatively, oh so tentatively, John took one tiny bite.

It was heaven. It was pleasure and peace and memory

encased in a delicate, delectable shell. John leaned against the frame and devoured the rest.

Leslie brushed his hands. "There now, that ought to do it."

"Ought to do what?" John asked dreamily.

"Take you off to la la land," replied the desk.

Except desks couldn't talk, John knew that. But the world was feeling so awfully funny.

"Bring him in and shut the door," instructed the desk.

John wanted to protest, lash out at Leslie with his newly acquired arts of self-defense, but the bones in his arms appeared to have liquefied. He could only smile sheepishly as Leslie hauled him into the room.

"He'll be out in a couple of minutes," said the desk. "I told you he'd go for the chocolate."

The warning bell that John had heard near the river now struck a solemn dong.

"Great-Aunt Beauregard," he slurred as his vision grew blurry.

A rain-slicked rock face came into view. "Thought you'd have more sense, John Peregrine Coggin. But what can you expect of the father's son?"

John twisted his tongue—a tongue that felt like it had been packed in ice cubes—into a few precious words. "What did you do to me?"

Leslie's laugh came from far, far away. "Not so dumb after all, eh, John? Who was it that got Maria out of the way? Who was it that thought of writing the notice? Who was it that packed the chocolate puffs with sleeping pills for little boys to eat?"

Great-Aunt Beauregard harrumphed.

"With a little direction," Leslie added.

A cold scurry of air fanned John into temporary consciousness. The outer door must have been opened.

"Where's Page?" A sickly odor of cologne told him that Leslie was the one dragging him toward the platform. "Boz, help me!"

"You shouldn't put your faith in friends," echoed his great-aunt. "They'll always let you down."

"But I don't want to go back to Pludgett!" John managed to croak.

The train whistle sounded a long, snickering shrill.

"Oh, you're not going back to Pludgett."

CHAPTER
27

JOHN AWOKE IN a coffin. And not any coffin, but a Coggin Family Number Eight Walnut Standard. He'd know that woodgrain anywhere.

Breathe, he told himself. Just breathe.

Breathing would have been a lot easier without the gag in his mouth. Or the putrid odor wafting through the coffin's airholes. Or the nips of midges crawling across his ankles. Or the insufferable sticky heat.

"Not a haunted house tour I'd pay for," someone grumped.

"Put it down here," a voice answered.

The coffin landed with a bang, and he heard no more.

When John came to, he was out of the coffin. Out of the coffin and shackled by three feet of heavy chain to the wall of a cozy dungeon cell.

A cozy and unfurnished dungeon cell, it should be said. Bed, chair, cot—using any of these to escape was out of the question, since they didn't exist. The only additions to the decor were a window with iron bars, a historic chamber pot, and an impenetrable wooden door.

Oh, and a ceiling that was dripping foul-smelling green goo, via his head, onto the floor. Smack dab into a pool of blood.

I'm dying, John thought, running his hands frantically over his body, searching for the fatal wound.

It wasn't until he reached his upper lip that he realized that the jolt from the coffin must also have given him the nosebleed of the century. Half of his shirtfront was covered in a delta of brownish red.

"Ugh," John said, and was astonished to discover he could hear himself. The gag had been removed.

"Help me!" he shouted. "Somebody help me!"

"I'm coming, I'm coming," came a faint cry.

Footsteps on the stairs were followed by the sound of a deadbolt being shot back and the jingle of keys. The door creaked open . . .

To once more reveal Leslie the Pig.

A pig that was looking much the worse for wear since the last time John had spoken to him. His cheeks were spotted, his belly sagged, and his eyes were puffy with fatigue.

"Let me go!" John demanded.

"I wish I could do that."

To his credit, Leslie appeared sincere. He fidgeted from one foot to the other, wiped his brow, shrugged at the bag on his shoulder. But he made no move to release John.

"Did you hear me? Let me go!" John repeated.

Leslie's reply was to reach into the bag and remove something extremely unpleasant.

"I want you to know this was not my idea."

John stared at the object in dismay. On the top, in letters as large and sinister as he remembered them, was the word

CONTRACT

"You great-aunt says you can't see your sister unless you sign this," Leslie said, fumbling in the bag for a fountain pen. "She says that family is family and a Coggin born means a coffin made." John's jailer was doing his best to fake an air of authority. "Until you accept your responsibilities as the heir apparent, she says you have to stay here with me."

Keeping well out of the range of John's arm, Leslie removed the last sheet of paper from the contract, wrapped the pen within it, and rolled the package across the floor. It hit the tip of John's shoe with a fluttering sigh.

"No! I told her I'd never sign it!" John seized the pen and hurled it at his jailer, wrenching his right arm in the process. The little black spear went rifling over Leslie's head and ricocheted off the stones behind him. "And I meant it!" John picked up the page and shredded it into confetti.

"Look," whined Leslie, "I don't like this situation any more than you do. I had the perfect plan for this place until you came along and ruined things. I won't have enough money for a golf ball until you agree to do what your great-aunt wants."

Unnerved by John's reaction, Leslie's remaining bluff and bluster had disappeared. The slightest feint would have been enough to send him shrieking from the room.

"Why don't I let you think about it until tomorrow?" He gathered up the contract papers, tiptoed backward into the hall, and hastily slammed the door.

This left John alone.

He glared at the chamber pot. The chamber pot glared back.

But in his woozy brain, questions were forming. To start with, where was he? Laboriously, John went through the details of the previous conversation. Leslie had mentioned golf balls . . .

That must mean he was in the castle at Howst! Entrapped in the piece of prize real estate that Leslie never could shut up about. John took a closer look at his surroundings and shrugged. Leslie was going to have a tough time turning this into a resort.

Okay, so he was in Howst. But where was Page? Was she back in Pludgett? Did Great-Aunt Beauregard really have her penned up in the workshop?

No, John suddenly realized, Page was with Boz! Boz would have seen him being captured. Boz would have rescued his sister and taken her back to Miss Doyle. This was simply a trick to make him sign his life away. Page was safe. Boz was safe.

And I have Colonel Joe's jackknife! With giddy triumph, John dug in his hand into his left pocket.

And came up empty. He tried the right. Empty.

Nuts! Leslie must have thoroughly searched him while he was unconscious. Unless John could wait for his fingernails to grow three inches long, picking the locks of his shackles was going to be impossible.

Breathe, just breathe. Nursing his sore right shoulder, John leaned back against the wall and repeated this mantra over and over to himself.

He repeated it so long he fell asleep.

Only to wake stiffer than a board, and twice as ravenous. In the white afternoon heat, he saw that a slice of bread and a couple of wizened apples had been tossed on the floor. Mindlessly, he wolfed them down.

And still the chamber pot glowered at him. This time,

he observed, it had acquired a bright new signature sheet as a companion.

For three hours, John stared at the piece of paper and contemplated alternatives. Until the moment came when he realized he was well and truly stuck.

It was then that he started to cry.

"Pssst . . . comrade."

John scanned the room. The voice was human, but there was nothing in the cell bar a discontented black beetle.

"Who's there?"

"No time for knock-knock jokes, my dear boy. We're facing an exponential crisis."

"Boz?"

"The one and only."

"What are you doing here?"

"I've come to rescue you."

John's laugh was loud enough to send the beetle scuttling into the ceiling cracks. "You're here to rescue *me*?"

"Indeed! Though I admit that the tactical execution left something to be desired."

"You were captured."

"Afraid so." Boz's voice was bizarrely cheerful. "Trussed and trundled as soon as I attempted admission through the back entrance of this fortification. I had expected the great Leslie, but not the additional security guards. Last thing I remember was an impressive display of knuckles heading straight for my superior orbital fissure. Or, in more prosaic terms, a fist in the eye."

"I'm surprised you're not dead."

"For an interim, I thought I was. Until it occurred to me that the waiting room of the afterlife would be more suitably furnished—antimacassars, to say the very least."

"Boz!"

"Yes?"

"I'm glad you're not dead."

"Why, thank you."

"But where are you?"

Boz coughed. "I appear to be ensconced in a stone cell, decorated in a minimalist style with a charming view of a sewage outflow pipe. Much like yourself, I imagine."

John looked at the ceiling. There he noticed one thing he had neglected to spot on his initial examination—a small vent high up in the corner of the interior wall.

"You're next door!"

"Am I? Remarkably civil of them to let us share a suite."

John smiled. Despite all that had happened, it was comforting to hear Boz's voice and picture him, unbowed and unbroken, sitting with his squashed face on the opposite side of the wall.

Until he realized that Boz was there. And not with his sister. "Boz. Where's Page?"

There was an uneasy silence.

"Ah."

John waited, but there was nothing after that. "Boz . . . ," he said threateningly.

Boz sighed. "Alas, my deepest regrets, but she is currently incarcerated in Pludgett with your Great-Aunt Beauregard."

"What?" John stood up, forgot that he was shackled by his ankles, and was yanked backward into the wall.

"I'm sorry to be the bearer of mercurial tidings, my dear boy, but it's true. As I lay lying near the tracks, I overheard her being berated in the carriage of the Pludgett express."

"Why didn't you stop the train? Create a diversion? Kidnap her back?"

Boz sighed again. "Don't think I didn't contemplate one of your death-defying feats. Only it did occur to me that I was not the best person to be assuming the reins of command."

"So you left her?"

"Well, relative cause and all that. In any case, I thought I'd better consult you before effecting a reunion. So instead I hitched a ride on the caboose, disembarked when Leslie did, and sniffed the scent of your captor to his lair. Do you realize, Jack Sprat, that we are currently entombed in a rather remarkable railway baron's folly?"

John could have torn apart the stones with his bare

hands. "You followed Leslie because you were afraid of Great-Aunt Beauregard and what she might do to you!"

Boz sighed a third time. "I suppose, if one were to examine the subconscious underpinnings of my primordial unconscious, then yes, that might be the honest-to-goodness truth."

"You're such a coward!"

"I'm afraid I am. We live in a cold, cruel world, and I, for one, find no reason to risk my delicate parts. Now I do not suggest that this is a commendable trait. Far from it. Your propensity to risk life and limb for your sister makes you a much more admirable—and, may I say, dashingly adventurous—character but sooey generis, as Leslie might say.

"No, it is my job to remain your humble scion, the poncho to your umbrella, the citrus to your tonic, the nitrogen to your manure—"

"Boz!"

"Yes?"

"I get it!"

Funnily enough, John did. He could smack his head against the wall all he wanted, but Boz was Boz, and would be forevermore. You can't change your friends any more than you can hold back the tide. There was little John could do but accept the situation for what it was.

Which was pretty grim. John could still see no avenue

of escape, and now he was being forced to imagine what Great-Aunt Beauregard might be doing to Page. Even at this moment, his sister could be painting the lips of a ninety-year-old corpse. It was enough to depress a hyena.

And himself. Exhausted, worried, and sick to death of thinking, he lay down and fell back to sleep.

He woke a few hours later, numb below the waist and slick with perspiration. A monotonous hum was reverberating in his right ear.

"Boz!"

"Yes, my dear boy?"

"Shut up!"

"Oh, I do beg your pardon. I had no idea it was fortissimo. I shall endeavor to be a piano."

John wiped his forehead with the edge of his sleeve and closed his eyes again. Less than a minute later, Boz coughed.

"I hate to be a perennial periwinkle, but would you, by any happy chance, care to know what I was thinking about?"

"No."

Either Boz didn't hear this, or he chose to ignore John altogether.

"While I have been lying here contemplating existence, the anemic atoms of my anorexic self have been instructing my interior that it would like a soupçon of sustenance."

"You're hungry," John said.

"Bang on the boutonniere. And do you know what the particles of my particulars are craving?"

"No."

"Well, now," Boz snuffled. "At this precise moment I am thinking of Maria's blueberry muffins."

John couldn't help it. He moaned and rolled over onto his stomach to try to squelch his hunger pangs. "Can we talk about something else?"

"But of course. First course? Primi? Secondi?

"I mean something besides food."

"I'm sorry, old chap, but at this pie-cise gâteau-ment, I can't seem to think of anything else."

"Then can you keep your cakes to yourself?"

"Certainly," Boz said, amiably enough. The hum started up again.

"Boz!"

"Sorry. Simply attempting to meditate into a higher astral plain. Wait a moment, wait one precious nanosecond, I have it! I know what prisoners are supposed to do in purgatory when they are starving and sleep deprived. Are you ready for my inspired suggestion?"

"Do I have a choice?"

"Not particularly."

"Then go ahead," John said, wincing at the barrage that was to come.

"Tell me a story."

"A story? Not now!"

"My dear boy, if not now, when? Seize the carp, John. Seize the carp."

John sighed and rolled over onto his back, just in time for a large, lukewarm glob of goo to go *SPLAT* in his left eye.

"I can't feel my legs," he said.

"Pah!" Boz bellowed. "That's no way to begin a story!"

John reached up to wipe the muck from his eye, and a bolt of pain cracked through his right arm.

"Why don't you tell one?" he groaned.

This time it was Boz who sighed. "Now, now, you know I have neither the facility nor—let's face it—the faculties; nutty as a maggot-infested fruitcake. No, I am merely a player that frets and struts his hour upon two arthritic limbs. You, on the other hand, are incurably optimistic and still breathing. The perfect job description for a storyteller."

John looked up through the bars of his window. The sun was setting, casting a steamy glow over the door of the cell. He could feel his sweat mixing with the dried blood on his shirt and returning it to liquid.

"I don't know how."

"Balderdash," Boz retorted. "It's very simple. You begin at the beginning and end at the end."

"And what's the end?"

"My dear boy, I haven't a clue."

John sighed again and closed his eyes. "Once upon a time, there was a boy who made coffins. . . ."

Boz chuckled.

"Now *that* is an excellent way to begin."

CHAPTER
28

And so John told the story of his improbable adventures, from the perils of Great-Aunt Beauregard to the wanderings with the Wayfarers to the bakery of Maria Persimmons to the dig with Miss Doyle. And for the most part, Boz stayed mercifully silent.

Until, that is, John reached the point in the tale where they lay shackled to a wall in Leslie's timeshare dream.

"You haven't finished!" Boz wailed.

"That's it. I don't know what comes next."

John peered between the window bars. Dawn was curdling in the sky. Suddenly, a tiny bug flitted in and landed on the floor near John's foot.

"Nonsense. You're simply not seeing the covert for the cover."

"The what?"

"The forest for the firs, the coppice for the copper beeches, the wood for the trees."

"That's because I'm chained to a stone wall."

John could tell what the insect was now—it wasn't the black beetle; it was a ladybug.

"My manacled young miscontent, you merely need to parse your story to see that the solution to our predicament is right in front of you."

"What do you mean?"

"How many times in your chronicle did you risk death and dismemberment in your escape? And how many times were you saved by your own inventive cunning and the kindness of chance?"

John watched the ladybug waddle onto his pants. "A lot."

"Egg-zact-edly. Pree-seye-sly. So if your narrative holds true—as any good narrative should—you will now put your nostrils to the grindstone and devise a cunning plan that will bust us both free."

"Sure, no problem, and I guess I'll rescue you with my feet dragging three tons of lead behind them," John blasted. The ladybug rose in fright and darted to the window.

"Well, it's an admirable aim, but I thought you'd prefer to use this."

There was a short silence, then a clatter, then another short silence, and then a *whump*, as a small, heavy object clonked John on the temple.

"Owwww." John rubbed his forehead.

"My apologies!" Boz called out. "My knuckleball is not what it used to be."

John sat up and peered into the gloom. Resting at his feet was Colonel Joe's jackknife.

"Where did you get this?"

"I may have borrowed it when we were lurking outside the station."

"You *what?*" John yelled.

"Well, you know, off to fight for kin and country and all that. And the thought arose that I might need to saw off some important limbs at a critical juncture, and wouldn't it be helpful to have a jackknife."

"So you stole mine?" John picked up the knife and held it gently in his palm.

"Borrowed, my dear boy. Borrowed. And aren't you glad I did? For I doubt you would have had the fore-sight to store it in your bum crack while you were being searched."

John dropped the knife.

"But why didn't you give it to me earlier?" he asked, using the cuff of his pants to wipe every inch of the knife's surface.

"Course, I meant to, but I became so caught up in the perils of your peculiar adventure that I completely forgot I had it until you mentioned the lock-picking lesson on the train. Have you finished extricating yourself yet?"

"Almost," John muttered. In the time it had taken for Boz to yammer, John had inserted the knifepoint into his lock and maneuvered his way around the interior mechanism. "There!" he called out. "I'm free."

"Excellent. Now what?"

"Shhh. I'm thinking."

Thinking was an understatement. Steam was seeping through every follicle in his head. The lock on his cell was impossible to reach from the inside. And even if he did succeed in releasing Boz, it was no use trying to fight their way back up the stairs—they'd be nabbed in two seconds flat. They needed an alternative route.

"Any luck?"

"Shhh! I'm still thinking."

"Capital," Boz replied. "I will sit here like patience on a monument and contemplate the outflow of sewage."

John looked up. "Boz. Did you say there was an outflow pipe outside your window?"

"I did. It appears to be issuing from the opposite wall. And the stench, I must say, is enough to choke a crocodile."

"Where does it go?"

"I assume it sallies forth into the canal that I passed on my approach."

John said nothing. If it wouldn't have sounded so crazy, he could have sworn he heard Boz turn white.

"My dear boy, please don't tell me you're cogitating an escape by that means."

John was, until he remembered the first problem. "It doesn't matter—I can't reach the cell door lock."

"Is that all?" Boz chuckled.

"Why?" John snapped back. "Do you have a brilliant suggestion?"

"Naturally, but I'm not sure I should relate it if you're going to be ornery."

"Boz!"

"Play dead."

"What?"

"Imitate one of your great-aunt's finer specimens. Pretend you are deceased—Leslie will not want a decaying corpse stinking up his tourist establishment. I will alert him to the issue, and when he comes to collect your remains, you can use the dark arts of defense to disarm him, snatch the keys, and release me. Then, ahem, we will attempt your descent."

John had to admit it was a good plan. Of course, it also involved him risking his life. Again.

"Why don't *you* take out Leslie?"

Boz laughed. "Truly, my dear boy? You wish me to be the one in charge?"

John paused, flexing his muscles to get the blood moving to his hands and feet. He hated to admit it, but any physical activity involving Boz ran a high risk of failure.

"Fine. I'll do it."

"Capital!" Boz cried. "Now, if you will arrange yourself in a position of prostration, I will alert Leslie. But remember to be nonreactive to any experiment I might attempt."

John hardly had time to roll himself into a ball before Boz let forth a screeching, ear-shattering wail, like six dozen cats being run through a meat grinder.

"Boz!" John raised his head and hissed. The caterwauling stopped. "What are you doing?"

"I'm keening, my dear boy."

"It sounds horrible."

"It's meant to. Now, if you don't mind awfully, you're supposed to be dead."

John put his head back down on his arm while Boz resumed his wailing, this time at triple the volume.

It didn't take long for the noise to achieve the desired result. *Thunk, thunk, thunk* went a pair of boots down the staircase.

"What are you doing?" Leslie shouted at Boz.

"Oh, alas and alack!" John heard Boz lament. "I believe John is dead! He was fading fast a few hours ago—suffering from dehydration, desolation, and a perforated glottis—and I have not heard from him for some time. He is gone, I'm sure of it. No longer will we walk the moonlit prairies. No longer will the bells of St. Helen's sing out with the feats of our felonies. Oh, perish the hour, perish the day—"

"Would you be quiet?"

The jangle of keys and a clang told John that Leslie had opened his cell door. He tensed as he heard the boots come nearer—

Thunk.

THUNK.

Then . . .

WHAM!

Just as he had with Miss Doyle, John brought his left foot out in a sweeping motion, neatly tripping Leslie. The Pig went down hard, hitting his head on the chamber pot with a thud.

"Oh, dear," Boz said through the vent. "That had every indication of being rather painful."

John jumped up and cautiously approached the figure sprawled out on the floor. For an anxious moment, John thought he had killed Leslie. But then he noticed the steady up-and-down movement of Leslie's chest.

"I think I knocked him out."

"Marvelous," Boz cried. "Then let us sally forth into—"

"Sewage," John completed. He heard Boz gag.

Leslie's key chain had ricocheted into a corner when Leslie went down. It took but a moment for John to release a rather bedraggled Boz. Along with his piratical black eye, Boz was sporting a gash in his knee and a crop of tight braids.

"What did you do to your hair?"

Boz sheepishly tugged on a braid. "I had some time on my hands."

"Let's go!"

Off they sprinted down the corridor, diving around a spiral staircase and through a dingy door. There was no time to waste—John could hear the thunk of more boots coming down the stairs.

Round a corner they hurtled, picking up speed on the straightaway. They were going so fast that they almost missed the access door to the sewage pipe. It was only the foul smell that alerted John.

"Wait!" he said, skiddering to a halt and feeling Boz smash into his back. "Look up there!" He pointed to the cast metal door in the side of the wall.

"My dear boy," Boz said, "you cannot truly expect me to descend by these means."

"We don't have much choice," John said, listening to the raised voices through the walls. "We're either dead roses or live stinkbugs."

Boz grinned. "What a wonderful turn of phrase—I find it immensely flattering that you are inheriting my oracular tendencies."

"Boz! Would you get in the pipe?"

"Of course, of course," Boz said, opening the door and gasping at the odor. John practically had to push him into the funnel as the footsteps grew louder and louder. After inserting one leg, Boz paused, swiveling his neck to look at John. "Did it ever occur to you that we spend far too much time with poop?"

"Go!"

Boz went, his lips clamped firmly together and his nose held delicately between his thumb and forefinger. John followed, but only in the nick of the moment. For right as he was going down, he felt someone grip his collar. With no time to think, he raised his hands and allowed his weight to pull him out of his shirt. Down he went, down into the dark.

CHAPTER 29

RICOCHETING DOWN A sewage pipe was not as uncomfortable as John had thought it might be.

Sure, it smelled like the inside of a dog's dinner and there was suspiciously squidgy stuff coating the interior, but the pipe was remarkably roomy. It rapidly dropped them down a story; then the steep gradient eased up a little.

PLOP!

They fell headfirst into the bubbling brown stew of the canal.

Gasping for air, John struggled to the surface and looked around for Boz's head. He spotted the braids first, then the squished-in eyes, then the freckled grin.

"I'd like to see your great-aunt try that one!" Boz shouted.

John paddled his way over to his friend. "Are you okay?"

Boz whipped his head around, smacking John in the mouth with his braids. They didn't taste nice.

"All parts intact. All systems are go."

John assessed their situation. The canal was drifting them downstream, down toward the town of Howst. Seen from a distance, Leslie's real estate purchase did nothing to inspire confidence. It was a squat, brutish thing, with a rickety stone tower and a crumbling foundation. John had a brief twinge of pity for his captor. Nobody in their right mind would want to live in that dump.

"How far are we from Pludgett?"

Boz turned toward the land, again catching John in the mouth with his hair. "Heading north on a horse? I'd guesstimate around a week or two."

"Do you have any money for the train?"

"None! But not to fret, my dear boy. We need only fetch Rosinante."

"Rosinante?"

"My latest love," Boz said, flailing toward the shore. "The lady who led me to your door. I confess she's not particularly pulchritudinous, but she has a sturdy heart and the loveliest pair of brown eyes."

John learned the truth of this statement a few minutes later, as the old brown horse tried to chew his pants off.

They made it to Howst in good time. It hadn't been

difficult to avoid people—wherever they had gone, their smell had gone ten feet before them. Strong-armed men and long-legged children fled in equal terror from the horrific stench.

Rosinante didn't seem to mind John's lack of personal hygiene. That was probably because she reeked just as badly.

"Isn't she a sweetheart?" Boz said, patting the back of the mare. "Borrowed her at the train station from a charming gentlemen. Said she'd only had one previous owner—an antiquarian lady who exercised her on Sundays."

John pushed Rosinante away and evaluated her stance. Her mangy coat and bowlegged hindquarters suggested she'd seen more than an occasional Sunday walk.

"I don't think she'll take the weight of both of us."

Boz scratched Rosinante's ears. "No, my darling, I don't suppose you will. But no matter." He turned to John. "As your faithful servant, I shall walk and you shall ride."

John jumped on the mare. A reaction, it seemed, Boz was not expecting.

"Do you mean you're content to let me trudge through the wasteland, even after I came to rescue you?"

John leaned down and, for once, said precisely what he wanted to say:

"Boz, after abandoning me in Hayseed, blowing up my invention, and leaving my sister with the worst woman on the planet, you think *you* should be the one to ride?"

Boz tapped his index finger on the side of his mouth. "Well, seen in that particular prismatic light, I suppose it would be more appropriate if you rode."

"Good choice," John said, tightening the reins and giving Rosinante a firm kick.

Their pace was about as quick as a snail in salt, but they reached the main north road faster than John had expected. He even judged Rosinante strong enough to allow Boz on the saddle.

"Froggy went a-sporting and he did ride, a-hum," cried Boz. In a single bound, he was up behind John. Rosinante reeled, staggered, and chomped her yellow-stained teeth together, but she hung on.

"Like the good old days with the mayor's baby!" cried Boz. "Onward and onward rode the six hundred."

"So you're ready to help me rescue Page?" John asked.

Boz swallowed. "Well, I suppose the situation might merit—"

He was cut off by the thundering hoofbeats of a horse. John tried to whip Rosinante around, but she only responded by blundering amiably toward a blackberry bush.

So it was too late to do much but panic when the stallion reared up in front of them. It was so close that some of the foam from its nostrils spattered John's face.

"You aren't going anywhere!" Leslie squawked. He was jiggling and joggling on the back of his mount, waving a riding crop, and trying his best to look menacing.

"Yes, we are!" John shouted back, bracing for the smack of the crop to the head.

Which never came. Baked by the sun, the leftover stench of the sewage pipe—combined with the already pungent fumes of Rosinante's hide—had turned the trio into the equivalent of an eight-legged stink bomb.

Having done his valiant best, Leslie's horse could take the smell no longer. He turned a sickly shade of pea green and fainted.

Down went Leslie, his body trapped under the considerable weight of his mount.

"Oh, I give up," moaned a voice from beneath the stallion.

With the mere hint of a sneer, John led Rosinante past the prostrate figure of his former captor.

"You're more trouble than you're worth, John Coggin!" Leslie croaked.

John's sneer cleared to a sunny smile. "Tell that to my great-aunt," he said.

And off they went.

John's good mood lingered for a long while, only fading as the effects of the sun and an empty belly began to take their toll. By the time he drew Rosinante to a halt at a consumptive creek, John had passed from hunger into a fugue state of willpower.

He wasn't defeated—that was the wrong word for

it. He was bound and determined to stand up to his Great-Aunt Beauregard. She could hammer on him until doomsday. John would not be broken.

He was, however, worried. He had Boz and an ancient horse—those weren't exactly the best assets to effect a daring rescue. If he was going to save Page, he would need a little bit of help from the heavens above.

"Don't count the end of the day out."

John lifted his head. That hadn't sounded like Boz. He looked toward the east. Rosinante was slurping sludge and Boz was sprawled, facedown and fast asleep, on the ground. He looked toward the west. The sun was creating puddles on the parched landscape.

It was the sun that did it. Suddenly John found himself back near the old yellow house at the edge of the sky-blue sea.

He and his father had been out for hours, searching for butterflies in the afternoon light. In hopes of better luck, they had gone farther and farther into the tall grass beyond the house.

As the late summer's sun began to wane, they reached a dirt road. Daring John to race him, his father headed off toward the west. It seemed to John they were playing chase with that great, glowing ball, trying to catch it before it fell to the earth.

They lost the game. The sun slipped below the trees, leaving only the memory of warmth behind.

"Why does it set so fast?"

"What?" asked his father. "You mean the sun?"

John nodded, watching the sky shade from orange to aquamarine.

"It goes real slow and then, *whack!*" John clapped his hands together. "It's gone. And there's nothing."

"Well . . ." His father gazed at the sunset. "I guess nature doesn't want you to take her for granted."

He smiled.

"But I'll tell you what, John my lad, there are consolations. You're not likely to forget a sky like this anytime soon." He pointed to the first star glinting above them. "And," he added, "I've always thought there's magic in the gloaming."

"The gloaming?" John asked.

"What you're looking at now. Twilight. The time before dark."

"I don't see any magic," John retorted.

His father refused to take the bait. "The world can surprise you. Wherever you may be, don't count the end of the day out."

Splossshhh!

A handful of muddy water slapped him in the face.

"Yoo-hoo! Earth to Planet John!" Boz sang. He was standing on the opposite side of the creek. Freed from the braids, his hair had morphed into a crimped mass of seaweed.

John kicked at the water.

"You were in the throes of deepest, darkest introspection. Something bothering my fine feathered companion?"

"Oh, I don't know," John said sarcastically. "Maybe because I don't know how I'm going to save Page? Maybe because I know it could end in disaster?"

Boz grinned. "My dear, dear boy, you seem to be laboring under the misapprehension that life is about success."

"Well, isn't it?"

"Of course not!" Boz leaped over the creek. "What a dull and dreary existence I might have led if I had encountered only fair winds." He stuck his fists on his hips and puffed out his chest. "If you are to get anywhere in this unquestionably ridiculous world, remember that life is about failure. As a bosom companion of mine once said, 'Fail. Try again. Fail again. Fail better.'"

"That's the dumbest idea I've ever heard."

Boz shrugged. "In my experience, dumb ideas are sometimes the best ones of all. But whatever you may decide, fearless leader, remember that I shall be here." Boz punched one of those fists into the air. "Maintain your sangfroid, my friend. It's not over until the obese rooster crows."

"And when will that be?"

"Maybe after you've b-b-both had a b-b-bath!"

CHAPTER 30

"You boys look like you've been in the wars," Colonel Joe said drily.

His father had been right, John thought. The world has a funny way of surprising you.

Thanks to his encounter with Alligator Dan—who had also arrived at the creek to refresh the horses—John, to his astonishment, now found himself back in the bosom of his old comrades.

Back, but not exactly embraced. Even in the considerable acreage of the field outside the big top, the Wayfarers were giving the runaways a wide berth.

"We're a little worse for the wear, sir. Had an encounter with a mass of mysterious malodorences," Boz said.

"I'll say," Porcine Pierre carped. "You smell like a cracked goose egg."

Pierre's pets appeared to agree. At the first sniff of Boz, Priscilla had dropped to the ground, shoved her head down, and crossed both paws over her nose.

"And Dung Boy over here stinks worse," Mister Missus Hank added, somewhat unnecessarily, John thought.

"I must say"—Boz tugged on a greasy forelock—"how fortunate we are to have encountered you all on the road to perdition. An unbiased observer might think that you too are journeying north to Pludgett."

"Course we are," said Colonel Joe. "Pludgett Day is in a fortnight."

"Well, bless my soul and tie up my guts for garters." Boz slapped his palm on his knee. "I'd forgotten your annual pilgrimage. Why, that does make things nice and neat."

"Where's Page?" interrupted Tiger Lil.

John explained—minus a few embarrassing details—how Page had fallen into the hands of his great-aunt.

"Pleased you found use for the jackknife." Colonel Joe gave John a nod of approval.

"I might have known she'd stoop to kidnapping!" said Gentle Giant George indignantly. "That woman is a menace to society!"

"She called us freaks!"

"She threatened to tweezer my beard!"

"She said Frank should be blistered into pork chops!"

Colonel Joe spat. "As you can see, your relative didn't

make much of an impression when she came to search our premises in Hayseed."

John felt a faint stirring of hope. A band of resentful Wayfarers might prove to be useful allies in the rescue attempt. If, that is, he could persuade them to forgive his little episode with the mayor's baby.

"Do you know where your sister's being kept in Pludgett?" persisted Tiger Lil.

"At the workshop," said John. "I was hoping you might help me rescue her."

The appeal hung in the air like one of Frank's belches. Every one of the Wayfarers, including Tiger Lil, sported a doubtful brow. John knew he was asking a lot. Going up against Great-Aunt Beauregard was an endeavor not to be taken lightly.

Finally, Colonel Joe spoke:

"Well, then, folks, howzabout it? Should we take John to Pludgett to save his sister?"

Again, there was a moment of silence. All that John could hear was the faint snores of somnolent grasshoppers.

"I can't think with that stink," said Alligator Dan petulantly. "And it's none of their right to hear what we've g-g-got to say anyway. Give 'em a b-b-bath while we decide."

"Yeah," said Mister Missus Hank. "Plunk 'em in a tub full of catsup. The boy pongs worse than a skunked camel."

John was tempted to tell her that living with the Wayfarers was no bed of lilies, but he kept his tongue clenched between his teeth. He had enough troubles.

"Follow me," said Colonel Joe. "But keep your distance," he warned. "My nose won't stand for any more insults."

John and Boz did as they were told, trudging around the caravans until they arrived at the back of the campsite.

Where John was gobsmacked to see the Autopsy!

He dashed over to inspect it. It had acquired a higgledy-piggledy assortment of accessories—a shaft for a team of horses, a circlet of fencing around the platform, a variety of dog dresses and pig hats and half-chewed rubber balls—but the engine compartment was precisely as John had left it.

"I—" John began.

"I told Pierre to make use of it as a nursery for Priscilla and Frank." Colonel Joe gave John a wink. "Old men never throw anything away."

A surge of joy pulsed through John. He knew what that meant. Colonel Joe hadn't kept the Autopsy for Pierre. He'd kept it in case John was able to come back and fix it. That could only mean one thing. Despite all that had happened, Colonel Joe still believed in him.

Believed in him, yes. Willing to stand near him, no. As John rounded the end of the Autopsy, Colonel Joe paused a good twenty feet from his charges and pointed to two giant barrels.

"John, you sink yourself in that for a bit. Boz, fetch a bucket of bicarbonate of soda from the chuck wagon."

John nodded. Boz curtsied and ran off for supplies.

"You'd better soak yourselves in your trousers while I rustle you up another shirt," Colonel Joe instructed John. "I'm afraid we can't spare any more water for washing duds." Then, hocking his beeswax over his left shoulder, he limped off toward his caravan.

John propped a rock against the barrel and heaved himself into the cool water. It felt like sinking into satin sheets. He ducked his head under and emerged as a shower of snow fell on his shoulders. Boz was back with the bicarbonate of soda.

"I'm dreaming of a white Christmas," Boz hummed, unleashing a blizzard on John's scalp. Then he righted the half-empty box and vaulted over toward his own barrel.

For a half hour, John poached in the warm fizzy water and thought. The appearance of the Autopsy had given him unexpected confidence. He didn't care what the Wayfarers thought. By the high road or the low, he was moving forward.

The problem, he reckoned, was getting inside the workshop to reach Page. Negotiation was impossible and ambush unlikely. If he knew his great-aunt, she would have turned the workshop into a veritable fortress. Perhaps he could get Priscilla to dig a tunnel under the door. Or ask Alligator Dan to bite his great-aunt in the backside. Or shoot Boz straight through the walls of Page's prison.

Nope, John corrected himself. Even Boz's head wasn't hard enough to level a building.

Wait! He sent a dollop of water sloshing over the barrel in elation. Not Boz—*Betsy!* She might not be equipped to launch cannonballs of any real weight, but she was certainly strong enough to punch through a wooden door. Even her shape was the same as a medieval battering ram. Get enough speed behind her metal prow, and she'd bust through the front of the workshop in no time.

But how would they get such speed? John settled back down in his tub and considered the options.

The Wayfarers could all hold on to Betsy and run at the building. Yet John strongly doubted they had enough force to batter through six-inch oak.

Using a conventional wagon was out—horses and harnesses would only get in the way of the cannon.

So that left . . .

With a triumphant spring, John leaped skyward and shouted:

"EUREKA!"

"Ahem." Boz was on the verge of coughing up a hairball. *"Ahem!"*

Dripping with excitement, John looked at his friend.

"We appear to have acquired an audience."

John turned in the direction of Boz's index finger. The Wayfarers were arranged in a dense battalion around their barrels, with Colonel Joe leading the fray.

"Come on out, Dung Boy."

Trousers streaming, John clambered out of the barrel and stood in front of the firing squad.

"We've talked it over and taken a vote."

John carefully examined the faces of the Wayfarers. Then he smiled.

"It was a close-run thing, but we went with our hearts. Come hounds or high water, you've got our support in rescuing your sister."

"You had my vote from the beginning!" Tiger Lil insisted.

"And mine!" Gentle Giant Georgie added.

"Not mine," Alligator Dan grumbled. John didn't blame him overmuch. Even the best of men can find it hard to forgive a snake in their underpants.

"It ain't going to be a walk among the cornflowers," Colonel Joe warned. "That woman is madder than a regiment of hornets. I'd imagine she has the whole of the Pludgett police force on the watch for you."

"Not to mention your sister locked up in the family

business," Gentle Giant Georgie rumbled like an earthquake.

"But I've got an idea about how to rescue her," John said eagerly, squelching his way forward. "Using a battering ram!"

With a stick to sketch the particulars, he proceeded to outline his idea. "We fasten Betsy to the front of the Autopsy, like the bowsprit on a ship. Colonel Joe steers the carriage while I take care of the boiler and switch the gears into reverse. Boz stands on the caboose to man the brakes and make sure the furnace is fed. With a good head of steam, I think we'll be able to bust down the door in one or two charges!"

The Wayfarers crowded around his diagram.

"Smart work," said Colonel Joe, examining the sketch. "But your great-aunt can't know what we're up to. Otherwise she'll scarper. And . . ." He sucked thoughtfully on his chipped left canine. "I don't know how we'll get it to the workshop on Pludgett Day. The streets will be clogged with the floats for the parade."

For the second time that day, the gift of Hom came to John's aid. He had a searing vision of a ladybug's wings retracting.

"Then we'll join the parade ourselves!" he said. "We'll make a shell and hide the battering ram in a parade float of our own design!"

"May I suggest a horse of a Trojan color?" Boz quipped.

Colonel Joe contemplatively twirled the end of his mustache. "You know, that might work. We have two weeks. The Wayfarers can work on the shell while you concentrate on fixing the Autopsy."

"I think it's the dumbest idea I've ever heard," snorted Mister Missus Hank.

"Sometimes dumb ideas are the best ones of all," John retorted. Then he grinned—what did it say about his mental state that he was quoting Boz?

"Well, it's the best we've got at the moment." Colonel Joe drew his foot across the sand, obliterating their traces. "So let's give it a go!"

CHAPTER 31

WITH A HEAVE, a *harrumph*, and a whole lot of dust, the Wayfarers hustled their way north. For the grand plan to work, everyone had to be in position and ready to launch the float on Pludgett Day. It didn't escape John's sense of the absurd that this also happened to be his birthday.

But the old familiar gusher of enthusiasm was rising inside him. As soon as Frank and Priscilla's slobbery toys had been removed, John took up residence in the Autopsy. He slept in the cabin and ate on the platform and worked his tail off in the engine compartment. It would take all of his brain and sinew to get his steam carriage working in time.

His previous failures now spurred him forward. Finally he knew why his boiler had split—he had used a solder that couldn't withstand the heat, just like the mortar on the generator of his oven. Happily, he saw why his chains had tangled—as he had seen on the mayor's baby, they needed to be tight to bite. His instructions to Boz about repairs were detailed and specific.

Fixing the Autopsy was one thing. Getting a bunch of nutty entertainers to build a float was another challenge altogether. As John was to discover, many of the Wayfarers didn't know one end of a screw from the other.

Moreover, they weren't used to being bossed around by an eleven-year-old. On the first day of float construction, they had argued over his blueprints incessantly. Even the shape of the thing was a source of contention.

"I think it should be a pirate ship!"

"An exploding birthday cake!"

"A humongous narwhal!"

But John was not the same boy as last year—the one who had attempted to appease everyone and ended up pleasing no one. This was *his* idea and *his* invention. And he knew exactly what he wanted.

"No," he said, remembering the eyes of the garter snake and the scream of the freight train and the serpent of fire that stalked his dreams in the desert. "It's going to be a mechanical dragon." He cut off Mister Missus Hank before she could protest. "And that's final."

And so the Wayfarers set to work. What with the sawing and the welding and the oil and the sweat, there was little time for socializing. Nevertheless, John noticed that

there was one member of the band who was spending a lot of time with the Autopsy.

And that man was Alligator Dan.

John couldn't understand it. His sworn enemy was hustling up wheels and wood with the speed of his reptilian ancestors. John would mutter aloud that he needed this or that, and the tool would be by his side the very next hour. Yet Alligator Dan never said a word.

Eventually John could stand the suspense no more. "Dan?"

Alligator Dan paused in the process of sanding the crankshaft.

"Why are you being so nice?"

Alligator Dan straightened his back and beat the sawdust from his trousers.

"I thought you were mad at me," John insisted.

Dan shook his head wearily. "I was. Then I was mad at myself."

John's answer was a silent gawk.

"Or jealous," Alligator Dan clarified. "I never had the b-b-brains or the g-g-guts to make inventions when I was younger. I was only the b-b-big ugly freak that kids liked to throw rocks at. Maybe p-p-people would have treated me b-b-better if I'd been smart like you."

In his mind, John conjured an image of a little boy curled up in a ball while stones rained down on his scales. It was funny, but he'd never thought of Dan as young. His childhood must have been terrifying. "I'm sorry about the way I treated you."

Alligator Dan twitched. "I'm sorry too. B-b-but you know what, John Coggin? I was wrong about your inventions." He ran his fingers longingly over the Autopsy's crankshaft. "You really g-g-got something." Then he pointed a finger at John. "And never let that b-b-bird-b-b-brained woman tell you different."

John contemplated his half-finished engine. Yes, he thought to himself. For all the kids with broken dreams, I'm going to make this right.

On the Wayfarers' caravans rumbled, on toward the stolid, solid wall that lay between the world and Page. Every day John refined the workings of his steam carriage. Every night he consulted with Colonel Joe on the progress of his fearsome float.

Happily, it was beginning to take shape. Granted, that

shape was more like a bloated caterpillar than a petrifying monster, but John was willing to be patient. Great creations, he had learned, take time.

"I can't get the jaws to retract!" griped Porcine Pierre.

"This stupid tail won't bend," fretted Mister Missus Hank.

"Exactly where do I put the nostrils?" queried Tiger Lil.

John never despaired. With hard work and cajoling, he assisted the Wayfarers in rebuilding their faulty constructions and reworking their clumsy errors. It was imperative that every detail of the dragon be right. Like the words in a story, he reminded them, even the smallest nail could have a key role to play.

And still they marched north. It was coming on early summer, the grass in the meadows and the peas in their pods. Cows appeared beside the roadside, gazing in astonishment as piles of disembodied claws and fangs trundled by.

Finally the Wayfarers arrived at the outskirts of Pludgett. John smelled his hometown before he saw it—a sulfurous odor that wafted down the road and stuck to his skin. For caution's sake, Colonel Joe halted them at a campsite a few miles before the city. Nobody in town should know about the battering ram.

This was the place where the field test would be conducted. With Pludgett Day only two days away, John was aware this was his sole chance to discover whether his boiler repairs had been effective. Whether his crankshaft could withstand the pressure of the piston. Whether, in other words, the Autopsy worked.

The trial took place at sunset. While Gentle Giant Georgie and Colonel Joe braced an eight-foot stack of logs—a reasonable facsimile of the front door to the workshop—the remaining Wayfarers assisted John in strapping Betsy to the front of the Autopsy. To carry the weight of the cannon, John had built a special extension. It was effective, but it also meant the engine was responsible for driving forward a heavy load.

John wriggled into the compartment with the critical mechanics. Colonel Joe took his post by the steering wheel. Boz scrambled onto the caboose. It was a bare-bones operation. John had decided to add the dragon frame closer to the time of the parade.

If, that was, the Autopsy ran.

"Okay, Boz." John sparked a match. "I'm lighting the coal! Be ready to add more fuel when I tell you to!" He watched as the fire slowly gnawed through the black lumps. "C'mon," he muttered to the furnace. "Heat!"

Slowly but surely, John felt warmth begin to emanate from the boiler. He pictured the water inside simmering, then popping, then exploding with energy. *Creak!* went the piston as it started its downward trajectory. *Crank!* went the chains as they turned the axle of the wheel.

"It's alive!" Boz shouted.

Tiger Lil let out a wolf whistle as the Autopsy trundled toward the log pile. It was holding steady, bumping and bustling over the uneven ground.

"More power!" Colonel Joe barked to John.

"More coal!" John called out to Boz.

"Drat the torpedoes, full steam ahead!" bellowed Boz.

BANG! went the nose of Betsy into the log pile. The axles shuddered, the boiler hissed, and the Autopsy came to a dead halt. John leaped out of the engine compartment to inspect the damage.

The test, to put it bluntly, was a dud. Some of the top logs had fallen off the pile, but the majority stood firm. What was more, John knew that the dragon frame would be adding extra weight. The Autopsy simply had to go faster.

"You achieved more than I estimated." Boz pole vaulted over one of the logs. "Don't be downhearted."

Yet John wasn't discouraged. He was thinking. How could he eke more power from the engine compartment? The coal obviously wasn't doing its job. He needed a more potent fuel. Like, say, the poo pellets from Henrietta hens.

But I don't have Henrietta hens, John reminded himself sternly. So I'll have to try something else.

He tossed back his shoulders and addressed Colonel Joe.

"I want to take a look at the workshop entrance. See if there's a way to gain some speed on the approach."

Colonel Joe rubbed the wax in his fake ear.

"Far too risky. Your great-aunt will either smuggle your sister out of town or sic the Pludgett constabulary on you. Or both."

John had learned from experience that it was useless to try to argue things out with a military man. Instead, he nodded and retreated to the Autopsy. If Colonel Joe couldn't see the merits of his position, then a little subterfuge was going to be necessary.

He found his opportunity at midnight. While the Wayfarers slept off the effects of potato hash, John cloaked himself in one of Tiger Lil's magic capes and tiptoed out toward the main north road.

He got as far as the fence before he was stopped in his tracks.

"To battle and glory we go!" Boz cried, skittering along the perimeter and hurling himself at John's feet. "Half a league, half a league, half a league onward!"

"Shhh!" John ducked his head instinctively. Boz followed suit.

"I want you to stay here while I check on the workshop," John whispered.

Boz clapped his hand over his heart. "I am wounded, sir, chiffonaded to the quick. I would have thought after our sojourn in the sewers that I would merit—"

"It's not you," John interrupted, attempting to apply a tourniquet to the flow of words. "Well, in a way, it is. It's because you're so . . . you. If my great-aunt hears about you in Pludgett, we'll have no chance of a sneak attack. I can't risk that now."

Boz appeared to take John's backhanded apology as an enormous compliment. "I *am* me, aren't I? And, as my brethren in tartan might brogue, there can be only one."

John smiled. "I won't be long."

"Aye, aye, mon capitaine." Boz tipped his elbow to his forehead in a salute and disappeared.

A long and jumpy jog ensued for John. At every bend, he scanned behind him to make sure Colonel Joe wasn't following. At every tree, he half expected his great-aunt to drop like a bobcat on him from above.

Upon reaching the city, however, he found his confidence returned with a vengeance. Ducking and weaving through the alleyways, John charged through the streets toward the wharves. Pludgett hadn't changed. The soot and grime were just the same.

In a couple of hours, he was at the burial ground that marked the center of Main Street. There, to his disgust, the streetlamps cast a nauseating halo on the sign at the end of the road:

COGGIN FAMILY COFFINS
Supreme Craftsmen of Death

He examined the family workshop. It was even worse than he had anticipated. The front door was chained. The windows were shuttered fast. It looked as fortified as . . . well, a fort.

John clenched his teeth. Unless the Wayfarers could build a massive artificial ramp, there was no way he would be able to get up enough speed to bust through the door and the chains. It was too late to enlarge the Autopsy's boiler or adjust the crankshaft. Without a super-powered pellet fuel, his invention was bound to be a failure.

"It's not going to work," he muttered.

"Optimistic as ever, I see."

John wheeled around. A singular form sporting a fetching red parasol was leaning against a spindly tree.

"Miss Doyle!"

"Shhhh." She pulled him behind a gravestone. "City authorities may be lurking."

"How did you get here?"

Miss Doyle flicked her tongue to the corner of her mouth. "After cobbling together a crutch, I limped after you to the station. Once I learned that you had been separated from your sibling, I was forced to make a decision. The boy, I said to myself, has his wits and my training. But the girl, I reasoned—the girl needs looking after."

Despite the fact that he had been second choice, John felt oddly pleased. It was encouraging to know that Miss Doyle trusted he could take care of himself.

"Is that strange excuse for a member of the human race with you?"

John nodded. "Boz is with the Wayfarers." he said. "He rescued me. Sort of," he added.

"Surprised he had the gumption."

"So have you seen Page?" asked John.

Miss Doyle shook her head. "Not a whit. Your great-aunt has her bottled up tight." She paused as she examined his face. "But judging by your lack of despair, I hypothesize that you already have a plan. Are the Marines in town?"

"Not exactly," John replied, imagining Betsy blowing the workshop door to splinters. "But I am."

Though he could see her trying to fight it, Miss Doyle's smile would not be beaten back. "Excellent." She twisted her parasol to protect her from the first drops of acid rain. "In that case, I recommend we retire to the safety of my lodgings. Then you can tell me about your grand plan."

A pang of misery twanged in John's chest. He'd forgotten. His grand plan was dependent on one key ingredient. An ingredient that he didn't have.

"Something wrong?" asked Miss Doyle.

"I do have a grand plan," John said, "but I need the poo from Henrietta hens for it to work."

"You might try asking Maria Persimmons," Miss Doyle said slyly. "I'm sure she'd be more than happy to lend you some—it's making a mess in the back garden."

"Maria's here?"

Miss Doyle nodded.

"How?"

"Simple." Miss Doyle smirked. "I found her."

CHAPTER 32

"Harry, John, oh my heart's ease, don't you ever do that to me again," Maria said, splashing tears onto his shoulder and soaking his shirt.

John hadn't been able to say a word. As soon as Miss Doyle had shown him into the front room, Maria had wrapped him up in a hug so tight that he couldn't breathe.

He didn't want to. He was too happy knowing that Maria truly had forgiven him for what he had done.

"Of course I've forgiven you," Maria said, after she'd finally released him and sat him down on the sofa. "You're family! And I was so worried about what had happened to you. The first thing I saw when I got home was a horrendous fire. Then Leslie told me that you and Nora—I'm sorry, you and Page—had run away.

"I didn't know if you had been injured or killed or

were somewhere in the cold starving to death. I had half of Littlemere out looking for you."

There were deep bags under Maria's eyes and her clothes were mussed where she had hugged him, but she was the most beautiful person John had ever seen.

"Then this awful woman with a stuffed passenger pigeon in her hat showed up. She wouldn't tell me who she was, but she kept demanding to know more about you. So I told her to go to . . . the place other than heaven."

"You didn't tell her you hated the sight of me?"

Maria looked shocked. "I'd never do that! As soon as I'd pulled together enough money, I sent Leslie south while I went north to look for you. I was searching for weeks." Maria smiled. "I'd almost given up when I remembered Page talking about Pludgett. It sounded like a place you both might have been. So I packed my bags and took the train. And that's where I met Miss Doyle."

"But the bakery is . . . ?"

Maria's eyes grew suspiciously bright. John thought she might be about to cry again.

"Not a bit left."

"I'm sorry, Maria." John hung his head.

"You were trying to help." Maria hugged him again. "And I love you for it." She drew her sleeve across her face and smiled. "In any case, I still have my Henrietta hens. Miss Doyle was insistent on having them shipped here. Said I couldn't leave them orphaned in Littlemere."

After hearing that, John almost wanted to hug Miss Doyle too, but he realized she might not take it as well as Maria had. Throughout the reunion, she had been sitting at a wobbly table, scribbling on a piece of paper.

Only now did she look up. "If you've finished coddling him, Maria, I think we'd best discuss our next steps. I deduce that John would like to focus on Page's retrieval."

John nodded.

"How many hens did you bring to Pludgett?" he asked Maria.

"All of them."

"Is that enough?" Miss Doyle inquired.

He nodded again. That would be more than enough fuel for the Autopsy's furnace.

"Capital." She brushed off her hands. "Then what are the next steps?"

The matter-of-fact way in which Miss Doyle said this gave John heart. He wasn't about to be beaten—not with the Wayfarers, Maria, and a woman of uncommon talents behind him.

"I've converted a steam-engine carriage into a battering ram. We're going to hide it inside a dragon float, head down Main Street during the parade, and bust through the front door."

John hadn't expected Miss Doyle to do sidesplits of

ecstasy when she heard his idea, but he had hoped she might congratulate him. Or at least give him a hint of approval.

Instead, she drummed her pencil against the table.

"There's only one door to the workshop?" she asked.

John nodded. "Made of oak. But a few hits should break it down."

Miss Doyle kept tappety-tapping the pencil.

"What?" John demanded.

"Don't take this the wrong way." Miss Doyle laid the pencil down with precision. "But I'm not sure you're fighting with your brains."

"Of course I'm not fighting with my brains," John shot back. "I'm fighting with the Autopsy!"

Miss Doyle held up her hand. "And a very effective weapon it is too. But I wonder . . . have you thought about your sister in this plan? She's in a highly vulnerable position."

John slumped against Maria's arm. What Miss Doyle said was true. With Page inside the workshop, his Great-Aunt Beauregard had the upper hand. Blasting a hole through the door was all well and good, but there was no guarantee what kind of damage might happen during the siege. Page might be hurt in the assault. Or used as a hostage for his great-aunt's release. Or a thousand and one things he hadn't considered in his initial enthusiasm.

"What else can we do? There's only one door in and

out of the workshop. And we have to get through it."

"Well," Miss Doyle said, picking up her pencil once more. "Instead of an obvious frontal assault, I suggest we mount a sneak attack."

"And may I be the first to volunteer for the estimable honor?"

Boz shot out from underneath the sofa, sending Miss Doyle's chair spinning in a tizzy.

"Boz! You scared me half to death," Maria said, clutching her chest.

"Ah, my dear mademoiselle." Boz yanked his balaclava from his head and kissed her hand. "How oft I have thought of you on my long and weary odyssey. How oft your sweet face has appeared to me in the dying light of a desert fire. How oft the words of contrition have hovered on my lips, only to have your sight whisked away by a comrade's hairy—"

"Boz!" she interrupted.

"Yes?"

"Do be quiet."

"I am yours to command." Boz sat down on the sofa. Then he jumped back up again. "But before I do, let me reiterate how anxious I am to ascend the highest heavens of self-sacrifice."

"You were supposed to stay with the Wayfarers!" John told him.

Boz tilted his head. "And there I was. But it occurred

to me that I had made a solemn vow to protect you from mortal danger. Would the gods forgive me if I let you walk blindfolded into the mouth of an inferno? No, thought I! I must follow him, wherever he may go—"

"Boz!" the company shouted in unison.

"Sorry."

"To continue," Miss Doyle said to John, "I suggest we mount a sneak attack."

"How?"

"Yes, how?" Boz twitted. He was busy massaging his hair into a gravity-defying Mohawk.

Miss Doyle poked Boz with her pencil. "You are coming with me to rescue Page."

Boz turned the color of blancmange, but he didn't flinch. "I daresay that Miss Beauregard Coggin will be less than pleased at the turn of events."

"She will not know," Miss Doyle replied.

"Ah," Boz said. "Then am I right in assuming you will be needing me for a little night ruse?"

"No." Miss Doyle smiled. "You'll be a Saint Bernard."

"What?" John and Boz exclaimed together.

Miss Doyle showed everyone the piece of paper she had been writing on. It was a list that included wool, needles, and linen. At the top, in large letters, were the words DOG SUIT.

"My trusty dog will accompany me when I make a delivery of groceries. While I unload the boxes, Boz can sniff out the whereabouts of Page."

"Why can't I be something more exciting?" Boz persisted. "Like an avocado?"

"Miss Doyle, it's brilliant!" Maria clapped her hands.

"Thank you," she said, leaning back into her chair. "I am a woman of uncommon talents."

But this time it was John's turn to be unconvinced. Although he admired the framework of Miss Doyle's plan, he could already see a number of large holes in the sheathing. Besides, if anyone was going to be involved in a daring rescue, it was going to be him.

"What's wrong?" asked Miss Doyle.

"Don't take this the wrong way, but it's not going to work."

"Why?"

"Mainly because Great-Aunt Beauregard doesn't know who you are. There's no way she'll let you in the front door. Plus you haven't thought about the parade. The streets around the workshop are roped off to traffic."

Miss Doyle took his criticisms with a practical good grace. "Fair points." She clasped her hands together. "So is there any opportunity when your great-aunt would be willing to admit a stranger?"

John considered the humdrum routine of his former life. The only outsiders he'd ever seen in the workshop were undertakers, lumber deliverymen, and—

"BYOP!"

The adults looked at him as if he had gone crackers.

"It's an event Great-Aunt Beauregard holds on Pludgett Day," John explained. "People are invited to bring parents or loved ones into the workshop to get them measured for coffins. It's very popular," he said, noting their skeptical expressions.

"This city is in desperate need of medication," Miss Doyle noted.

"But we can't dress up Boz like an old person," Maria said. "Your great-aunt would see right through that."

"She would," John agreed. "Which is why Miss Doyle will be in the market for a *pet* coffin." One that's just the right size for an avenging Coggin, he thought to himself.

Miss Doyle chuckled. "Inspired, John. Inspired."

Maria was still worrying at a piece of dough stuck on her arm. "Are you sure the event is going to happen? She's wrapped up that place so tight."

"Not tight enough!" Boz crowed, yanking a Pludgett Day poster from the inside of his jacket. "BYOP takes top billing this year."

John examined the printed poster. Boz was right. There the BYOP was, lording over the parade and the fireworks and the pickle-eating contest. His great-aunt must be running low on funds—for the first time in John's memory, she was charging a hefty admission fee.

"Then it's settled." Miss Doyle picked up her list. "Boz and I will gain entrance to the workshop disguised as a befuddled pet owner and her aging Saint Bernard."

"And what am I required to do after that?" Boz asked Miss Doyle.

"Simple," she said. "The most rational place for Page during BYOP is in a strong locked room. Is there one in the building?" She paused to look at John.

John nodded. "The ground-floor storeroom has a good lock. That's where Great-Aunt Beauregard keeps the safe." Simple enough for me to gain access to, he noted silently.

"So your job, Boz, is to pick the lock, help Page into your costume, and send her back to me."

On hearing this last instruction, Boz's Mohawk flopped limply to one side. "I hate to interject, but won't that leave me in a rather unenviable position?"

"Only for a quarter of an hour or so," Miss Doyle replied. "Once we have Page safely in hand, you can sneak or fly or hopscotch out through the front door."

Boz bit his lip. "Even so, it seems a rather hazardous undertaking for one diminutive daredevil."

"You don't have to worry about escaping," John interrupted. The moment had come to lay down the law.

"Why?" Miss Doyle's tone sharpened.

"Because Boz isn't going." John stood up. "I am."

Maria grasped his arm. "No, John. We cannot risk you."

"She's my sister!" John shook himself free.

303

"As we well appreciate," Miss Doyle said with infuriating calm, "but Maria is correct. As I said before, we can't risk you being captured by your great-aunt. And should this first plan fail—which, I will admit, is a slim possibility—we'll need you on the outside to save us."

John was livid. Here they were, only a couple of days away from the parade, and Miss Doyle wanted to chop off his limbs. He had let Page down so many times, he couldn't bear to sit on his backside and watch Boz waltz into danger.

Practically breathing fire, he stomped outside and squatted on the front steps. A fog of queasy odors swirled around him.

The front door opened, and a set of footsteps approached. Then a dried red sponge bloomed in John's left eye.

"My dear boy, you appear to be wrestling with cherubim and seraphim," Boz said.

"I want to go!"

Boz sat down. "I know you do. But Miss Doyle is right. We may yet need your services. This part is not yours to play."

"Yes, it is!"

"No," Boz said, "it's mine." He ran his fingers through his hair and pulled out a pinecone. "I'm aware I have not been what one might call the most exemplary of friends. Yet despite having loins that are the consistency of a jellied eel, I am going to make it up to you. So I will brook no opposition. I hereby vow to hoist your great-aunt Beauregard with a Saint Bernard—my final penance for a misspent maturity."

John examined Boz carefully. In all the days he had known his friend, he realized, Boz's squished-in face was the closest it had ever been to looking serious.

"You're not going to let me go, are you?"

Boz shook his head. "No, my dear boy, I'm not. And I'm afraid that if you try, you will wake to discover yourself chained to the nearest radiator."

John sighed. "You promise you'll find her?"

Boz smiled. "As sure as the sun sets upon the salty sea."

John reached into his pocket. "Then I'll guess you'll be needing this."

And he handed Boz his jackknife.

CHAPTER
33

ON THE GRAY, glumpen morning of Pludgett Day, two improbable creatures had come to life under the shelter of the big top. A magnificent steam-driven dragon, and a rather obnoxious dog.

"I thought I was destined to scratch my way to glory as a Saint Bernard. This is the wrong color," Boz griped to Maria. She was stitching an elaborate bundle of corded wool to his costume.

"Listen, Boz," she said, planting her needle in his false eyebrow, "if you'd like to devise a Saint Bernard costume that will pass the muster of Great-Aunt Beauregard, you go right ahead. But my primary concern is to get Page out of there alive and well."

"I have every appearance of a sheep with a Rapunzel complex. Does my hair have to be this lengthy?"

"Yes," Maria said, "because that's what mutts look like. And they don't talk, so be quiet while I finish your headdress."

"I—"

"Zip it."

Boz zipped it.

Maria could be forgiven for being a little testy. The last two days had been a litany of hiccups, holdups, and plain exasperation.

To begin with, there had been a right royal battle between Miss Doyle and Colonel Joe.

"You can't send Boz into the workshop," Colonel Joe had fired at Miss Doyle on their first meeting. "Anyone with two peas for wits will know what he is!"

"I am here to assure you, Colonel, that I am fully capable of anything I set out to do," Miss Doyle had countered, skewering a wad of his discarded beeswax with the tip of her umbrella and examining it critically. "I'm not sure I can say the same for your family."

"You, madam, are a . . ." Colonel Joe was spitting brass tacks. "A spoilsport!"

The only way John could keep both parties from going to war was to suggest a temporary truce. The Wayfarers would work on putting the final touches to the dragon float while Maria and Miss Doyle sewed the dog suit. If the sneak attack failed, Colonel Joe and John would bust through the door as per the original scheme.

Needless to say, this compromise made neither party happy.

"Fight with your brains," Miss Doyle hissed at him constantly, "and you won't go wrong."

"In times of war," Colonel Joe insisted on mumbling every hour or so, "walk softly and carry a ruddy big cannon."

Personally, John was torn. While his brain argued for the practicality of Miss Doyle's plan, his heart was firmly on the side of Colonel Joe. He knew—he just *knew*—that his invention could save his sister.

If, that is, he could get the Wayfarers to stop moaning and finish attaching the wings to the Autopsy.

"I'm only here for the girl," mumbled Minny.

"I hate paint," grunted Porcine Pierre.

"My sideburns ache," pipped Mister Missus Hank.

And yet . . .

Despite the spats and the split seams and the pressure of the too-short hours, things came together. Tasks got done. Progress was made.

So much so that by the time Maria was putting the last touches on Boz's costume, John was feeling a minuscule flutter of hope.

The engine compartment was stocked with coal for the trip into town. The chicken poo pellets were stacked by the feed pipe in readiness for the potential charge. And the float, by the grace of the gods, was finished.

Not only finished, but looking a lot like the fairy-tale dragons of John's fantasies. Coats of silvery-blue paint, very similar to the color of Alligator Dan's chest, covered the scales. Jagged wings were caught in midflight with thin wire ties. A clever lever in the caboose controlled the swish, swish of the forked tail.

But everyone agreed that the real glory was the head. To give the Autopsy riders an unobstructed view of the workshop door, John had created lookout spots in the narrow slits of the eyes. The toothy jaws were clamped shut in grim determination. And there, nestled in the secret hollow of the mouth, Betsy lay sheathed in a red velvet sleeve.

"Hurrah!" Colonel Joe shouted. "We'll give your great-aunt reveille, all right! We'll shake her bed so hard she'll have to ask the bedbugs to hold it together!"

"You won't need to," Miss Doyle countered, emerging from behind the curtain. "Because we're going to get there first."

John had to do a double take. The woman of uncommon talents was now a hard-bitten ninety-year-old hag. Her long dress was cinched together with a yellowing apron. Her bottle-cap glasses made her pupils bulge in an amphibian manner. A crocheted hat was jammed firmly on her head.

And there was Boz. Except there he wasn't. Boz had disappeared completely into a snarl of wool coils.

"Will we do?" Miss Doyle rasped. Boz merely panted.

"You're perfect!" said Maria.

"Boz, are you okay in there?" asked John.

Boz barked.

"Good, then we should proceed," Miss Doyle said, still speaking in a manner John found quite unsettling. "BYOP begins at nine a.m. sharp."

Giving Boz a pat, Miss Doyle strode past Colonel Joe with a brisk tread and a slight swagger. John's insides turned to jelly when he found Rosinante hitched up to a cart outside the big top. Suddenly, the possibility of failure seemed very real.

"Please be careful."

Miss Doyle peered at John through distorted glasses. "I'll bring her back, John. I promise."

But this was not enough for John. He grabbed Boz by his dog collar and led him aside.

"Boz," he whispered, "are you sure you want to go through with this?"

Boz barked again. John yanked on the collar. "I'm serious. I can still go."

Boz rose on his hind paws and removed his head. "No, my dear boy. As I said before, this is my mastodon to conquer. Besides," he added, "we need you in command of the Autopsy."

"Boz!" Miss Doyle called out. "Whenever your highness is ready."

Boz raised his left paw and took John's hand. "Ours not to reason why, ours but to do or die." He shook the hand vigorously. "My dear boy, it's been an honor serving you."

Replacing his head, Boz clambered up on the wagon seat next to Miss Doyle and sniffed her shoe.

"I'll leave Rosinante by the town limits," Miss Doyle noted, "and from there we'll proceed on foot to the workshop."

And with a slap of the reins, they were off, trundling toward Pludgett with hearts full of deception.

"Now," said Colonel Joe, coming to stand behind John, "there's not a moment to waste. Parade starts at noon, and we need to move that beast into place." He handed John a box of matches. "Get that steam engine fired up, and quit your moping."

Alligator Dan paused on his way toward the caboose. As an act of respect, John had chosen him to be the brakeman. "Try not to worry. We'll know b-b-b-by eleven or so if they've made it out."

This was supposed to be a comforting thought, but for John it was sheer torture. As he took his place beside Gentle Giant Georgie in the engine compartment, he found himself counting seconds, then milliseconds, growing more and more nervous as he watched the coal burn. The closer the Autopsy got to the city, the more apprehensive he became. What if Boz was recognized?

"Georgie."

"Yep?"

"Take over for a bit."

While Georgie tended to the furnace, John inched his way through the cabin and into the head of his dragon. Flanked by Tiger Lil and Maria, Colonel Joe stood in command of the steering wheel. Acting as his lookouts, Porcine Pierre and Mister Missus Hank had taken positions in the right eye, Mabel and Minny in the left. Even Frank and Priscilla had found a place underfoot.

John squeezed beside Mabel and surveyed the territory. Minny cocked her head at him. "If this is a public holiday, I'd hate to see the funerals," she joked.

Minny was right. As John had anticipated, Pludgett was making a very poor show of celebrations. A few scraggly flags, edges torn and tips stained, lay draped from the windows. Decaying flowers were twined around the lampposts. A moldy bandstand had sprouted in the park.

Yet these were miracles of beauty compared to the floats. John had witnessed some depressing Pludgett Day parade spectacles in his time, but this was embarrassing. The city's asthmatic buildings, her putrid flora, her grumpy gulls—each float's theme was more pathetic than the last. A model of the clock tower was present, complete with the precarious lean. Six overweight men representing the original founders accompanied it.

So it was not surprising that a wave of excitement rippled through the organizers as John's dragon trundled into place.

"Gwwahh, look at that!"

"It's better than a picture!"

"They must have a team of eight horses under that thing!"

Safe inside the head, John found himself chuckling. Pludgett truly had no idea what he was capable of.

Phrrrumpp.

As Alligator Dan applied the brakes, the Autopsy came to a graceful halt behind the seagull float. From his perch in the dragon's eye, John could see a small section of the street in front of him. Page was not on it.

"What time is it?" he asked Colonel Joe.

Colonel Joe consulted his pocket watch. "Half past eleven."

"Mabel, can you check if Miss Doyle has arrived yet?"

Mabel saluted and ducked under the dragon's wing. She was back in a jiffy. "I asked around. Not a sign of her or her dog."

John worst fears flamed into life.

"It's your decision, Dung Boy," Colonel Joe said brusquely. "Give the order and I'll sound the charge."

"But what if Page is still in the workshop? What if she gets hurt?"

"We may have no choice."

This was a risk John was not yet ready to contemplate. He held up his hand. "Nobody goes without my say-so. Maria, make sure everybody stays here." John was out of the Autopsy before any of the Wayfarers could protest.

Rumors of the dragon had reached the crowds. To get a good view, people had already begun to line up along the sidewalks, waiting for noon to strike. Only then would the floats make their procession down Main Street and past the workshops that fronted the sea.

A steady, relentless drizzle began to fall as John pushed his way toward the pier where the family business stood. He felt as if he were hurtling down a waterfall, with no ability to stop himself from plummeting over the edge and smack into Great-Aunt Beauregard.

But he did stop. At the burial ground, he pulled himself up short and ducked to the side. Scrambling on top of a tomb, he peered over the misty heads of the spectators.

His shoulders fell. The workshop was unchanged. The windows were shuttered, the front door was chained. A poster for BYOP, half ripped, festooned the wall. From his vantage point, John could also see the hands of the city clock creeping toward midday.

After ten minutes of watching, he gave up. Miss Doyle and Boz had been captured, he knew it. Not only was Page still in danger, but now two of his best friends were caught in Great-Aunt Beauregard's clutches. He would have to tell Colonel Joe to hold off on the attack. They couldn't risk an assault, not with Page trapped inside.

Over the graves John leaped, and out through the back of the burial ground. He was panting so hard from the force of his run that he hardly heard the footsteps behind him.

"John Coggin, I have little hope for your future if you can't trust a woman of uncommon talents."

CHAPTER 34

"IF YOU'D CARE to shut that gawp of yours, you'll notice that I've brought someone with me," Miss Doyle said, giving her dog a friendly pat on the head.

Stiff and slow, the shaggy dog trotted to John's side. Stiff and slow, the dog stood beside him. Stiff and slow, it shed its wooly overcoat.

"Page!" John said, and threw himself into Page's arms. "Are you okay? Did she hurt you?" he asked his sister.

Page shook her head no.

"And Boz?" asked John.

Miss Doyle shrugged. "I let him loose as soon as we got into the workshop. Your great-aunt was pleased to see the back of him—he kept trying to lick her armpits. She was frisking everybody who came in, but she didn't think to search a dog. I've ordered him a brand-new casket in curly cherry, by the by."

John turned to his sister, who had been listening intently to all that had been said. "Page, do you know what happened to Boz? Where did he go?"

Page looked like she was about to cry. "He broke into the storeroom and told me to pretend to be the weird old lady's pet. He said he was going to follow me as soon as he was sure I was out of the workshop alive. But he hasn't come!"

"Okay, okay," John said, giving her a hug. "I'm sure he's going to escape. Don't worry."

As if to mock him, the sky began to thicken into a black-and-blue stew. Heavy Gloomy Gus clouds were drifting over the city, coating the rooftops. The clock began to toll twelve.

Bong. Bong. Bong. Bong. Bong. Bong. Bong. Bong. Bong. Bong. Bong. Bon—

"JOHN PEREGRINE COGGIN!"

John jumped.

"John Peregrine Coggin, if you are within range of this confounded bullhorn, hear this! You may have your sister, but I have your Boz. Do you hear me? I have Boz locked up tight as a ten-gallon drum. And I'm never going to let him out, do you hear me? I'm never, EVER, going to let him out. So stick that in your craw and chew on it!"

"Oh, nuts," said Miss Doyle, squinting in the direction of the sound. "We may need Colonel Joe after all."

So this was it, thought John. The time had come, once and for all, to show his Great-Aunt Beauregard what a Coggin boy could do.

"Page!" Maria's voice rang out. She was sprinting down the road, her skirts gathered up high around her knees. She screeched to a stop in front of Page and swept her into a twirling hug. "Page! Oh, Page!"

Page was bawling, tears running in rivulets down the cobblestones.

"We can't wait," Miss Doyle said hastily. "Boz is in there."

"I know," Maria said, setting Page down on her feet. "That's what I came to tell you. Colonel Joe heard the bullhorn. He has the engine running and said it was now or never."

"Then let's make it now!" John shouted.

Together, the group sprinted back to the Autopsy. Colonel Joe was standing outside the dragon, tapping out a step so fast it would have earned him a job with the Mimsy Twins.

"We're primed to go," he said to John, pointing to the floats that were creaking and crunching their way past the starting line. "We'll blast that workshop to bits if that's what it takes. Everyone's in position. Alligator Dan has the chicken poo pellets at the ready. Your sister can stay here with Maria."

Page stomped her foot and pointed to the dragon.

"I'm coming," she insisted.

"Can't be done."

"I won't leave her," warned John.

"You'd do well to listen to them, Colonel," Miss Doyle instructed. "Page has just as much right to see it through. Unless"—she tilted her chin—"you think we feminine types need looking after."

Colonel Joe spat in impatience. "Land sakes alive. You try to show a little bit of chivalry in a rough-and-tumble age, and you're hanged, drawn, and quartered for your troubles. Course the Sprout can come, but . . ." He pointed at John. "She's in your charge."

"I want to come too," Maria said. "I'm not letting these two out of my sight."

"Fine. But let's move!" Colonel Joe roared.

And move they did. By the time the seagull float had inched itself out of the starting blocks, the entire crew was on board and the Autopsy's engine was humming like a train.

"Release the chicken poo pellets!" John called to Alligator Dan.

As Dan obeyed instructions, John caught the faint *plunk plunk* of his super fuel sliding down the chute into the furnace. He pictured the pellets lying on top of the red-hot coals, paralyzed by confusion. He imagined their internal temperature climbing higher and higher, their skin stretching tighter and tighter, their guts growing hotter and hotter until—

Phhhwweeesshh! A screeching jet of steam shot straight through the bony spine of the dragon. Stunned by the noise, horses and floats scattered to the sides of the street in confusion.

"Forward!" John cried.

Bump, thump, VROOM!!

The Autopsy took off like it had been shot from a cannon. Down the center of Main Street it rumbled, snowballing in speed as it went. Rain had begun to fall steadily, but the dragon flew on, flipping its tail in glee.

The inhabitants of Pludgett, used to the dingy spectacles of yesteryear, could not believe their eyes. They sent up a deafening cheer as John's creation barreled along the parade route. Men and women and children rose to their feet and applauded.

"It's working, John, it's working!" Tiger Lil shouted.

It *was* working! John hardly trusted the evidence of his own senses. All the muddles and mistakes and catastrophes of the previous year no longer mattered. He had done it. He had accomplished the impossible.

"To your stations!" he yelled to the Mimsy Twins.

Mabel and Minny hurtled themselves toward opposite sides of the dragon's head. Mabel grabbed one small flywheel and Minny another.

"Unleash the secret weapon!"

Heaving with effort, Mabel and Minny turned the

wheels. An inch of daylight appeared in the space between the fangs of the dragon. Then a foot. Then a yard. The massive jaws creaked backward, collapsing in on themselves like the folds of an accordion.

"Wooohoooo!" Porcine Pierre yodeled, grabbing hold of Tiger Lil to stop himself from tumbling off the front of the platform. "Do you see that? I helped build that!"

With the mouth of the dragon now wide open, John had a superb view of the workshop's front door. It was approaching the tip of Betsy's forked red tongue at a frightening rate.

"Fire in the hole!" Alligator Dan bellowed from the caboose. "Chicken poo pellets away!"

"We got her now!" Colonel Joe cried. "A skeeter couldn't squeeze out of this jam jar!" He spat a gob of beeswax over his left shoulder and into Mister Missus Hank's beard. "Ten seconds to impact! Brace positions!"

The Wayfarers scampered to the relative safety of the cabin. In the shuddering, shivering light of the dragon's heart, John looked at his sister. She was gripping his right hand so tightly the blood had drained from her fingers.

"It's okay." He squeezed. "This is the moment when everything comes right."

BOOOMMMM!

Betsy smashed into the front door with the full force of a meteor. There was a tremendous crack as the center beam split down the middle. Feet and hands and heads inside the dragon went flying.

"Everyone alive?" Colonel Joe demanded.

John stumbled to his feet and picked up his sister. She was smiling.

"Are we through?" he asked as the Wayfarers crowded out onto the platform.

"Almost!" Miss Doyle said. Her hooded eyes were dancing with impatience. "One more push should do it!"

"Back her up!" John shouted to Georgie. The dragon trundled tail first away from the door.

"Pour on the poo, Dan. We've got a mighty short run!" instructed Colonel Joe.

BANG! went the heavy metal shutters as Great-Aunt Beauregard appeared in the workshop's third-story window. The once-proud face of granite now resembled rancid cottage cheese.

"Afternoon, Beauregard!" Colonel Joe patted the left side of the cannon. "Remember me?"

Great-Aunt Beauregard could hardly speak for anger, but she managed. "What have you done with my niece?" she brayed.

"Same thing we've done with your nephew. Let 'em have their way," Colonel Joe replied.

"JOHN PEREGRINE COGGIN!" hollered Great-

Aunt Beauregard. "Get off that silly contraption and return to the family business immediately!"

John stepped to the right side of Betsy.

"No!"

"So that's the thanks I get for my care?" Great-Aunt Beauregard leaned out a little farther. "Well, let me tell you something, John Peregrine Coggin. If you leave me, you'll never amount to anything. Just like your father. You and your sister were born slack-jawed dreamers and you'll die slack-jawed dreamers, and I for one will not shed a tear!"

"Why, that uppity peppercorn!" John heard Miss Doyle sputter behind him. "Let her have it!"

"Wait." John tugged on Colonel Joe's jacket. "See if she's willing to let Boz go in return for the workshop."

Colonel Joe nodded. "Beauregard!" He cupped his hands to ensure his words were heard loud and clear. "This is your last chance. You open the door and hand us the ginger imp, and we'll spare your precious business. Otherwise we're coming through!"

Great-Aunt Beauregard guffawed.

"You've gone off your rocker! What are you going to knock me down with, hot air? A rickety contraption that looks like it's about to break into pieces? Next you'll be talking about rainbows and butterflies. The only way Boz is coming out is feetfirst in a Number Three Special!"

And with that, she slammed shut the shutters.

"That's the last straw!" Colonel Joe bellowed. "It's time that woman learned to respect the law of Betsy!"

John couldn't agree more. Every miserable moment of his life in Pludgett, every hour of soul-crushing work, every insult and cuff and sneer, seemed to run through the grain of that impassable front door. He was going to blow it to kingdom come.

"CHARGE!" roared John.

BOOOOOOOMMMMM!

The Autopsy broke through the remaining beams like the coming of doom. A tumult of dust and debris rose from the wreckage, cloaking the interior from view. Whooping wildly, John and the Wayfarers jumped off the platform and stormed toward the workshop.

And stopped on a dime.

The door was gone, yes.

But the portcullis was not. A brand-new gate of criss-crossed steel barred the way.

Great-Aunt Beauregard reappeared at the window. "Didn't expect that, did you?" she crowed. Her face was flushed with triumph. "Didn't expect your stuck-in-the-mud great-aunt to be smart enough to hide a security gate behind the front door? You think you're so imaginative? Let's see you deal with two tons of industrial steel!"

John was crushed. How could they get through a port-cullis?

"Is that all you've got, Colonel? Is that all your army of freaks has to show for itself?" By now, his great-aunt Beauregard was laughing maniacally. "Serves you right for putting your trust in one of my great-nephew's inventions!" She looked down from distorted nostrils at her relative.

"You should have listened to me, John Peregrine Coggin. When will you ever learn? Wherever you go and whatever you do, YOU WILL ALWAYS BELONG TO THE FAMILY—"

KABOOOM!

Great-Aunt Beauregard never finished her sentence. The entire top floor of the workshop ripped wide open, sending a torrent of color into the air.

John stepped back to admire his birthday show. Sky-rockets, Roman candles and Catherine wheels were bursting across the sky, staining the clouds with gold and red and purple sparks. Horsetails and waterfalls spiked and shimmered, falling in glittering cataracts over the sides of the workshop. Every flower that John could think of—from chrysanthemums to peonies to dahlias—seemed to bloom simultaneously.

But wait!

There was one single dud amid the glory—a thick brown rectangle that rose in a magnificent arch, belting through the colors like a humongous piece of chicken poo.

"What *is* that?" John shouted, pointing to the speeding object.

"It's a turd!" Colonel Joe said.

"It's a crane!" Miss Doyle countered.

"It's Great-Aunt Beauregard!" shrieked Page.

Great-Aunt Beauregard it was, sitting bolt upright in a coffin and advancing with considerable speed toward the clouds.

"Is she going to come down?" asked Page.

"Look!" Alligator Dan shouted. "There she g-g-goes!"

And there she went.

Having reached the apex of its climb, the coffin now began its descent, plummeting ever faster down the curve of its arc. Great-Aunt Beauregard appeared to be completely unaffected. Straight and grim she sat, moving not a muscle as the coffin bridged the buildings along the waterfront and disappeared into the harbor.

"After her!" Colonel Joe yelled, running toward the water. Page and John followed, with Maria and Miss Doyle close on their heels. They reached the edge of the pier at the same time as the rest of Pludgett's population.

"There she is!" John cried, pointing to a figure that was bobbing along in the bay.

"She's headed for the cut," Colonel Joe said. "The current will have her any minute!"

The current did have her. It was sweeping the coffin along in a smooth and seamless ride, pulling Great-Aunt Beauregard faster and faster out to open sea.

"She'll be picked up by that sailboat!" Miss Doyle said.

"She's going to hit the rocks!" Maria exclaimed.

Only John knew that she was going to do nothing of the kind. Only John knew that she was leaving Pludgett in the way she had always wanted—in a Limited Edition Chestnut with optional silver-plated handles.

"Do you think she'll be back?" Page asked as Great-Aunt Beauregard slipped over the horizon and disappeared from view.

"I don't know," John answered, turning around to face the workshop. "But I don't think we have to worry about the family business anymore."

Indeed, they didn't. For there *was* no family business anymore. All that was left of Great-Aunt Beauregard's one true love was a heap of sizzling lumber, a bunch of twisted steel, and the indestructible office safe.

But no Boz.

Colonel Joe grimaced.

"I'm sorry, John. He may have gone down with the ship."

Page squeezed his hand. "What's that?"

John cocked his ear. Then he heard it—a faint *thump, thump, thump,* like the ghost of a one-legged pirate roaming the wreckage.

Miss Doyle pointed at the safe. "My acute hearing would indicate that the sound is coming from inside that item."

John crouched down next to it. "Hello?"

The door of the safe flung open. *WHUMMMP!* John was sent tumbling over the ashes of the wreckage and headfirst into the crumpled legs of a vise.

"My dear boy, my most profuse apologies. Have I knocked the bats out of your belfry?"

John looked up. Dressed in his long underwear and clutching a raggedy bear, there was the squashed melon of a face he knew so well.

"Hello, Boz," John said as Maria and Page gently freed his skull from the vise. "I'm glad you're not dead."

THE
END
OF THE
BEGINNING

"IT WAS A minor matter of insurance," Boz explained that evening.

John grinned. Being under house arrest was proving remarkably entertaining.

The city elders were in a tizzy of indecision. Great-Aunt Beauregard may not have been the most amiable woman in Pludgett, but she had been the rightful owner of the workshop. And as much as the police were unhappy about the horror stories that John and Maria and Colonel Joe told them, they weren't quite prepared to sanction Boz's explosive conclusion.

Their solution, like the best work of bureaucrats, was to stuff the problem in a convenient corner while they bickered among themselves.

That left the heroes of the hour—including each and every Wayfarer—smushed tooth by jowl in Miss Doyle's rented residence. Not that they were complaining. They kept themselves busy warming their hands by the fire and licking the cinnamon-nut frosting off Maria's sticky buns. Maria herself was in the kitchen, preparing a second batch.

"While I trusted John would fulfill his promise of taking down the portico," Boz continued, "I did have a modicum of hesitation about whether he would succeed in persuading his great-aunt to see reason."

He paused to help himself to another sticky bun.

"So when I happened upon the supply of fireworks for the parade," he mumbled through a mouthful, "I took the liberty of liberating them." He pulled something out of his pocket and tossed it to John. "As ever, my dear boy, I'm indebted to you for the temporary acquisition of your possessions."

John looked at his jackknife. There was hardly a scratch on it.

"Weren't you scared?" Page asked, hugging her bear.

"Not at all," Boz said, airily waving his hand. "I merely followed the admirable instructions: 'Light Fuse and Retire Promptly.'"

"Into the safe," John completed.

"What safer place?" Boz smiled, leaned back, and rested his feet on an end table.

"Boz," Miss Doyle trumpeted.

"Yes?" he answered, removing his heels and shrinking into his chair.

"I would like to say . . ." She paused, appearing to struggle with the words. "Thank. You."

"Not at all, my estimable comrade. Merely a down payment on favors in arrears. Speaking of arrears," said Boz, teasing a gold coin from his shoe. "I might add that the safe provided me with an admirable cushion of currency.

"And . . ." He brought forth a white tome from his shirt. "An interesting volume of light reading."

John scowled at the stack of paper. Would he never be free? Seizing his great-aunt's contract, he made for the fire.

"Before you contribute to our carbon footprint," Boz said, gently restraining John's arm, "you may wish to peruse the contents."

"I already know what it says," John countered. "It says I have to work with Great-Aunt Beauregard in the family business for the next twenty years."

"I am no jurisprudent." Boz took the contract from John's hands. "But from what I have gleaned, it says nothing of the sort."

"Here, let me look at that," said Miss Doyle.

While she and the Colonel examined the contents, Boz inhaled another sticky bun and quizzed the Wayfarers on the precise details of his rescue. "So you were part of the little engine that could?" he said to Alligator Dan. "I must say I find that intensely flattering."

Alligator Dan plucked a scale off his elbow and skimmed it over Boz's head. "I did it for the kid, not you."

"Next time you should try making that thing *really* fly," griped Mister Missus Hank. She was massaging her bruises with a potent mixture of mint and calf's-foot jelly.

John swiveled around from his place by the fire. "What did you say?"

"I said you should make the dragon fly," Mister Missus Hank repeated. "I'm getting too old for battering rams."

From her seat on the sofa, Page glanced at her brother. "Uh-oh."

"Uh-oh, what?" asked Tiger Lil.

"He's got his thinking look on."

"He'll be needing it," interrupted Colonel Joe, "if this contract is anything to go by."

"What do you mean?" asked Page.

"Well"—a mischievous twitch appeared in the corner of Miss Doyle's smile—"there's enough hooey in here to choke a chimney, but one thing is dead certain." She took John's hand in hers and shook it firmly. "I'd like to be the first to offer my congratulations. You, John Peregrine Coggin, are the legal owner of Coggin Family Coffins."

"How can that be?" John croaked. "Great-Aunt Beauregard owned it. She said she was making me the heir."

Colonel Joe consulted the middle section of the contract.

"But the workshop didn't legally belong to your great-aunt. It belonged to your father. When he died, he deeded it to you. The business was to be held in trust until you reached maturity on your twelfth birthday—that happen recently?"

"Just yesterday."

Colonel Joe nodded.

"That would explain Beauregard busting a gut to get her hands on your signature. She must have been worried you'd toss her straight out on her tush."

All that effort by his great-aunt, thought John, a whole year of chasing him around the country, simply for the chance to stay buried in her business. Dreams are funny things.

"A copy will be filed in Pludgett's registry of deeds," Miss Doyle said. "We can go there tomorrow with the police to prove your ownership."

"And then what do I do?" John asked the Colonel.

Colonel Joe smiled. "With the gold from that safe? Anything you darn well please."

"I'd say he's p-p-passed his induction. He can stick with the Wayfarers if he doesn't b-b-bring B-B-Boz," Alligator Dan interjected.

"Who are you to be issuing invitations?" pipped Mabel from her perch on the windowsill.

"I'll take care of the girl if John can—" began Tiger Lil.

"He gives Frank hives," Porcine Pierre interjected. "And I don't like his taste in company."

"It's a lot better than yours," Mister Missus Hank snapped.

"Well, at least I'm not running a private flea motel, like some I wouldn't care to mention."

"Are you calling me dirty?" The patches of skin behind Mister Missus Hank's beard were turning crimson.

"He calls it as he sees it!" Minny sniped.

Wham! Wham! Wham!

Miss Doyle's umbrella beat a rhythm section on any number of skulls. "Put a cork in it! I want to hear what the boy says."

The Wayfarers sank back into their seats.

That's me, thought John. They're waiting for me to speak.

But he didn't know what to say. Where should he start? A workshop of his own in Pludgett? A life on the open road with the Wayfarers? A new beginning with the help of the redoubtable Miss Doyle?

He had the money. He had the brains. He had the freedom. He felt like he was back behind the wheel of the mayor's baby. The world was once again a limitless horizon. A whim might take him anywhere.

"Johnny? What should we do?"

Page's trusting face—the same face as their mother—looked up at him from under her halo of golden hair. In the kitchen, he could hear Maria kicking at the oven door. She was humming the tune of "Ladybugs' Picnic."

And just like that, John knew *exactly* what he wanted to do.

"We're going to live with Maria," he told his sister. "We're going to find a town with an old yellow house by the sky-blue sea and we're going to build a new bakery—a real family business." He paused. "And then I'm going to make the dragon fly."

Page grasped his hand eagerly. "Will there be rainbows again?"

"I'm sure of it," John replied.

"We'll miss you," Gentle Giant Georgie said wistfully.

"Stop b-b-blubbering, G-G-Georgie," groused Alligator Dan. "We can stop b-b-by their new home at the end of each summer."

"Will your famous oven be in residence?" There was a chuckle lurking in Miss Doyle's query.

John smiled. "Yes," he said. "And if I can come up with the right pellet mixture, a poo-powered automobile to take everyone around town."

"Suits me fine," Colonel Joe stated. "More than happy to lend a hand with the prototype when I stop by."

"Will you come and see us?" John asked Miss Doyle.

"I might," Miss Doyle said. "As long as you promise to visit me on one of my digs."

"Do you think we can do that, Page?"

"Only if we can ride in a train with real toilets."

John laughed and hugged her close.

"What did I miss?" Maria asked, brushing her floury hands on her apron as she came through the door.

"We're going to build you a new bakery," Page said, running over to grab her around the legs.

"With a chicken poo oven that works!" John shouted, joining his sister.

"With the hearts and hands of the Wayfarers," Colonel Joe added gallantly.

"In a town by the edge of the sky-blue sea," Miss Doyle finished.

Maria laughed loudly, but her eyes grew suspiciously red as she knelt down and drew John and Page close to her heart.

"I think I'd like that. But haven't you forgotten someone in your grand plans? What does he think?"

John turned to Boz's chair.

But Boz, it seemed, was no longer there.

ACKNOWLEDGMENTS

Special thanks to:

My mum & dad, for giving John his brain.

Steven Chudney, my literary agent, for giving John his heart.

Jordan Brown, my editor, for giving John the courage of his convictions.

I'd also like to thank Ben Whitehouse, my illustrator, for making every cog and Coggin come alive; Renée Cafiero and Laaren Brown, my copyeditors, for their patience and humor; the editorial and marketing teams at Walden Pond Press and HarperCollins—including Debbie Kovacs and Viana Siniscalchi—for their unfailing support; and my siblings, for fostering my inanities.

Finally, I'd like to express my heartfelt gratitude to Miriam Marecek, who has always believed in the power of children's literature to save the world.

ELINOR TEELE

is an author and playwright who graduated with a PhD from the University of Cambridge in 2005. She lives with her family in New England. You can visit her online at www.elinorteele.com.